Praise for *Street*

STREET

CALUMET EDITIONS

Minneapolis

First Edition December 2023
Street. Copyright © 2023 by A.D. Metcalfe.
All rights reserved.

This is a work of fiction. All of the characters, names, incidents, organizations, and dialogue are either the products of the author's imagination or are used fictitiously.

10 9 8 7 6 5 4 3 2 1

ISBN: 978-1-962834-03-2

Cover and book design by Gary Lindberg
Cover art by Nathalie Erika Langner

STREET

A.D. METCALFE

CALUMET EDITIONS

Minneapolis

For Sally

CHAPTER ONE

Run. Just fucking run.

The slapping of sneakers on pavement matched the rhythm of Johnny's breath. Palm trees, parked cars and bungalows bounced in his peripheral vision, obscured by sweat. When headlights approached, he ducked his wiry frame behind a telephone pole. He used the opportunity to wipe his face on his T-shirt, then realigned the shoulder straps of his backpack. Once the car passed, Johnny hurried along the sidewalk. But run where? He searched the sky. Miami's summer haze had muted the moon's glow, along with the blinking lights of a descending jumbo jet. He remembered there was a bus station near the airport a few miles away.

When Johnny got to the depot, he watched from across the street. Moths ricocheted off the big picture windows, drawn to the fluorescent lights. Inside looked desolate. A few people paced while others lay on benches. Blue-shirted employees slumped over counters, smoking cigarettes and chatting.

It was still too empty. In a few hours it would be light, there would be more people to blend in with. Johnny saw a parking lot on the next block. It was surrounded by hedges and a flimsy chain-link fence. He ducked inside an opening and found a secluded corner behind some cars. Shaking off his pack, which was stuffed with as many clothes as it could fit, he sat down to wait. *Please let me be gone before my parents wake up.*

When Johnny checked again, there was more activity in the terminal, so he went inside. He moved slower than he wanted, keeping his head down while looking for anyone who might be looking back. He stood under the list of departures. From what he could tell, the next bus leaving was going to New York City. That would be far enough. He went to a counter.

"How can I help you?" asked the gray-haired clerk.

"One way to New York, please."

"Where are your parents?"

Johnny's eyes swept the room until he found a suitable couple near the convenience store and pointed to them. "Over there, but I've got the money. I go to New York every summer to visit my grandmother. She meets me at the other end."

"You don't need a round trip?"

"No. She's driving me back."

The man yawned into his fist. "That'll be thirty-six dollars."

Johnny sorted through the bills he had swiped from his mother's purse and handed over two twenties.

The clerk gave him change and a ticket. "Your bus is boarding in ten minutes from gate seventeen."

"Thank you." Johnny headed toward the suitable couple to polish off the ruse.

Near the magazines and books, he saw *The Traveler's Guide to New York City*. It was outdated—printed in 1969—but he figured things would not have changed that much in three years. He brought it to the register, with some snacks and a drink, before drifting to the gate where the empty coach was parked.

When the driver opened the doors, Johnny walked straight to the back and slouched by the window. The heels of both feet bounced as other passengers filed on. It was not until they were coasting north on the highway that Johnny felt his panic subside. But in its absence came the thoughts. The doubt. How was a twelve-year-old kid supposed to care for himself in such a big, unfamiliar city? He rubbed the raw skin around his wrists. He would have to figure it out. There was no choice.

Johnny stared out the window, watching his reflection skim over the passing scenery. He had his Colombian father's good looks, with dark eyes and jet-black hair that hung in a mop of loose curls. His mother's Turkish heritage was represented in his smooth olive skin. He wondered if his parents would even bother reporting him missing. Probably not, but the neighbors might.

The bus stopped in Jacksonville for a short layover. People got out to stretch their legs or purchase snacks, but Johnny hunkered down, putting his backpack and a jacket on the seats next to him to deter new passengers from sitting there.

Once they crossed the state line, Johnny gave in to the exhaustion and fell asleep. Between naps, he eased his anxiety by studying the guidebook. He read about New York City's historic sites and neighborhoods and surveyed street maps of all the boroughs. He found some comfort learning that the city was on a grid system, like Miami.

The next afternoon, the coach descended into the bowels of the Port Authority Bus Terminal. It parked beside dozens of others. Johnny slipped on his backpack to follow the line of slow-moving passengers into the exhaust-filled garage, side-stepping the people waiting by the luggage compartment. The station was bigger and dirtier than Miami's, with people hurrying in all directions, and there were more vagrants. Johnny rode up an escalator, following the exit signs through the colossal terminal. He scanned passing faces, checking if anyone seemed concerned that a kid was wandering alone. But nobody even looked at him.

After another flight of stairs, Johnny stepped onto 8th Avenue. The blistering heat hit him hard. Florida was hot in late July, too, but the air was different here. It was thicker and fouler, a combination of diesel, simmering asphalt and dog shit. Chaotic humanity rushed and dawdled, with tourists trying to zigzag their luggage through beelining commuters. Johnny followed a random flow of pedestrians until it spit him onto the curb at 42nd Street.

Since he had read about Times Square, he walked east to Broadway to check it out. At the corner, his eyes widened. It was just like in the movies. Johnny wandered around, taking it all in. The energy was exhilarating and minimized whatever apprehension he had been feeling. Different aromas from food vendor carts steamed into the street, momentarily overpowering the exhaust.

Folding tables tempted passers-by to play their games of Three-card Monte, while others sold cassettes and 8-track tapes. Made-up ladies in high heels, short shorts and tube tops tried to lure men into peep shows and XXX-rated movies. Mixed with the hustlers, people in three-piece suits and fancy dresses weaved through the streets.

Johnny bought juice and a hotdog from a cart before walking to 59th Street and into Central Park. From what he had read, he thought he might find some good places to hide overnight, but he would have to scope things out before it got dark. He meandered through a lush, winding footpath until he came to a large field with several baseball diamonds. The exuberant cheers of the players echoed as bats hit balls, filling Johnny with excitement. He could have stopped to watch any one of the games but knew there would be time for that another day.

Continuing, the faint sound of a rolling, off-key organ enticed Johnny, so he headed toward it until the path opened up to an octagonal brick building. Inside was a big carousel with colorful wooden horses bobbing up and down. Kids clung to poles laughing while their mounts circled to the blaring, disjointed music. Johnny stepped through the barricade, sharing in the excitement of the ride until he felt a tap on his shoulder. He turned to see a man in a uniform and froze.

"You got a ticket?" the man asked.

Johnny relaxed when he realized it was just the carousel attendant. "No, I don't."

"Then you're gonna have to step aside. In here is for ticket holders. You can get one over there." He pointed to a booth several yards away.

"Okay." Johnny scrambled back to the footpath, determined to stay focused on his mission.

By dusk, he saw a small bridge near a wall of rocks. He climbed up and discovered a gap hidden from the path. There were food wrappers, a booze bottle and cigarette butts scattered around. He was not the first person to use the place. Brushing out the litter with his foot, he shook off his pack and wedged it in the back of the tiny cave, then lay against it and closed his eyes.

Johnny was startled awake by men yelling. He sat up. It was much darker now, and the moon was high in the sky. He tipped an ear toward the voices. Drunks. After a while, the incoherent exchange wound down, with one man shuffling away, but another sounded like he was crawling up the rocks. Johnny pushed up and stood in a shadow, watching the man's silhouette weave and grunt with every step. *Old, fat and hammered as a motherfucker.*

"Hey! Is someone in there?" the drunk said. "This is *my* spot!"

Johnny groped around until his hand found a rock. It wasn't big, but it was better than nothing. He lowered the register of his voice. "Move along, old man."

"*You* move along."

"Don't make me fuck you up!"

The bum swayed near the entrance. "Fine, you don't gotta get all assed up about it. There're other places to crash." He picked his way back down the rocks, mumbling obscenities into the night.

The next time Johnny woke, it was just before dawn. He stretched, inhaling the moist air. It was earthy, with a touch of spice, cloves maybe, and a hint of horse manure. He collected his things and set off into the park. He found a water fountain, took a long drink, and rinsed his face and hands. The public restrooms were closed overnight, so he picked a sheltered spot to drain his bladder and change into cleaner clothes. Exploring the city would be hard if he had to hump his backpack around. He needed to find a place to stash it.

As the sun rose, Johnny entered a wooded area where the trees were tall and leafy. He stopped and looked up. "If I can climb a palm tree, I should make it up one of these things." He found the fullest one and clambered up its hearty limbs. He got pretty high before sitting on a branch to make a note of the landmarks. On the perimeter of the park was a playground and a yellow high-rise across the street. That would be easy enough to remember. Johnny shook off his backpack and removed the rest of his money, everything he had saved over the last few years, mowing lawns and helping neighbors clean out garages. He stuffed a few bills in his pocket and slid the rest into his socks. Johnny stood up to loop one of the pack's straps over a more flexible branch, then wedged it tightly between two limbs. Satisfied, he climbed down.

He exited the park at 68th Street and walked south. After a few blocks, he saw a sign for the YMCA. He had been going to a branch in Miami, where he lifted weights and took karate classes to better defend himself against his crazy brother. If this one were similar, there would be lockers and showers.

At the counter, a stodgy-looking woman peered at Johnny over her bifocals. "Can I help you?"

"How much for a membership?"

"Twelve dollars a month, but you need a parent to sign."

"They're both at work today, but I've got the money." He pulled the cash from his pocket and showed it to her, then brushed an errant curl from his forehead and batted his brown eyes.

She squinted and bit her lower lip before pulling a form from a drawer. "Okay for today. Just make sure this is signed the next time you come, or you won't be let in." She took his money and grabbed a pen. "What's your name?"

Johnny looked at her blankly. His real name, the one the police might already be looking for, was Javier Alejandro Álvarez, but he'd been called Johnny for years. His kindergarten teacher used to struggle with the name Javier, so she called him Javi, which, over time, had morphed into Johnny. By first grade, everyone outside his household called him that, and when things started to get really bad at home, he preferred it. John was common enough to be safe, and what popped into his head for a last name was that kindergarten teacher's. "Avalon, Johnny Avalon."

"Date of birth?"

Pick something easy to remember. "April first, 1959."

She smirked. "You're born on April Fools'?"

"I know, crazy, right?" He grinned, shaking his head. "My parents never let me live it down."

Shrugging it off, she went back to completing the form. Johnny's actual birthday was July twenty-fifth, the day he had run away. By subtracting a year, he made himself thirteen instead of twelve. A slight improvement.

The woman handed him the form and a temporary membership card. "Here you go."

"Thank you." He stuffed the card into his back pocket and smiled. It was his first official document with a new identity.

Johnny toured around the building, checking out the pool and weight room before heading to the lockers. He undressed, wrapped a discarded towel around himself, and went to the showers. There was a stall with a small cake of soap left behind, which he used to wash and lather up his hair. After, he dressed and went outside, pausing on the steps to feel the sun on his clean face.

The Y would be a good place to meet people and shower, but he had to get the form filled out. Forging a signature was easy, but they also wanted an address. If he made something up, an employee might know it was fake and get suspicious. He needed a believable location, and he wanted to find some other places to sleep anyway, so he decided to start at the top of Manhattan and work his way down.

At Columbus Circle, he ventured into the subway station. He had never ridden a train before, much less one underground. He stood aside to watch what everyone else was doing, then went to the booth and purchased a token for thirty-five cents. He pushed through the turnstile.

On the way to the platform, he stopped at a poster-sized subway map. It looked like a veiny mess, but after some review, Johnny opted for the A train. It was crowded, but he squeezed inside and grabbed onto a pole with a handful of other folks. As he glanced at the surrounding faces, he noticed everyone was either looking down or staring vacantly at the ads on the walls. Others read books or strategically folded newspapers. A few even dared to nap. It seemed that the subway must have some generally accepted no-eye-contact rule. *Works for me.* Johnny smiled, dipping his head to the floor.

The train's last stop was 207th Street. Johnny walked out of the station and headed downtown on Broadway. The neighborhood was different from what he had seen so far—less crowded, smaller buildings and the stores didn't look as fancy. People were hanging out on stoops or tinkering with cars. Many spoke Spanish, and Salsa music played in the distance. He would be able to blend in around here.

Johnny walked south, past row after row of six-story brick apartment buildings over varying storefronts, looking for a place he could call home. It was such a contrast from the bungalows and ranches he had grown up around.

Though young, Johnny was not naïve. To avoid his family, he had spent a lot of time wandering around Miami. He could tell this was a neglected part of town. Some buildings he passed had been gutted by fire. Others were in general disrepair. He could recognize a drug hand-off and knew the guy slumped in a doorway wasn't just resting. But none of it felt threatening.

At 180th Street, Johnny turned east to get off the busy avenue. Parked cars were flanked by piles of trash and broken furniture. After a few blocks, he stopped at a six-story, U-shaped apartment building that seemed more desolate than others. It was bisected by a courtyard with broken cement stairs that led to the entrance. He peeked through the dirty smoked glass to make sure it was clear before pulling on the door. It was locked.

Johnny backtracked to look for another way in. A few people sat on stoops down the block but weren't paying attention, so he sidled up to a trapdoor in the sidewalk. He lifted one of the twin hatches to look inside. A flight of diamond-plated steps led to an unlit concrete hallway. Johnny climbed in and shut the cover, which made it pitch black. He put out his hands, feeling the narrow walls as he moved forward, sometimes stepping in puddles of what he hoped was just water. Focusing on a distant strip of light, he tried to ignore the squeaking and shadows darting in front of his feet. Why were basements always so damn creepy?

Eventually, he came to a half-opened steel door. Behind it were some dimly lit stairs leading to the rear part of the lobby. It had probably been attractive once, with its sand-pattern tiled floors and decorative moldings, but everything was soiled from age and neglect. An alcove with battered mailboxes sat opposite the main door, surrounded by cracked walls marked with graffiti.

Johnny ventured around the ground floor's hallways. Half the apartments appeared lived in, based on the faint sound of televisions and voices, but others had holes where the locks had been removed. A few of the doors could not close at all, so Johnny looked inside. Those units were bare and had been stripped of all appliances. Some had litter, liquor bottles and candle remnants. One had an old mattress, but the building wasn't terrible; it smelled okay and had functioning sinks and toilets, which kept trespassers like him from pissing in the corners.

He tracked back through the lobby and climbed the main staircase, which had a fancy grooved handrail and worn, scuffed marble steps. Each floor had evidence of tenancy, but it seemed that illicit use diminished the higher he climbed. On the sixth floor, all but two of the units looked vacant. Fewer nosy neighbors to contend with up here. Johnny selected an apartment at the end of the hall, farthest from the legit renters.

The door opened to a short hallway leading to an L-shaped kitchen with paisley linoleum tiles. Several sections had peeled off, exposing dried glue underneath. Further in was a living room and a single bedroom with a walk-in closet. Only the bedroom windows faced the street. The others overlooked the courtyard. Most of the apartment had wall-to-wall carpeting, but the original color, whatever it was, had long ago been trampled into an unsightly gray. The plaster walls were cracked and thick with layers of paint.

Johnny checked the bathroom. Its white hexagonal tiles were yellowed and chipped, the toilet seat remained attached by only one hinge, and the clawfoot bathtub was blackened from decades of hard-water stains. He pursed his bottom lip. "This ain't too bad." When he turned on the faucets, the water came out brownish and lukewarm. "It'll do. At least for now." Johnny walked around, flicking light switches, but nothing happened. "That's okay. I can live without electricity. As long as I got a place to crash and clean up."

It was getting late, and Johnny wanted to go out for some supplies before dark. He trotted down the six flights of stairs and pushed open the front door. A white girl sat on the steps, tossing tiny pebbles into the gutter. Johnny guessed she was a few years older than him, even though she was short and slight. Her mousy hair was unkempt, and she wore cut-off shorts with a tank top and flip-flops.

"You looking for something?" she asked as he passed.

Johnny turned. "Excuse me?"

"I saw you sneak in." She pointed to a second-floor window. "I live up there."

"Oh, that, yeah." Johnny waved the air. "I thought one of my friends lived here, but it must be the wrong building."

"Sure, you did." Her eyes narrowed. "You were probably gonna rob an apartment or something."

Johnny cringed. "What? No. I'm not robbing anyone."

"Relax." She rolled her eyes. "I'm just fucking with you. Homeless people and druggies drift through that skanky basement all the time." She bit her cheek. "They're just not usually so cute."

"Hmm." Johnny smiled and sat on the step next to her.

"So, which one are you?"

"Huh?"

"Homeless, or looking for a place to get high?"

"Neither." Johnny shook his head. "I was just poking around." He flicked at the tongue of his sneaker. "You know, seeing if there was someplace I could hang out sometimes."

She perked up. "Are you running away from home?"

Damn, this girl is pushy. Johnny coughed out a laugh. "No. God no. Nothing like that. It's just that sometimes I need to get out of my house for a bit, get some space. It's too crowded there, and my family argues all the time." He chuckled. "But I might consider running away if shit doesn't change."

She clicked her tongue. "I wish *I* could. It's miserable here now." She tossed another pebble harder than the others. It bounced through the courtyard and across the sidewalk, hitting a parked car's hubcap. "This block used to be full of families, and I had friends, but they all moved away."

"That sucks. How long have you been here?"

"My whole life. In that same crappy apartment. Me, my mom, and my grandma. She moved in to help look after me when my dad left."

"What's your name?"

"Lily Anderson."

"I'm Johnny."

She nodded. "You must not live nearby 'cause I'm *always* here, and I definitely would've noticed you."

Think fast. Be vague. "You're right, I don't. I'm further downtown, and before that, we lived in a bunch of different places." He wagged his head. "We move so much it's hard to keep track."

"I wish *I* could because this neighborhood is really going to shit. A bunch of apartment buildings have already been abandoned because the owners weren't making enough. My mom says it's only a matter of time before that happens to ours. They fired the regular super a year ago, so now it takes forever to get shit fixed, and there's never enough heat or hot water in the winter. She says they're doing it on purpose, to force us out. Then they can just close and be done with it."

"That's rough."

"But we can't afford to live anywhere else. My mom barely makes enough to get by, even with my grandmother's social security. Most of the other tenants have the same story. It's why we pitch in to keep shit clean, so the city won't condemn the building."

"You clean up after the bums?"

"Kind of. If you report them, it might give the management an excuse to close down sooner. We don't get too many because there's plenty of vacant buildings around." She sighed and looked at Johnny. "So that's basically my life, listening to a bunch of adults bitch about the conditions all the fucking time."

He grinned. "So, I guess it won't be a problem if I hang out in there."

Lily laughed. "Are you kidding?" She untied a shoelace that hung around her neck and handed him one of the keys strung on it. "Here. It's for the front door. Then you don't have to keep going through that scary basement."

Johnny shrunk back. "You don't have to do that."

She pushed it into his hand. "It's okay, really. I'll just tell my mother that I lost it, and she'll get another cut."

"But you don't even know me."

"You don't look too threatening, and you're a lot nicer to talk to than the other squatters."

"Wow, thanks." He slid the key in a pocket. "So, like, if I wanted to get a few things to eat, you know, for when I'm just hanging out in there, where would I go?"

Lily popped up. "There's a supermarket on Broadway. C'mon, I'll show you."

In the store, Johnny grabbed a basket, which he filled with toiletries, candles, matches and some food.

"You're gonna need roach spray," Lily said, following behind him.

"Huh?"

"There's a lot of roaches. Rats too, but they mostly stay in the basement." She took his arm and pulled him toward the correct aisle.

After checking out, they headed back to the building. Lily carried one of the bags. "You got a big family, huh?"

Johnny focused on the sidewalk. "Yeah."

"And they fight a lot?"

"Um-hm, a *lot*."

"My parents used to, too. It's probably why my dad left. My mom can be a real cunt. Now she just yells at me instead." She expelled a disgruntled cough. "So, I get it, the whole wanting to get away thing. And I'm not gonna tell anyone."

Johnny looked at her. "Thanks. I mean it."

They climbed to the top floor and into the apartment, where Johnny set the bags on the counter.

"Good choice," said Lily, doing a quick tour. "This is definitely one of the better ones because the bums won't usually climb this high. And the guy at the end of the hall? He must have a job where he needs to travel or something because I hardly ever see him. There's a lady up here, too, but she's pretty old, so she only goes out when she has to. Sometimes she'll toss me a buck for helping her schlep her groceries up the stairs."

"You know everybody, don't you?"

Lily shrugged. "You gonna stay here all night?"

"I haven't decided." He bit his lip. "Maybe."

Lily's face lit up. "I'll be right back." She ran out of the apartment.

Jesus, what is up with that girl? While she was gone, Johnny lit a candle and set it on the living room floor, then brought his soap, toothbrush and paste to the bathroom sink.

Lily returned moments later with a blanket and a towel. "Here, I snuck these out of the house. My mother won't miss them, you know, just *in case* you decide to stay."

"Are you sure?"

She foisted the items into Johnny's arms. "Yeah, but I gotta go 'cause I'm supposed to be in by eight."

"Okay, thanks. I guess I'll see you around."

"Oh, one quick thing."

"What?"

"How old are you?"

"Thirteen."

"Good."

"Why is that good?"

"Because I'm fifteen, and I didn't want it to be awkward."

"What would be awkward?"

Lily walked over and kissed Johnny's mouth. "That," she said, turning to leave with a bounce in her step.

Johnny stood a moment, trying to sort out his emotions. They were all good. Eventually, his hunger snapped him out of it. He ate some bread and peanut butter with a can of Yoo-hoo while pacing around. Bending over, he peeked into the hallway through the hole where the front door's cylinder lock had been removed. He balled up a piece of the paper grocery bag and wedged it into the opening. Since the bathroom had the only door with a lock, he decided to sleep there. He moved the candle to the toilet tank, washed, brushed his teeth, then folded Lily's blanket lengthwise to make a thin mattress inside the tub. The towel he used as a pillow.

After opening the window, he blew out the candle and lay listening to the sounds of the city. It was not quiet, like his neighborhood in Miami. Here, there was always some distant siren, traffic noise or loud conversation going on, but Johnny found it comforting. His old house was too quiet—a forced quiet, because his parents, Miguel and Aylin, had no tolerance for disruptions. Johnny relished whatever was the opposite of that.

CHAPTER TWO

The jolt of anxiety that normally smacked Johnny awake every morning was notably absent as his eyes fluttered open inside his porcelain bed. He sat up to see a large blond-colored cockroach perched on the rim of the sink by the toothpaste. It seemed to be looking right at him with antennas swirling. "Oh yeah? You think so?" He climbed out of the tub, tore off a piece of toilet paper and crushed it. After tossing the carcass in the toilet, he peed on it. "You, I can handle."

Johnny hung the blanket over the door and turned on the faucets. There was no shower curtain, but he managed to bathe without spilling too much water. It would be nice to have clean clothes, but he planned to grab his things from the park later.

Toweling off, Johnny looked around for a good place to hide some money. He found a broken floorboard in the bedroom closet where he stuffed several twenties. The smaller denominations he folded and slid in his pocket.

More roaches were crawling around on the counter near his food. He sprayed them with Raid, but some of the bigger ones managed to withstand a direct hit and staggered behind the counter. As he was spritzing into the crevices, there was a tapping on the apartment's door, and Johnny tensed up. He set down the spray and tiptoed closer.

"Are you up?" Lily's hushed voice was saying.

He exhaled and opened the door.

She stood in the hall. Her hair looked washed and combed, and she had chosen a prettier blouse and shorts than the day before. She held a small stack of books. "I was wondering when you'd wake up."

"Why, what time is it?"

"Like nine-something."

"That late? I musta slept good. Come in."

She followed Johnny inside. "I brought you these books to read in case you get bored up here with no TV and stuff. There's a puzzle book, too, and a pen." She set them all on the floor in the living room. "Don't worry about marking it up. I've got plenty. My favorites are the circle-a-word."

"Wow, thanks. That's really nice of you."

"No sweat. I gotta help my grandmother with the shopping right now, but I'll be back later, in case you want to do something. Just come by my apartment if you don't see me. It's 2C."

"Okay. Cool." And off she went, leaving Johnny standing there. As nice as she was, Johnny would still have to be careful. He shook off the thought, pulled the YMCA application from his pocket, and began filling it out with Lily's pen. He got stuck where it wanted his parents' names. Avalon, the name he'd spit out when the clerk asked, could come from many different places, but he guessed his parents should at least have Latin-sounding first names. They also needed to be ones he'd remember if quizzed on the fly. He settled on Juan and Maria.

On the ground floor, he stopped at the rows of mailboxes. Some were intact, but others had been vandalized. The one for 6F had a broken lock, a bent door, and a missing hinge, but it could still close. Johnny thought it was perfect. Mail could be delivered, and he could retrieve it without a key. He tore off a piece of paper, wrote Avalon, and slipped it in the slot. Satisfied and on a mission, he jumped on a downtown A train.

At 59th Street, Johnny headed back to the YMCA, but there was a different woman at the desk. He handed her the application and flashed his card, but she barely looked at him, so he went inside to find the karate classes. There was a session already in progress, but it was all adults. Some wore the traditional uniform with purple or brown belts. Way above his league. Johnny slipped in and sat on the floor in the back to watch.

The next class was Johnny's age group, so he joined in. The instructor was not as enthusiastic as the one he had known in Miami, but some of the students were entertaining, razzing each other with insults during the warmup. Johnny joined in with their banter and earned respect because he threw powerful kicks and was good at deflection.

When the session was over, he went to the lobby to get a copy of the scheduled classes. As he was leaving, he passed two white boys sitting on the steps. One was thin, with layered brown hair highlighted by the sun. The other was a bit taller, with darker hair and eyes.

"Hey, that's the guy from karate," said the taller one.

"You got some good moves, man," said the other.

Johnny faced them. "Thanks, it was fun."

"Are you new? I haven't seen you before."

"Kind of. I was going to a different branch for a while." *Not really a lie.* "Do you guys come here a lot?"

"Mostly in the summer," he said. "My name is Jarrod. This is Clyde." Clyde waved.

"I'm Johnny."

Jarrod's brown eyes looked wiser than his years, and he spoke with confidence. Clyde seemed less hardened.

"Do you live around here?" asked Clyde.

"No, I'm up on one-eighty."

"Shit, that's far," said Jarrod. "Isn't there a Y further uptown?"

Johnny shrugged.

"We both live in Chelsea," said Clyde. "There's a branch on 14th, but we like this instructor better."

Johnny wasn't sure what Chelsea was.

"We're gonna go smoke a joint. You wanna come?"

Johnny had tried marijuana twice before in Miami and liked how it made everything seem less important, but it was never worth the added paranoia he would feel when returning home. "Sure, why not?"

The trio walked across the street into Central Park and lined up on a bench. Clyde lit up, took a puff and passed it to Jarrod.

"Jesus, right here in the open?" Johnny whispered. "Don't you worry about someone seeing?"

Jarrod coughed out a puff of smoke before passing the joint to Johnny. "In *this* city? Nobody gives a fuck."

"It's true," said Clyde. "I see people lighting up everywhere. Even on the subway."

16

Johnny took a small hit before handing it back. "You guys do this a lot?"

Clyde smirked. "To be honest, we just discovered it last week."

Jarrod burst out laughing. "Yeah! His slutty older sister had three joints in a pack of cigarettes in her pants pocket, but she put that shit in the hamper. It was Clyde's turn to do the laundry, so we scored!" They all laughed. It seemed much funnier than it should have been.

"This is the last one, though," said Clyde. "But it's been entertaining as hell to watch her tear up the apartment looking for it." He stubbed out the roach and stored it in the matchbook.

"How long have you known each other?" asked Johnny.

"Not long," said Jarrod. "We go to the same junior high, so we've seen each other around, but we didn't really start hanging out together until this summer."

"Where do you go to school?" asked Clyde. "Uptown?"

Lying required more effort because Johnny's brain was muffled. "I was, but I'm looking to transfer."

"What grade are you going into?"

"Seventh."

"Cool," said Jarrod. "Us too."

They sat on the bench for a while, telling jokes and making fun of the people passing by until Clyde realized it was getting late. "Shit. I'm supposed to be home to babysit my little sister." He stood and looked at Jarrod. "You riding downtown with me?"

"Yeah. I'll hang at your place while you watch her." Jarrod turned to Johnny. "You wanna come?"

Johnny was tempted but wanted to retrieve his backpack before dark. "I'd like to, but I probably better be getting home myself."

"That's cool. What're you doing tomorrow?" asked Jarrod. "You want to meet up?"

"Sure. Where?"

"Let's go to Washington Square Park," said Clyde. "You know it, right? Off 4th Street."

"Yeah." Johnny would look it up in the guidebook. "What time?"

"Like eleven? We'll call you when we're leaving."

17

"My phone doesn't always work," said Johnny. "Like, when my parents don't pay the bill. Can I call you guys?"

"You better call Clyde's house. My parents are too drunk to answer the phone." Jarrod rolled his eyes. "It's a long story."

"Whatever you say." Johnny handed a pen to Clyde, who wrote his number on the YMCA flier before they said their goodbyes.

Still buzzed from the joint, Johnny smiled as he walked uptown along the park's thoroughfare, which was bustling with cars, bikes and joggers. He liked this city, the crowds, the chaos and the anonymity, how everyone was too busy with their own shit to be concerned about him.

After a few minutes, he veered onto the bridle path, where the foliage was thicker, and spotted the tree with his backpack. Beneath it was a woman with a Great Dane as tall as her waist. It sniffed and circled at the end of the leash before squatting to defecate. Johnny made a wide berth and then doubled back. The dog kicked a flurry of leaves over its mountainous excrement until it noticed Johnny and lunged, almost pulling the woman off her feet.

"Zelda! No!" She jerked the leash to engage the choke collar, and the dog settled. "It's okay, she's friendly."

Johnny stood still. "Yeah. I'm sure."

Once the dog started following a scent down the path with the woman in tow, Johnny shimmied up the tree. He looped the backpack's straps through his arms and climbed down, careful to avoid the dog shit.

He cut across to a narrower, more secluded footpath that looked like it led to the street. As he walked, he sensed someone behind him. He marched faster, but the person quickened their pace. Johnny stole a glance. It was a sickly-looking teenager.

"Hey, kid, can you spare a few bucks?"

Johnny lengthened his stride. "I don't have any money."

"What's in the bag?"

"Nothing. Just clothes."

He grabbed Johnny's T-shirt. "C'mon, kid, gimme some change?"

"Get your fucking hands off me!" As Johnny faced the kid, he was hit with a familiar jolt of emotions: claustrophobia, terror, vulnerability—everything he hadn't felt since leaving home. The panic made him worry he might black out. But as Johnny looked at the twitchy adolescent, he had a realization. His hands weren't tied, he wasn't trapped in a cellar, and this was not his psychotic brother.

Johnny dropped his backpack and swung his fist into the teen's forehead. Before the guy could respond, Johnny kicked him in the shin. The junkie snapped out of it and swung a fist. Johnny ducked but caught the teen's fingernails on his cheek. The guy pivoted back, windmilling his arms. A flailing fist caught Johnny's temple, more by accident than intent, so Johnny grabbed the assailant's elbow, using his own momentum to flip him to the ground. *Wow, that worked!*

The junkie scrambled to his feet and ambled away, cursing. Johnny picked up his pack and looked around to see if anyone was watching. The path was empty, so he continued on.

On the train, Johnny recalled the incident. Even though the violence paled in comparison to what he had faced at home, it was still troubling. But he liked how it felt to hit someone. Still, he couldn't stop worrying about that moment of panic. He didn't want to start losing chunks of time again, especially here, where he risked being caught by authorities and sent back home.

On his block, he hugged the buildings' shadows, hoping Lily had already settled in for the night, but as he rounded the corner to the courtyard, there she was, sitting on the front steps.

Johnny sat next to her. "Hey."

"Hey." She barely looked up.

"Aren't you supposed to be home for dinner?"

"My mother's in one of her moods. Screamed at me for being under her feet while she was trying to cook."

"That sucks."

"I was just trying to help, ask about her day, but she treats me like a fucking mosquito." Lily picked at some crud on her shoe. "So, where've *you* been all day?"

"Around."

"I didn't see you."

"Yeah, well…"

"I was worried."

Johnny sighed. "Look, I come, I go. You don't need to be waiting around for me all the time." He realized it sounded harsh as he said it, especially after what had just happened with her mother. But he hadn't run all the way from Miami only to be answering to a fifteen-year-old girl with a crush.

She pouted.

"Lily, I didn't mean it that way."

"You *said* it that way."

"I did." *She's honest. I gotta respect that.* "I'm sorry. I had a bad day."

"I can see that by your face."

"Is it that noticeable?"

"Yeah. Pretty noticeable." She turned away like she didn't care.

"Some guy tried to mug me."

Her concern appeared. "Are you okay?"

"Yeah. I chased him away, but I'm still pissed off about it. I didn't mean to take it out on you."

"I guess I'm just everyone's little fucking mosquito."

"Stop it." Johnny took her hand. "You've been helping me out a lot, and I really appreciate it. And we'll hang out, I promise."

She perked up. "What are you doing tomorrow?"

Johnny grimaced. "Tomorrow's not good. I got shit to do."

"Right. Of course, you do." Lily took her hand away and got up. "It's probably safe for me to go back in now."

"Wait." He stood to block her path, putting his hands on her elbows. When she didn't pull away, he stepped closer. It had been so long since human contact didn't elicit fear and revulsion that he barely recognized the urge for it. He wrapped his arms around Lily. Unsure what to do with his head, he turned it away to rest an ear on her shoulder. She did likewise. When it became awkward, they both shed each other off, and she left.

CHAPTER THREE

Johnny got out of the subway at West 4th Street and walked around to get a feel for the area. Sixth Avenue was busy and loud, with four lanes of traffic, but the side streets were quieter, dotted with shops, restaurants and nightclubs. He noted how each section of this city had its own character and vibe, and he liked the contrast. A person could disappear a hundred times over.

He stopped at a phone booth and dialed Clyde's number. A female voice answered.

"Is Clyde there?"

"Hang on." The phone dropped, and she hollered, "Hey, asswipe, it's for you!"

After some muffled background sounds, Clyde picked up. "Hello?"

"Your mom sure sounds polite."

Clyde laughed. "You dick, that's my sister—one of them, anyway."

"You coming out?"

"You're there already?"

"Yeah."

"Cool. I'll grab Jarrod, and we'll be over in a bit."

While Johnny waited, he took a lap around the park. Washington Square spanned ten acres, with a seventy-seven-foot, free-standing marble arch by the Fifth Avenue entrance and a large fountain in the center that was shallow enough for kids to splash around. Tree-lined pathways flanked with benches shot off toward all four corners, leading to a public bathroom and two kids' playgrounds. Being a Sunday, lots of folks began trickling in to enjoy the warm sun. Johnny noticed that they ranged from wealthy to homeless, tourists and bikers, Jesus freaks and hustlers, all of varying ages and ethnicities. *And not a single one of them gives a flying fuck about me.*

A half-hour later, Clyde and Jarrod showed up by the fountain. "Yo, what happened to you?" said Jarrod, pointing at Johnny's face.

"I had a little scuffle on the way home yesterday."

"No shit," said Clyde. "Are you okay?"

Johnny laughed. "Yeah. I dealt with it."

"This city's getting crazy," said Jarrod. "If you wanna protect yourself, you gotta act loonier than the loonies." He flailed around, wagging his tongue, making the other two laugh.

A middle-aged Jamaican with waist-long dreads and a red, green and yellow cap ambled over. "Loose joints, Colombian gold, got good sinse', good sinse'. What you kids need?"

Johnny cocked his head. "Excuse me?"

Jarrod waved the man away. "We're all set. Thanks."

"What the fuck was that?" Johnny asked.

"You better get used to it," said Clyde. "Dealers are like cockroaches in this park."

Within a minute, a pudgy white guy in a tie-dyed shirt walked past, mumbling, "Window Pane, blotter, mescaline."

Clyde outstretched his arms. "What'd I tell you?"

Johnny grinned. "At least we know where to get another joint."

"My sister says the Rastas have the best weed."

"The same sister who called you an asswipe?"

Jarrod hissed. "That's mild for her. His sister's got a mouth and a half." He grinned. "At least that's what half the men in Hoboken say."

"You're talking shit about *my* family?" Clyde turned to Johnny. "This dude's parents drink *all* the time."

"He's not lying," said Jarrod.

"And when his mother's tipsy, she gets affectionate. It's creepy."

"What's your father do about it?" Johnny asked.

"He's too messed up to leave the recliner." Jarrod rolled his eyes. "I got an uncle—my mother's brother—he lives with us, too, but it's only a two-bedroom apartment, so he sleeps on the couch. And he's on the methadone program, so he's nodding out half the fucking time. I hate it. It's like living in a house full of zombies." He patted Clyde's shoulder. "That's why I'm over at his place so much."

"He should just move in full-time," said Clyde. "My mother wouldn't notice."

"Why? Does she drink a lot, too?" Johnny asked.

"No," said Jarrod. "She's just out busting her ass for her kids. I love her!"

"She's got three jobs," Clyde explained, "so me and my sisters help out as much as we can."

"Where's your dad?"

"That asshole fucked off years ago, but we're better off without him. He was useless."

"I joke about his family," Jarrod said. "But the truth is they're pretty tight, and at least *they* can get out of bed in the morning."

"You must have a big place."

"It's only a three-bedroom, but we make it work. Tiffany—the seventeen-year-old slut—and Claire, who's fifteen, share one room. Cecily's ten and sleeps in my mom's room, but she has it to herself half the time because my mother's always at work. I lucked out by having a dick because I get my own room."

"That's right," said Jarrod. "You don't want to be frightening those girls with your no-hair little ball sac, now, do you?"

"You must be talking about your own shit because I'm like a yeti down there!" Clyde grabbed his crotch. "A yeti crossed with an anaconda!"

"Yeah, right." Jarrod turned to Johnny. "So? What's your deal? You got some sad-ass broken home story, too?"

"My parents work a lot, too, and they're always crabby, so basically, I avoid them."

"Are they Puerto Rican?"

Johnny didn't think the truth would hurt him here. "They're both from Colombia, but my mother's half-Turkish."

"You speak fluent Spanish?"

"Yeah, Turkish, too. My parents want me to know as many languages as possible, so they always spoke to me in one or the other since I was a baby. I guess it's easier to pick up that way."

23

"How'd you learn English then," asked Clyde, "in school?"

Johnny nodded. "C'mon, let's take a walk, move around a bit."

They wandered the neighborhood, nosing around the head shops and electronics stores. Johnny stopped in front of Blimpie's. "You guys hungry?"

"Yeah, kinda," said Clyde. "But I don't have any money."

"Me neither," said Jarrod.

Johnny pulled a ten from his pocket. "I can get it."

"How'd you get money?"

"I helped a neighbor move a bunch of shit, and he gave me this."

"Cool. We'll get you back one of these days."

"I'm not worried about it. I know you will."

They each ordered subs and drinks, then sat at a table to eat and talk. When they got on the topic of music and who their favorite bands were, Clyde mentioned that he had been taking guitar lessons the last few years and that Jarrod played the drums. "But *my* parents won't cut into their booze money for *me* to get lessons." Jarrod rolled his eyes. "Still, I save my allowance and get some now and again, or I'll nab money from my mother's purse when she's passed out."

"He keeps a snare at my place so we can have these half-assed jam sessions." Clyde laughed. "And he's not above using some pots and pans."

Jarrod looked at Johnny. "You play something?"

"I used to take piano lessons, but it's been a while."

It was late afternoon when they returned to the park through the southeast corner. There was a circular area shaded by trees, with benches and a dozen granite tables with inlaid chessboards. A homeless woman surrounded by bags had usurped one table to rest her head. A family was having a picnic on another, but the majority were being used by people who had brought their own timers and pieces and sat playing, rapt in concentration.

A crowd had gathered around one table, and the three friends squeezed in to watch. A black man in his fifties with a cropped salt-and-pepper afro was playing a young Japanese guy in an NYU T-shirt.

"Come on, my brother," said the black man, capturing a rook with his pawn. "How'd you not see that coming?" He tapped the timer. "Motherfuckers saw *that* move coming up in the Bronx!"

24

The crowd chuckled, but his opponent remained focused, sliding a bishop across the board.

"Okay. I see how you do. You wanna come at the Brick like that? Make me work defense?" He slid a knight over to protect his king. "Not bad for a grad student."

Clyde tapped Johnny's arm. "We've seen this guy before. He's good."

"He's a trash-talker."

"Yep. His matches are never boring."

A murmur erupted from the crowd, and Clyde and Johnny turned back to see the student's king under attack.

"HAH!" said the Brick after a few more moves. "I hope you brought your footy pajamas 'cause I just put your ass to bed!"

The opponent smiled, shaking his head. "You got me again, B." He reached over to shake the Brick's hand before throwing down a twenty.

The Brick stood up to stretch and pocketed the bill, then brushed off his apricot slacks and straightened the wide lapels of his brown paisley shirt. A man in a tracksuit with a darker complexion and corn-rolled hair handed him a tall can in a brown paper bag. "Thank you, Russ." The Brick took a long pull as the crowd dissipated, but when two women walked by, his head turned. "Mm *hmm*, you ladies are looking *fine* today."

They smiled at him and kept walking.

"That was fun," said Jarrod. "But we should probably be getting home for dinner."

"He's right," said Clyde. "But let's meet at my place tomorrow. I've gotta babysit in the morning, but we could hang out after." He looked at Johnny. "I'm on West 28th. Call when you get out of the subway. I'll give you directions."

Johnny nodded. "Sounds good."

Once Clyde and Jarrod left, Johnny doubled back to the chess tables. It was dusk, and the vibe in the park was shifting as families and sunbathers were replaced by the derelict fringe. Still, Johnny wanted to watch some more of the Brick's matches. He was as curious about the social scene surrounding the tables as the game itself.

The crowd was thinner, and the game was not as animated as he played his friend, Russ. Different people breezed by, slapping skin with the Brick or putting a word in his ear, and all of them referred to him in the third person, calling him the Brick or simply B. Johnny noticed that Russ was the only one who called him Rick.

After a while, the Brick's eyes singled out Johnny in the group of observers. "What's your name, son?"

Johnny looked around. "Me?"

"*Sí, amigo,*" he said, capturing Russ's bishop with a knight "*¿Cómo te llamas?*"

"Johnny."

"That ain't your real name."

A ripple of fear shot through Johnny. *How would he know that?*

The Brick's eyes narrowed. "I mean, that's a pretty Anglo-Saxon name, and you look a little"—he paused—"other than that."

He smiled as he said it, which made Johnny relax. "Maybe I *am* a little 'other.'"

"I hear you, man. Where you from?"

Say anything but Miami. "Colombia."

"Ah, Colombiano. That's cool. I got a lot of Colombian friends. Maybe I know your parents." He picked off one of Russ's pawns.

"I doubt it."

The Brick feigned insult. "You don't know who I know." He hissed through his teeth.

Johnny remained straight-faced. "I don't think you know them because they're dead."

"Oh, shit, son. I'm sorry. I was just messing with you."

Johnny maintained a sullen expression, letting him have a moment of regret, but then grinned. "Nah, I'm messing with you, too. They're not dead, just boring. They wouldn't know anyone cool like you."

The Brick looked at him with a knitted brow, then laughed and hard. "No shit! You got me, you little motherfucker. You're all right with me, Colombiano." He went back to defeating his friend, chuckling and shaking his head. When the match was done, he stood up and put a hand on Johnny's shoulder. "See ya 'round, kid." He sauntered out of the park.

CHAPTER FOUR

Johnny woke in the dark, pressed in the kitchen corner, hugging his knees. The shadowy details of a dream dangled just beyond reach, but the feelings it generated were very real. They soured Johnny's stomach so intensely that he scrambled to the toilet. There wasn't much to throw up, but after dry heaving several times, he stepped into the shower. The water on his face made him feel a little better, but there was still an urge to get out of the apartment and into the street.

The sun was rising as Johnny boarded the number 1 train. He rode it to the last stop at South Ferry and wandered around Battery Park. After a while, he bought a bagel and coffee from a vendor, hoping the caffeine would wrest him from his fatigue. He sat on a bench overlooking the water and ate.

The last thing he remembered was falling asleep in the tub. Did he leave the apartment? How long was he in the kitchen? The frustration of not knowing made his head hurt. He knew his family was responsible for these amnesic episodes. But he was gone now, so why was it still happening?

Johnny tried to push the thoughts away, but his mind kept drifting back to the first time it happened.

It was the last day of fourth grade, and Johnny was excited for summer vacation. He walked the handful of blocks from his school, passing under the expressway toward 28th Avenue. The grades on his report card were perfect, the teachers' comments glowing, and he couldn't wait to show his parents.

As Johnny rounded the corner of his street, his pace faltered. It wasn't even conscious anymore, just something his body did, like blinking or swallowing. It had started six or so months before when things with his brother got even worse.

Johnny walked by the modest homes that lined the narrow road, with their ornamental mailboxes, flowerpots and lawn statues in an attempt to dress up the scorched Miami grass. But not the Álvarezes'. Their ranch-style house, which sat on a cul-de-sac at the bottom of the dead end, had the potential to complement the rest of the neighborhood, but Johnny's parents had no interest in wasting money on landscaping and paint. The overgrown yard backed up to an empty lot. Johnny and his brother, Orlando, who was six years older, used to play there. They would chase each other around and shoot targets with slingshots, but that was before.

Though the exterior of the house was neglected, inside was meticulous. Almost sterile in its simplicity. Johnny's parents didn't tolerate clutter or dirt, and he and his brother had been made aware of that early on. The floors were spotless, the furniture dusted and everything was obsessively symmetrical. No paintings or family photos hung on the walls, nor were there any other decorative items.

Johnny opened the front door, taking a moment to read the mood. He could tell by sounds and shadows that his father, Miguel, was at his usual spot at the kitchen table reading the paper. His mother, Aylin, was preparing a meal for him to take to his second job as a gas station attendant. There was no sign of Orlando, which meant he must still be locked in the cellar. How many months had it been since Johnny had seen him? Four? He used to be allowed up if he behaved, but his impulsive tendencies had grown hard to control.

Johnny removed his backpack and hung it up before pulling out his report card. The feeling of pride pushed away the other thoughts as he marched into the kitchen.

"Mama, Papá, I got my grades," he said in Spanish. "All *As*."

Miguel lowered the paper, but his expression did not mirror Johnny's news. His dark eyes were hardened into slits. He would be so handsome if his face wasn't always distorted by anger. "Javier, how many times have I told you not to leave your wet bath towel on the bed?"

Johnny's stomach clenched. "I—I'm sorry. I was rushing to get to school this morning and forgot." He switched to Turkish to repeat his plea to his mother, but Aylin turned away to face the counter.

Miguel folded the newspaper in half, making sure all the pages were even, and set it on the Formica table. "This is the third time this month. What did I tell you the last time?"

Johnny choked back a convulsive breath. "You s-said that if—if it happened again, there would be consequences."

"That's right, Javier." His lips squeezed into a distorted smile. "I told you there would be consequences." Miguel's open hand smacked the table hard. The sound echoed through the kitchen. "Aylin! Put the boy in the cellar!"

Johnny's eyes widened. "What?"

Aylin looked at Miguel, confused.

"Do it now!" He slapped the table a second time.

Aylin dropped the food she was preparing and stormed to where her paralyzed son was standing. She grabbed him by his shirt sleeve and dragged him away, his report card falling where he stood. Aylin pulled him across the living room and to the hallway, holding on with one hand while unlatching the cellar door's deadbolt with the other.

Johnny begged her in Turkish to please give him one more chance as he struggled to get away, but she was stronger. She swung open the door to put him on the other side, but Johnny resisted, so she shoved him. The cellar had no landing, only rickety stairs constructed by planks, with two-by-fours for handrails. Johnny tumbled backward down the first few steps before grabbing the railing, stopping himself midway to the bottom. The door slammed shut, and the bolt latched.

Johnny regained his balance, shaking off the shock of what just happened, only to realize that his sixteen-year-old brother was standing at the bottom of the stairs. His arms were folded, and his round face lifted in a combination of curiosity and glee. He was paler and doughier than the last time Johnny had seen him.

Orlando coughed out a laugh. "What the fuck is this?"

Johnny plopped down on the middle step. "I guess I pissed Dad off."

"No shit? Are you here for good? Does this mean I have a roommate?"

The thought rattled Johnny to the core. "He didn't say."

"Great. I could use a little company."

"Yeah, I mean, I guess. How've you been doing down here?"

The glimmer in Orlando's light brown eyes intensified. "Thank you for asking, little brother. I'm fan-fucking-tastic!" He threw a hand over his heart. "But now that *you're* here, you can share in the delights of the Casa de Miguel, too!"

Johnny pushed up a step to put a little more distance between him and his brother.

"Why don't you come on down? Let me give you the grand tour, you know, since you never *bothered* to visit me before."

"I would have, really, but Mom and Dad wouldn't let me." The lie didn't help. Orlando bounded up the stairs, grabbed Johnny by the arm and yanked him down. Johnny clung to the railing with his free hand to reduce the impact. Once they reached the cement floor, Orlando released his grip, and Johnny rolled to a standing position, bracing himself for whatever was coming.

Orlando spun around, flailing his arms like a showroom model. "Welcome to the palatial estate that our considerate father constructed. He works at a textile mill all day and pumps gas all night, yet he still made time to turn what used to be a dumpy shithole of a cellar into a dumpy shithole of a prison!"

Orlando laughed. Johnny's eyes swept the room. It was never very inviting before, just a damp, dusty space made of crudely poured cement, where his parents stored some old, mismatched pieces of furniture, but that had all been removed, and the one ground-level window was now cemented over. Miguel had also hung a few pieces of plywood and hired a plumber to install a sink, tub and toilet.

Orlando followed Johnny's gaze. "Yes, my own bathroom! Can you believe it? And our parents are such innovators. They went with the daring white-tile motif in there." He stuck his face in Johnny's to recapture his attention. "And look!" He then straightened to indicate his bed, a dresser and a small TV on a wooden box. Nearby sat a mini refrigerator and several stacks of books. "The master boudoir. Isn't it lovely? I'm sure you'll recognize some of the accoutrements from my former abode." He knitted his brows, pressing a fist on his chin. "What have they done with my bedroom anyway?"

Johnny shrugged. "Nothing, really. It's still kinda half empty. But Mom put a bunch of those foreign books in there from when her family lived in other countries."

A smile appeared on Orlando's face. "Those nursery rhymes and stories she collected?"

"Yeah. The ones she'd read to us all the time and have us read back."

"When she still gave a shit about teaching us languages." Orlando's frown returned. "Before she became just as big an asshole as Dad."

Johnny sighed. "Yeah."

"She brought some down here, too, with these other books, so I can brush up on my French and Portuguese." Orlando rolled his eyes. "You know, just *in case* I'm visited by any foreign dignitaries."

Sadness eclipsed Johnny's fear as he remembered how special it used to feel to have Aylin's attention. "I still read them sometimes when I'm alone and don't have anything else to do."

Orlando's eyes narrowed. "You mean when you're being ignored and neglected? Call it what it is, little brother. All our mother does for *me* is set meals on the stairs and come down once a week to clean, while our loving father stands by with a baseball bat to make sure I don't try to kill them."

Orlando laughed in a tone Johnny had never heard before, and it made him shiver.

"But enough of this memory lane crap." Orlando waved the air. "Over here is the best part." Orlando walked to a hand-built workbench that was set against a wall. It used to hold an assortment of tools, but Miguel had removed anything Orlando could have used to break out. All that remained were some mismatched nuts and bolts and odd pieces of chain and rope.

Orlando turned to Johnny with his arms akimbo. "What could we *possibly* do with all of this?"

Johnny swallowed hard. "I don't know."

"Ah-HA!" Orlando grabbed a coil of solid-braid cotton rope. "I have a great idea!"

Johnny backed toward the stairs. "Orlando, please—don't."

He lurched at Johnny and tackled him to the ground. It wasn't hard. He was much larger and outweighed him by fifty pounds. He held Johnny down while groping for his wrists and tied them together in front of his waist.

"You're *my* prisoner now." He scratched his head. "But what should we *do*?"

Johnny pleaded to be untied, but Orlando ignored him, perusing the workbench instead. He grabbed a piece of chain and whipped it over an exposed beam running across the unfinished, seven-foot-high ceiling, then secured the end links with the top half of an S hook. He picked up his brother with one arm, lifted him toward the chain, and looped the rope over the bottom half of the hook. He stood back to admire his work as his brother dangled by his bound hands.

Orlando pushed him and watched him swing. Johnny yelled for help. "That's a brilliant idea. Scream some more. We both know how our parents *love* noise! They'll never let you out now!" Orlando started whooping and yelling too.

Johnny knew his brother was right. If he stood any chance of being released, he needed to be quiet. "Okay. I'll stop if you will."

"I thought you'd see it my way. Whatever games we *do* play down here, you'd better keep your fucking mouth shut, understand?"

Johnny nodded. Orlando drew back his fist and punched him in the stomach. Spit flew from Johnny's mouth, but he managed to stifle the noise fighting to accompany it. Orlando stood back and grinned. "Smart boy."

Johnny watched his brother rifle around the cluttered workbench while muttering in a medley of languages. The rope cut into his wrists. His shoulders ached, and he became light-headed. Johnny closed his eyes, wishing to be anywhere else. Because it was the last day of school, no one would miss him for a long time. And if any friends came looking for him, his parents would probably tell them that he went to stay with cousins in Tampa. The same thing they had told Orlando's teachers.

"Yes! Perfect!"

Johnny opened his eyes to see that his brother was displaying an old X-Acto knife. "What are you going to do with that?"

"First, I need to see if it works." He lifted Johnny's T-shirt and drew the box cutter toward his stomach. The blade looked sharp despite its worn aluminum handle. Johnny kicked out, knocking the knife from his brother's grip. It flew across the room, landing by the bed. Orlando looked up at Johnny with rage as all the energy in the room shifted. At least, when he was being sarcastic, it indicated some attachment to reality. Now Orlando just looked devoid of human emotion. Johnny's terror overwhelmed him; warm urine trickled down his leg.

Orlando grabbed some grease-stained rags from the workbench to cover the puddle, then went to retrieve the knife. His movements were slow and deliberate. He stood where Johnny was suspended and sliced his shirt from neck to waist, exposing his torso. Johnny could barely breathe; his brain couldn't handle it. His thoughts and hearing became muffled, and his skin tingled. He noticed a crack in the cement wall a few yards away and marveled at how it looked like a lightning bolt. He allowed it to draw all of his attention while the rest of his senses evaporated.

The next thing Johnny remembered was sitting on the top step of the cellar, hunched in a ball. The cut halves of his shirt were pulled around him, and he could feel that the fabric was crisp with dried blood. It wasn't cold, yet he couldn't stop shaking.

Johnny heard heavy breathing from below and figured his brother had fallen asleep. The only light still on came from the bathroom, but it barely illuminated the stairwell. He ran a finger over his chest and felt several welts. It caused him to convulse, which made his breathing louder, so he stopped. He needed to be silent.

After a while, he heard footsteps that stopped on the other side of the threshold. The lock unlatched, and the door opened. Light flooded into the cellar as Aylin stood looking down at him. Johnny was afraid to move, not knowing what she expected. But then she motioned with her head for him to come out. He rose and stepped into the hallway behind her as she bolted the door. "Get cleaned up and go to bed," she said in Turkish before marching to her and Miguel's room.

Johnny tiptoed across the hall to the bathroom. He would have liked to soak in the bath but couldn't risk the noise it would make. Instead, he took a cloth, soaked it in cold water and patted the dried blood. He counted eleven slices on his chest and torso, but his brother had used care. The cuts weren't that serious, just deep enough to make him bleed. The greater pain was on his raw wrists from hanging by the rope and from being pulled down the stairs. Finally, he pulled off his pants to mop his soiled legs.

He crept to his room, gently closed the door and changed into pajama pants. He put a black T-shirt on under the pajama top. If he bled during the night, he didn't want to anger his mother by soiling the sheets. He threw the sliced shirt into his trash can, put the pants in the hamper, and lay in bed. His clock showed it was almost midnight. How much time had he lost? He was thrown in the cellar around five o'clock, maybe another hour of listening to Orlando rant, but then what? Was he hanging from the rafters all that time? Why couldn't he recall being untied or going to sit by the door? He pushed his brain to remember, but it only caused anxiety, so he let it go.

CHAPTER FIVE

Johnny called Clyde as he neared 28th Street and was told to come to number 548, just east of 11th Avenue. He found the six-story walk-up and pushed through the heavy door. Inside was a small vestibule with rows of names and buzzers. Johnny found the name DeMarco beside 4G and pushed the button. Seconds later, a shrill, metallic rattle echoed throughout the space, startling him so badly that he barely opened the door in time. Once inside, he bounded upstairs and down a narrow hall to Clyde's apartment, where the door had been left ajar.

Clyde stood at the kitchen counter buttering some toast. "What's up? You want something?"

"No thanks, I'm cool." Johnny sat at the dining table that barely fit between the counters and cabinets. In the adjacent living room, a young girl sat on the floor watching cartoons and eating cereal. Another girl, who looked a bit older than Clyde, was at the far end of the apartment, blasting a radio and walking between rooms. The overlapping sounds were chaotic but welcoming.

Clyde sat next to Johnny with his plate. "Her down there? That's Claire. She's got some stupid birthday party to go to." He chomped on his toast as he spoke. "The one in front of the boob tube is Cecily. My even older sister, Tiffany, doesn't get home from work till two, so I'm stuck here babysitting till then."

"That's fine." Johnny looked around. The apartment was cluttered, with carpets and furniture worn from use. Otherwise, it was very clean.

The buzzer sounded, and Clyde stood. "That's Jarrod." He glided down the hallway in his socks to ring him up and then returned to the table. Moments later, Jarrod came through the door and plunked down across from Johnny. "What the fuck happened to you?"

"What?"

"You look like you haven't slept at all."

The comment made Johnny hesitate, which only heightened Jarrod's suspicion.

"Were you partying all night without us?"

"I hang out with the neighbor girl sometimes," Johnny said to deflect. "I think she's got a crush on me."

Jarrod slapped his hands on the table. "I was being sarcastic, but damn, you were up all night getting laid?"

Johnny couldn't help but grin. "Shut up, asshole, it's not like that!"

Clyde and Jarrod were poised to hear every detail when Claire emerged wearing a black-and-white striped dress. "Okay, freaks, I'm leaving. Don't forget to check Cecily once in a while to make sure she's breathing."

"I'll watch her with the same attention *you* did when babysitting." He turned to his friends. "Did I ever tell you about the time she left me in an elevator? In a department store."

"Poor Cecily is doomed," Claire said, shaking her head as she walked out the door.

"For fifteen minutes!" Clyde continued, loud enough so she'd still hear him in the hallway.

"Really? She left you in an elevator *that* long?" asked Jarrod.

Clyde waved off the question. "I want to hear what happened to Johnny and his hot neighbor last night."

Johnny grinned. "It was no big deal, really."

"I'll bet that's what *she* said," Jarrod blurted. He and Clyde slouched over the table, laughing.

Johnny rolled his eyes. "She's fifteen and lives in my building. We kissed once. "

"You're my hero," said Clyde. "Did she slip you the tongue?"

Jarrod patted his chest. "I've touched some tittie before."

"Bullshit," said Clyde. "When?"

"At school."

"Damn, I gotta get into some of your classes."

"The girl didn't *mean* for me to touch them. I did it when she wasn't paying attention and then pretended it was an accident."

"That still counts," said Clyde, and the others agreed.

When the conversation turned to music, Cecily got ushered to another room so the boys could commandeer the stereo. They brought out the guitar and drum and jammed along with Clyde's rock albums, swapping riffs and singing along until Tiffany plowed through the door, tossing her bags on the kitchen table. She was tall and thin, wearing a cut-off shirt with tight pants and high heels. Her face was accented with colorful makeup, and her bleached-blonde hair was teased up high.

"Who the fuck's this?" Tiffany jutted her chin at Johnny. "A third turd for your retarded little posse?"

Johnny smirked as Clyde made the introduction. "Johnny, this is Tiffany, the girl you've read about on every skanky bathroom wall from here to the Bronx."

"Eat shit, you little fuck. Where's Cess?"

"In Mom's room. And still breathing, last I checked."

"Are you nutsacks here for dinner? Mom left cash for take-out."

Clyde looked at his friends, and they nodded. "Yeah, we're all eating here."

"I'll order pizzas for six-thirty. If you're late, you're shit out of luck."

After Tiffany clomped off to her room, Clyde gave Johnny the scoop as they put everything away. "When my father left, she dropped out of school and got a cosmetology license to help pay the bills. She works at a salon and does some neighbors' hair on the side for cash." Clyde lowered his voice. "But she *does* like to party, which is why she's always so snarky. The bitch needs a nap!"

The three friends headed outside, where they peeked in stores and traded karate moves, migrating downtown toward Washington Square.

"You guys want to get some weed?" said Johnny.

"Sure," said Clyde. "It's the paying-for-it part I have trouble with."

"I got money."

"How've you always got money?" asked Jarrod.

37

"I had some saved up, but I'm gonna run out soon."

Clyde chuckled. "Then what?"

"Maybe I could snatch a few bucks from people in the park."

"We could help," said Jarrod.

Johnny nodded. "Sure, if we worked together, maybe we could pull off some scams."

"Cool," said Clyde. "Who would you hit? The musicians who play out here, with all that cash in their cases?"

"No musicians or poor people. I'd grab it from the ones who won't miss it so much. But I'd rather work for it. What if *we* learned some songs? I'll bet people would throw a lot of money at a bunch of kids, even if we were crap. We could get one of those little keyboards and some more drums."

"I'd be down for that," said Jarrod. "I don't mind sucking in front of a bunch of strangers if it gets us paid."

Clyde scrunched his face. "That would be an act for *Times* Square, not *Washington* Square."

Jarrod shoved him. "Shut up, you twat. You know what I meant."

Inside the park, they sat near the arch. "I got enough for a few joints," Johnny said. "Then we can share some with your sister."

"Why?" asked Clyde.

"Because she's gonna feed me and Jarrod, and we don't even live there."

"But that's my mother's money she's using anyway."

"So what? We should take care of the people who take care of us, right?"

"When did you become such a fucking philosopher?" said Jarrod.

"I'm not. There haven't been too many people in my life who gave a shit about me. When it happens, I want to do the right thing." He smirked. "Even if it means tossing a thin joint to a skanky ho."

While they sat, the Brick sauntered by. He noticed Johnny and swung over. "Hey Colombiano, what's shakin'?" He held out his palm, and Johnny slapped him five.

"Not much."

"Are these your brothers?" He sized up Clyde and Jarrod, who both looked puzzled.

"No, man, they're my friends." He introduced them.

"That's cool. In fact, it's better. Your friends are your family by choice. Most times, your blood relatives are just a royal pain in the ass anyway."

"I hear you."

"All right then, you cats take it easy now." And he continued on his path.

Johnny beamed as he strutted away. "Now *there's* a fucking philosopher."

"How do you suddenly know that guy?" Clyde asked.

"He's the dude from the chess tables, right?" said Jarrod.

"That's him. The Brick." Johnny kept watching the man as he stopped to consult with one of the black teenage joint-slingers making rounds in the park.

"What the fuck do you do when you're not with us?" Clyde asked.

"I network."

"You network?" said Jarrod.

"Network this!" Clyde sprang up, grabbing his crotch. "So, who are we copping from?"

Johnny gestured toward the Brick's young associate. "Him. I'll be right back."

He walked over and offered the teen some tightly folded singles. The kid slipped him three joints in return. Johnny returned to his friends. "Who's got matches?"

Clyde shrugged.

"We can bum a light from someone," said Jarrod.

"Really?" Johnny raised an eyebrow. "Some stranger's gonna help a bunch of kids light a fucking joint?"

Jarrod laughed. "I don't know what it's like in your neighborhood, but around here, nobody gives a fuck." He wagged his fingers. "Gimme one of those."

Johnny handed a joint to Jarrod, who circled around before giving a head nod toward a shirtless white guy in American flag shorts with a blue bandana wrapped around his head. A lit cigarette dangled between his lips. Jarrod intercepted him, holding up the joint. "Yo, can I get a light?"

The guy handed him his butt, which Jarrod used to spark up the weed. "Thanks, man. I appreciate it." He drew in a long puff, holding it in as he returned to his friends. "What'd I tell you?"

They passed the joint between them as they strolled down one of the more secluded finger paths. By University and Waverly Places, they stubbed out the roach and stopped to watch a young woman playing classical music on the violin. A handful of people were standing around to listen. Jarrod slinked by them to peek at the sheet music on the metal stand, then sidled back over to Johnny and Clyde. "Tchaikovsky," he whispered, jutting his chin toward the bills and coins in her violin case. "If you ask me, this music sounds like chaos and a headache, but look at all that damn money."

Clyde nodded. "I've seen a homeless guy on the subway playing a bunch of plastic buckets, and people throw him money, too."

They cut over toward NYU, where three Latinos were jamming to salsa with a guitar, congas and a sax. Their draw was much bigger, and a few couples were dancing. "Now we're talking," said Johnny. He craned his neck to look in the metal pail set up in front of them. "That shit's like half full."

"We could definitely do this," said Clyde. "We've got nothing to lose."

Back at the apartment, they shut themselves in Clyde's room. He had a single bed and bureau against one wall, with an old orange sofa opposite. It was where Jarrod slept when he stayed over. A desk sat beneath some windows, flanked by shelves cluttered with books and record albums. All four walls were plastered with posters of sexy models and rock stars.

Johnny tossed the two remaining joints on the desk. "I'm gonna go get your sister."

Clyde wagged his head. "At your own peril."

Johnny walked across the hall to peek in the other bedroom and saw Tiffany lying on one of the two beds, reading a magazine. He leaned in the doorway and rapped on the wooden frame.

She looked up. "What the hell do you want, whatever-your-name-is?"

He liked her crassness. People who were loud and in-your-face were much easier to read than quiet types. "It's Johnny," he reminded her. "So, how's your day going?"

She rolled her eyes. "Is this a joke that Clyde put you up to?"

Johnny walked over and sat on her bed. "You think you could do me a favor?" He looked at her as seductively as a twelve-year-old could pull off.

She sat up. "Spit it out."

"We got a few joints, but we don't have a lighter. If you could hook us up, we'll share."

She was speechless for a moment but then burst out laughing. "Oh my God, *that's* what you idiots are doing in there? Where the hell did you get them?"

"The park."

"You copped on the street? I'll bet it's a bag of oregano."

"It's not. I know a guy."

Tiffany scrunched her face. "You know a guy. Right. I gotta see *this*." She pushed Johnny aside and stormed into Clyde's room. Johnny followed. Her eyes zeroed in on the two joints on Clyde's desk. "This is the cow shit you paid good money for?"

Clyde nodded.

"How much?" She sniffed one.

"Buck a piece," said Jarrod.

Her expression changed from skeptical to curious. "It smells decent, but Jesus Christ, you three aren't stupid enough? You have to smoke dope on top of it?" She reached in her pocket for a Bic and lit the joint, drawing in a big puff of smoke. "It's not bad," she said, holding her breath, and passed the joint to her brother. He looked at her like it was a bonding moment or a grand rite of passage and took a hit.

They finished the joint as Clyde wafted the lingering smoke out the window.

"Shit, I need to order pizzas," Tiffany said and headed out. The three stoned friends lay around Clyde's room listening to the radio.

"I get why you stay here all the time," Johnny said to Jarrod. "I could totally move in."

41

"Why don't you sleep over? I'm planning to," said Jarrod. "I mean, Clyde, is that cool?"

"Of course, it is. I got a foam mattress we can put on the floor."

"You mean I don't get to sleep with your sister?" Johnny said.

"Ew, gross. Besides, Tiff only dates *old* losers."

"Tiffany? I was talking about Cecily." They laughed.

After they ate the pizza and cleared the table, the group of kids spread around the living room to watch some variety shows. Johnny hadn't seen much TV growing up, but he found it amusing, and sharing the experience with friends gave him a warm feeling in the chest.

At ten, Tiffany put Cecily to bed before she and Claire headed to their room. "You gonna wait up for Mom?" she said to Clyde before ducking down the hall.

"Yeah. I missed her the last couple of nights."

"I'm sure she'll appreciate that."

"She's a nursing assistant at St. Vincent's," Clyde explained after Tiffany had gone. "But she also waits tables at a diner and works as a home health aide on weekends, so I hardly get to see her."

"I guess not," said Johnny.

"She's really sweet," said Jarrod. "You'll see."

"How's my sweet boy?" Diana DeMarco said, appearing in the living room.

They all looked up from where they lay, Johnny and Jarrod on the floor with some throw pillows, and Clyde, who was sprawled on the couch. Diana's complexion reflected her Italian heritage. She had thick brown hair tied up in a ponytail and dark eyes that looked cheerful but weary. She sat beside her son and squeezed him tight. He smiled and hugged back.

She released Clyde and turned to Jarrod. "I see you're staying over again. Do your parents even remember what you look like?"

"Probably not," said Jarrod. "But that ain't because I'm here. It's because they drink too much."

Diana chuckled and looked at Johnny. "You must be the new friend I've been hearing about."

"Mom, this is Johnny," said Clyde. "I told him he could sleep over, too."

Johnny smiled. "Hello, Mrs. DeMarco. Are you sure it's okay?"

"Please, call me Diana. And it's fine with me as long as your parents know you're here. I wouldn't want them worrying about you."

"They won't worry, Diana. Thank you."

"Not a problem. You're always welcome, but it's late. You should be getting to bed." Diana stood up, and the kids did too. She pulled Clyde close and kissed him again. Afterward, she extended her arms to embrace Jarrod. "Johnny, I know we just met, but you look like you could use a goodnight hug too."

Diana wrapped herself around Johnny in a warm, maternal way. At first, he tensed up but then realized it was a normal display of affection. A wave of sadness washed over him before he relaxed in her grip. She straightened up, ruffled his hair and bade them all a good night.

CHAPTER SIX

One afternoon, the three friends were lazing around in Clyde's room when Johnny put down his magazine and sat up on the couch. "Hey, can I ask you guys something?"

Clyde and Jarrod looked up.

"If some shit ever went down, would you have my back?"

"Of course," they said in unison.

"You'd protect me? No matter what?"

"Are you in some kind of trouble?" Clyde asked.

"No, but I haven't been honest about a few things. Like, some stuff about my family."

"We thought things were pretty fucked up," said Jarrod.

"You did?"

"Yeah." Jarrod pointed to the disfigured skin around Johnny's wrists. "People don't usually get shit like that without a story."

Johnny looked at the scars and took a deep breath. "When I said I lived uptown, that was partially true. I sleep in a vacant apartment and keep some clothes there, but I left home at the end of July. Just before I met you guys."

"Why?" Clyde got up from his bed and sat on the other end of the couch. Jarrod scooted his chair closer.

"I had an older brother…" Those few words were enough to cause a wave of revulsion that Johnny had to swallow down. "Much older. Six years. He was psychotic. He got so crazy that my parents yanked him out of school and locked him in the cellar. When I'd do something wrong, they'd punish me by putting me down there with him."

"And he would hurt you?" asked Clyde.

Johnny coughed at the understatement. "He liked to tie me up, punch me, cut me…" He stood, lifting his shirt to expose the reddened lash marks across his back and ribs and the raised scars from the razor knife.

Clyde and Jarrod's eyes widened. "Holy shit," Jarrod whispered.

"A lot of stuff I don't remember."

"Because he knocked you unconscious?" Clyde asked.

"Maybe. I'm not sure. I just know I got a lot of blank spots."

"That's some heavy shit," said Jarrod. "Good thing you got out."

"No doubt," said Clyde. "Are the cops looking for you?"

Johnny sat back down. "I don't know. I came here from Florida, so maybe they're looking down there, but part of me thinks my parents wouldn't even report it."

"That's fucked up," said Jarrod. "How could you not look for your own missing kid?"

"My parents are probably happy I'm gone. But some of my friends or neighbors might have suspected something. Maybe it made the news and one day someone will recognize me. I've seen stories like that before."

"True," said Clyde. "If I ever hear they're looking for a twelve-year-old named Johnny Avalon, I'll warn you."

"About that." Johnny clenched his teeth. "That's not my real name."

"For fuck's sake." Jarrod slapped his thigh. "What *is* your real name, Lou Stoole? Dick Hertz?"

They all laughed. "My real name is Javier Álvarez, but my friends have always called me Johnny. Only my family calls me Javier, so I'd appreciate it if you never do."

"You got it," said Clyde.

"Are you sure you're twelve?" asked Jarrod. "Or did you lie about that?"

"I told a few people I was thirteen," said Johnny. "Like at the Y because I thought it sounded less suspicious, but I'm twelve. And I'm gonna have to be really careful till I turn legal because I'd rather live in a rat-infested subway tunnel than go back to that house—or the pedophiles they stick you with in foster care."

Clyde and Jarrod agreed.

"If I could get in your school, it would be a good cover, keep me away from the truant officers, let me get a hot meal or two. You guys could show me how to get around so I look like I belong."

"I would totally be down for that," said Jarrod.

"If I go in with you the first day, I can just pretend my paperwork got lost."

"That shit happens all the time," said Clyde.

"Exactly," said Jarrod. "And the administration office won't question you because how many kids are trying to sneak *into* school?" He grinned.

Clyde nodded. "And you can sleep over a bunch, borrow some clothes if you want. It's just if you're here every night, Tiff and my mother will get suspicious."

"You can crash at my place, too," said Jarrod. "It's not half as fun as this, but it's better than the street."

"Don't worry," said Clyde. "We'll look out for you."

Johnny smiled. "Thanks."

CHAPTER SEVEN

The Saturday before school was set to start, Tiffany arranged to take her siblings back-to-school shopping. Jarrod and Johnny wanted to tag along and get some things, too, so everyone convened in front of Macy's on 34th Street. Inside, Johnny was mesmerized by its enormity. It seemed like all the department stores in Miami could have fit in the lobby alone. Every pillar was adorned with fancy floral decorations and surrounded by families of mannequins assembled in their own little scenes. Magnificent chandeliers hung above glass display cases the length of subway cars, selling everything from makeup to handbags to perfume and luggage. Johnny's head couldn't turn fast enough to see it all.

"Hey, kid!" barked Tiffany. "Gawk on your own time. We got shit to do."

Clyde and Jarrod laughed as Johnny jogged to catch them on the escalator.

At the girls' department, Tiffany corralled Cecily and Claire before turning to Clyde. "We're gonna be here a while, so go to the boys' section and try on what you need. When we're done, I'll meet you up there to pay. Got it?"

Clyde saluted. "Yes, Ma'am!"

"And no fucking around. You better be by the register. I'm not spending half the day hunting for a prepubescent gang of twits." She stormed off with the girls.

Clyde directed them to the upper level. Johnny needed lots of things but was only willing to spend enough for two pairs of jeans, some long-sleeved shirts and a jacket. Jarrod selected some similar garments.

"Your parents actually *gave* you money?" asked Clyde.

Jarrod coughed out a laugh. "More like I had to shake them down for it. And it's not nearly enough to cover what I need."

Johnny and Jarrod paid for their items, which the clerk placed in large paper bags, then they went to mill around the dressing room where Clyde was trying on stuff. As they circled a display table with an array of multi-colored T-shirts, Jarrod smirked at Johnny. "What if some things *accidentally* fell into these bags?"

"Don't they have people watching?"

"Maybe, but I doubt they're looking for kids."

Johnny bit his lip. "If I show up at school wearing the same shit every day, that's gonna be suspicious, right?"

Jarrod shrugged, but after a few shoppers walked by, he brushed a shirt off the table into his bag and then looked around. When nothing happened, Johnny did the same with two. They ambled over to the underwear section, and Johnny slipped a six-pack of socks and some briefs into his bag while Jarrod kept watch. Johnny returned the favor so Jarrod could get another pair of pants.

Behind a rack of winter coats, they reshuffled their bags to put the stolen stuff under the purchased items. When they surfaced, a security guard was weaving in and out of the displays. "Shit," Jarrod whispered, "Gimme your bag."

"Huh?"

"Just gimme it." He grabbed Johnny's shopping bag and shoved him into the coats. "Stay here."

Johnny couldn't see much from his position but watched as Jarrod worked too hard to make it look like he was perusing the merchandise, even stroking his chin as if deep in thought. *Jesus Christ, Jarrod, tone it down.* Johnny craned from behind a fur-trimmed hood to see that the only thing between Jarrod and the guard was a circular rack of sweatpants. He cringed, pulling himself deeper into the coats while expecting Jarrod to make a run for it.

"You lost? Separated from your parents?" the guard was saying.

"Nah," Jarrod said. "Didn't the long johns used to be around here?"

"Long johns? Probably over by the undershirts and stuff."

The crackling of a walkie-talkie rang out, and Johnny stole a glance to see the man unholster his handheld and lift it to his face.

"You gotta what?" The guard's eyes locked on Jarrod while he deciphered the scratchy transmission. "Ten-four." He put a hand on Jarrod's shoulder but then moved him aside and jogged to the aisle, where he disappeared.

"What the fuck are you doing?"

Johnny looked up from between two parkas to see Clyde, clothing draped over both arms. "I saw that guard, so I hid."

"He's probably going to help the old geezer who tripped on the escalator over there."

Johnny straightened up to see a small crowd gathered in the distance.

Jarrod handed Johnny his bag and turned in the opposite direction. "C'mon. Let's boogie."

"What's up with you two?" asked Clyde.

Jarrod lowered his voice. "We took a few things, but I think we're cool. We just want to keep moving."

"You what?"

"Let's just go wait for your sister," said Johnny. "She should be here soon, right?"

Clyde halted. "Listen, if you guys need stuff, put it in my pile, and Tiffany will pay for it with my mom's credit card."

"Your mother has a hard enough time making ends meet. She can't be buying our shit, too."

"We're wearing each other's clothes, so what difference does it make?"

"The difference is," Jarrod outstretched an arm, "Macy's can afford it a lot more than she can."

They spotted Tiffany and the girls laden with shopping bags and met them at the register. While she and Clyde waited in line, Johnny leaned into Jarrod. "Thanks for covering me back there."

"No sweat." Jarrod waved him off. "If I get caught shoplifting, all they're gonna do is slap me on the wrist and call my parents, who'll forget they even *got* a call by the time I get home." He patted Johnny on the back. "Besides, we promised to look out for you."

"I know, but—"

"But what? We promised."

Once Clyde's things were paid for, it was off for school supplies before Tiffany declared the mission complete and terminated all shopping activities.

At the DeMarcos', everyone retreated to their respective rooms except Tiffany, who threw on high heels and a mini dress and promptly left the apartment. Clyde made space in a drawer for Johnny to keep his clothes, but then he and Jarrod seemed bent on lounging inside.

"Don't you guys wanna wander around?" said Johnny.

"Not really," said Clyde. "I'm tired from all that shopping."

"Me, too," said Jarrod.

"But it's the last weekend before school starts."

Clyde opened an issue of *Tiger Beat* magazine. "Maybe that's why I can't find any enthusiasm. I always get depressed this time of year."

"I hear you, but it's making me restless, so I'm gonna go out. Maybe I'll check on my apartment, too, since I've been sleeping over here so much."

"Okay," said Jarrod. "But come back later if you want, or call. Maybe we'll be up for going out by then."

"Cool."

When Johnny arrived at Washington Square Park, the Brick was playing chess with Russ, but there was no bantering. The Brick looked dapper in a light blue peacock paisley short-sleeved shirt, with beige slacks and a matching fedora. Russ was donned in his regular Yankee apparel. Because the vibe seemed so serious, Johnny didn't interrupt. Instead, he slipped onto a nearby bench to see if the mood would change.

Two men entered the park and stood at the table. One was slender with a full beard; the other had a wide mustache and the beefy body of a wrestler.

The Brick perked up. "Mustafa's associates?"

"Yes," answered the thin one, dropping a small duffel bag at his feet.

"It is a nice game, chess," said the other in an accent that felt familiar to Johnny. "Strategic. Good for sharpening the mind."

As they all made small talk, Johnny sized up the strangers. *First impressions could save your life,* he'd once heard the Brick say to an opponent mid-match. These guys had kinky hair and olive complexions, but they weren't Latin. Johnny thought they could be Middle Eastern or Russian, and the heavier one was obviously in charge by the way he spoke. He also sensed that they weren't just there to chat about chess.

"So?" The boss man softened his voice. "It is all set?"

The Brick did likewise. "Yeah, man, it's good." He looked around before signaling to one of his teenage soldiers, who was waiting in the distance, also holding a bag. The kid walked outside the park to a phone booth on the corner, where he pretended to fumble through his pockets for a dime.

The thin man gave the bag to his associate, and the pair headed toward the park's exit. As they passed by Johnny, they muttered to each other in their native language, and he realized he understood everything. The men spoke Turkish. A sick feeling settled in Johnny's stomach, not only because the language was attached to memories of his family but because he grasped that the men planned to screw over the Brick.

Johnny's head toggled between the chess table and the phone booth. What should he do? If he didn't say anything, the Brick could get beat on the deal—whatever the fuck it was. And if he *did* say something, would the man even listen? *Trust your instincts. They've been good so far.*

Johnny slid off his bench, crept behind the Brick, and cupped a hand to his ear. "They're gonna cheat you."

The Brick's neck snapped toward him. "Say what now?"

"I just heard what they said. You gotta stop them."

"That didn't sound like no motherfucking Spanish to me, boy." The Brick looked furious.

Johnny's glance split between him and Russ. "It wasn't. It was Turkish, but I understood it. They're trying to screw you."

"What'd they say?"

Johnny grimaced. "It wasn't very nice."

"Boy, I don't give a fuck." Even though he was whispering, the words resonated. "Tell me what they said."

51

Johnny looked down at the table. "The big one said, 'These fancy black cocksuckers will buy anything. They're so dumb.' Then the beard agreed and said, 'Chess is for faggots.'" To reassure him, Johnny repeated the phrases in Turkish.

The Brick's mouth tightened, and he threw a glance at Russ, who shrugged. He then stood and blew a whistle with his thumb and forefinger. The teen at the phone booth was just about to swap bags but looked up. The Brick waved his flat hand across his throat, then gave a side nod for him to get out of there. The kid took off down the block.

"What the fuck?" Johnny heard the mustachioed man yell. He threw the bag at his partner's chest and marched back.

Johnny scurried to a bench across the path as the Brick sat back down and lit a Newport.

The Turk stood at the chess table, hands on his hips. "What are you doing? It's all set."

The Brick took a slow drag off his cigarette. "You know something, man? I'm having a change of heart."

"What?"

"I'm gonna pass on this transaction, but do give Mustafa my regards."

"You are crazy! It's all set."

"Yeah, well, things change." The Brick stretched both arms across the backrest.

"This is fucked! *You* are fucked!" His face contorted as he struggled to regain control, then spit a large gob of phlegm on the ground before storming off.

The Brick exhaled, swiping a hand over his face. "Russ, do me a favor and go make a beer run."

Russ gave a nod, then got up from the table and exited the park. Johnny sat folded forward, leg bouncing, sneaking peeks at the Brick as he finished his cigarette.

"Colombiano!" He flicked his butt into the grass. "Get your ass over here."

Johnny slinked over, head bowed, hands in his pockets.

"Sit the fuck down." The Brick patted the bench beside him, and Johnny obeyed. "I must be fucking crazy to listen to a kid like you."

"But they were gonna—"

"Yeah. You already said." He looked up, circling the tension from his neck. "How many goddamn languages you speak?"

"A few."

"A few," he echoed.

"Turkish, English and Spanish fluently, but I also know a little French, Portuguese and Ger—"

"Boy, shut the fuck up."

Johnny recoiled but kept his eyes on the man as he stared out at the park.

"He really called me a fancy cocksucker?"

Johnny winced. "Yeah."

"And stupid." Half a smirk raised one side of his goatee. "Well, Colombiano, we'll see who looks stupid now, won't we?"

"Definitely."

The Brick snickered, turning to Johnny. "Listen, kid, I don't know what the fuck you *think* you know, but you don't know shit, okay?"

Johnny nodded.

"I took a big risk listening to you." The Brick stroked his chin. "But it was a bigger risk not to. I had a shady feeling about those two from the get-go. Now all that's left to do is wait and see." The Brick put a hand on Johnny's shoulder and squeezed it. "All right, go on. When I see you next—or if I see you at all—I'll let you know if you were right."

"You'll see me, Rick. I'm no coward."

The Brick scowled. "What'd you call me?"

Johnny hadn't meant to use the man's real name; it slipped out, but he backed it up. "I called you Rick."

"Hmm, that's a bold move, boy. I hope that ass of yours can cash the check your mouth's been writing."

Johnny stood up and held out his palm. The Brick looked at it a moment but then smiled and slapped him five.

CHAPTER EIGHT

When Johnny entered his building, he was tired and couldn't stop second-guessing himself for meddling in the Brick's business. As he lumbered up the stairs, Lily was sitting between the first and second floors, working on a crossword puzzle book. She looked up. "Haven't seen you in a while."

"Yeah, I've been kinda busy." Johnny sighed, picking at the chipped paint on the banister. "Shopping for school, visiting relatives before summer's over… What's new with you?"

"Nothing. Still running errands with my grandma, trying to avoid my mom. Oh, but you got some mail."

"Really?" He perked up and spun back to the lobby. Lily followed.

In his broken box were two letters addressed to Mr. Juan Avalon: a renewal application from the YMCA and a flyer for a hardware store. Johnny thought it was a good thing if his fake parents could get real mail.

Lily peeked over his shoulder. "Can't you get mail in your own building?"

"I just wanted to see if I could get stuff here, too." He flapped the letters. "It worked."

"They've been there a while."

"Oh yeah?"

"I started to wonder if you would ever come get them."

"Hmm."

"I thought I might have to go to the police to make sure you were still alive."

Johnny grabbed Lily's tricep. "Don't mention me to the fucking police, okay?"

She ripped her arm away. "Jesus, what's the big deal?"

They both looked at the ground.

"Lily, I'm sorry. Will you come to my place so we can talk?" She pouted but then headed up the stairs.

In the apartment, Lily sat on the floor with her back against the wall while Johnny lit some candles, then paced back and forth. "Look, we're friends, right?"

"Yeah."

"And I'm glad we're friends. But don't keep getting freaked out because I don't come around. I told you that I only stay here when shit is bad at home."

"We could still hang out, even if you don't sleep here."

"That's true, but I've been busy, and I really don't want you asking about me, especially to the cops."

"How come you never tell me where you live?"

"Maybe because it's a bad neighborhood, with shootings, stabbings." He looked at the ceiling. "The other day, I got jacked up for my allowance. Two guys shoved me down for a lousy dollar, can you believe that?" He looked into her eyes. "If you ever got hurt because of *me*, I'd never forgive myself."

Lily picked at her shoelace. "It just feels like everyone avoids me, so when you don't come around..."

"I'm not avoiding you. Really. Why don't we hang out tomorrow?"

She looked up. "You sure?"

"Yeah, why not? I'll swing by your apartment in the morning."

"Cool." Lily got up. "I guess I'll see you tomorrow."

As she pranced out of the apartment, Johnny swiped his hands over his face. *That was easier than it should've been.*

The next morning, Lily directed Johnny to Bennett Avenue and Broadway, where she cut into Fort Tryon Park. "This looks like a good place to get mugged," said Johnny.

"You'll protect us." She smiled and pulled him down the path.

The park spanned from 192nd Street to Dyckman and Broadway to Riverside Drive. It was hilly, with large ivy-covered rocks and tall trees. Thick shrubs and assorted flowers lined the twisting walkways as they hiked. Only a few other people were walking around, but Lily seemed unconcerned and chatted non-stop. "When I was little, my mom used to bring me here a lot before she got so fucking crabby. My Gramma, also, but now she's too arthritic." She looped her arm in Johnny's. "When I was thirteen, I had a sixteen-year-old boyfriend who lived on the block. Sometimes we'd come here to smoke pot and fool around, but he got sent to juvie." She flicked her hair like it was no big deal. "I've had a few flings since then, but nothing serious. How about you? You date much?"

Is she lying to impress me? "Um, not really."

She batted her eyes. "Probably still waiting for the right woman."

On the path, the trees gave way to expose a stone archway and steps that led to a spacious overlook with benches. Johnny broke away from Lily to lean over the rock retaining wall where he could see across the Hudson River to New Jersey. "Wow, this is really cool."

"Not so scary now, is it?"

"No. It's beautiful. Thanks for bringing me." They strolled along the perimeter, stopping to admire the George Washington Bridge and the views of Washington Heights. "What's that castle thing over there?"

"That's the Cloisters."

"The what?"

"It's a museum. C'mon, I'll show you." Lily took Johnny back to the path. "There used to be beautiful gardens along here, but the city can't afford to keep them up anymore. The last few times I've been here, the museum hasn't been open either. But it's still fun to walk around outside." Lily spotted a dandelion and picked it. She sniffed it before tossing it into the scorched grass. "My mom says New York has become one big shithole and that it's only gonna get worse. But it's all I know, and some stuff is still nice." She took Johnny's hand and squeezed it. "Like this."

A tingling urged Johnny closer to her, but he was afraid to act on it and looked at the ground.

"What's wrong?"

"Huh?"

"You're so uptight." Laughing, she yanked Johnny closer, cupped his ass and squeezed.

"Don't!" He whipped around, smacking her hand away.

"What the fuck?" Lily stomped a foot. "What's your damn problem?"

Johnny pressed his flushed face into both palms. "I don't have a fucking problem. You're just so—" He walked a small circle. "Jesus."

She glared at him, arms akimbo. "Do you even *like* girls?"

The comment caused a wave of rage to blister Johnny's insides, choking his ability to articulate a reply. The frustration made him want to hit her, but he fought back the feeling. If she had kept talking, it would have been harder, but instead, Lily folded to the ground, pouting, and it deflated his anger.

"Or maybe you just don't like *me*," she mumbled.

Wow. Everything's always all about you. Johnny released a long breath and sat cross-legged. "If I didn't like you, I wouldn't be here."

She poked at the dirt with a twig.

"And yeah, I like girls, okay? Just slow the fuck down. Don't be grabbing me and shit."

Lily cocked her head to look at him. "My last boyfriend didn't like it either."

"See?"

"It's just that sometimes I feel like if I slow down, I'm gonna miss out. Like everything will pass me by. Like everything already *is* passing me by. I guess that's why I come on kinda strong. Does that make sense?"

It didn't, but Johnny had no intention of going into it. Instead, he plastered on a smile. "Well, right now, I feel like *I'm* missing out on a really cool tour of that oyster thingy."

"Cloister, not oyster." Lily laughed, standing, then held out a hand to help Johnny up. "I do give excellent tours, don't I?"

"You sure do." He brushed off his pants. "Lead the way."

As predicted, the building was closed, and the surrounding grounds were overgrown with weeds, but the pair still circled the stone structure, marveling at the huge Gothic windows and sculpted pillars. When they had seen what they could, they began their descent toward the playground at Dyckman Street.

"Where do you go to school?" Lily asked as they headed back.

"Downtown." *Please don't ask for details.* "How about you?"

"Over there." She pointed east. "Inwood High School. It'll be my first year."

"Are you excited?"

"No." Lily scrunched her face. "All it means is I'll get bullied by older kids."

"But I thought you liked older guys." Johnny grinned and gave her a nudge.

Lily booted a crushed soda can in her path. "It's never the guys who fuck with me. It's always girls. Girls are evil and cruel, just like my mom."

"Maybe this school will be different." *Jesus, this girl's mood shifts like a fart in the tide.* "Hey, are you hungry? We could get some sandwiches to eat at my place."

"Yeah, I guess."

Back at the apartment, Johnny spread the blanket on the bedroom floor, where the light was best. They sat on it to eat, then stretched out to work on Lily's crosswords. They lay side by side, on their stomachs, taking turns filling in the answers. Johnny could feel the heat from where Lily's shoulder pressed against his. She turned to look at him, and he kissed her. Her lips were soft and warm, and it sent a tingling throughout his body.

When they pulled apart, Johnny rolled onto his back, and she straddled him. She kissed him again, this time with her mouth open and with her tongue. It made Johnny's head spin. As she caressed his neck, he wrapped his arms around her waist. She kissed him deeper, and he followed her lead.

The sun beamed through the open windows, warming their skin. Muffled sounds of traffic and street noise wafted in until one sound poked through the others. It was a single voice and hard to ignore because it was repetitive and kept getting louder.

"Oh shit! That's my mother. I'm supposed to go school shopping with her." Lily jumped up. "I don't want to go, really, but if I don't, that cunt will make my life miserable." She blew a kiss and ran out of the apartment.

Johnny rolled over, clutching the swelling in his pants. "That girl is gonna drive me nuts."

CHAPTER NINE

"She did not," said Jarrod, jumping to swat a parking sign before crossing at the corner of 23rd Street and 8th Avenue. A smattering of pedestrians turned to look.

"I swear," said Johnny. "If her mother hadn't yelled, we would've done it."

"You wish," said Clyde.

"I'm telling you. This girl acts like a thirty-year-old trapped in a fifteen-year-old's body. It's wild, but also kinda sad, you know what I mean?" Johnny leap-frogged over a fire hydrant. "Hey, let's go in that supermarket," he said, shaking off the thought.

"What for?" said Clyde.

"To get money."

Jarrod stopped short. "You planning on holding up the place?"

Johnny grabbed Jarrod's shirt to drag him along. "No, you ding-dong. Shoppers wander around, not paying attention, with their bags and wallets sitting right in the cart. I've seen it. Two of us could act as a distraction while the other pinches what they can."

"I don't know," Clyde grimaced. "Are you sure?"

"No, but I *do* know that I'm gonna run out of cash soon. School starts tomorrow, so your parents will probably get a lot stricter about me eating and sleeping over all the time."

"If I have to sneak food out of the house, I will," said Clyde.

"Yeah, me, too," said Jarrod. "Except all my drunk-ass parents buy are TV dinners, so that doesn't help if you don't have an oven." He shrugged. "But I *could* sneak out a bottle of rum. At least it'll keep you warm at night."

Johnny tsked. "Look, you can't both be helping me so much that it blows my cover."

"And *you* can't be doing shit that gets you arrested," said Clyde.

Johnny stopped at the store's entrance to look his friends in the face. "I'm not doing anything to get caught by the cops. As long as we're careful and don't take stupid risks, maybe we could pull something off." He spun to walk through the automatic door. "But we'll never know until we try."

Inside, Clyde grabbed a box of Fruit Loops from an endcap before they ambled around, pretending to peruse the merchandise. Most of the aisles were too crowded, but they kept meandering until they saw a young mother alone in the paper towel section. Her baby lay in a carrier, wedged into the child seat of her almost full shopping cart. Her purse was set beside it.

At the end of the aisle, Johnny stopped. "She'd be an easy target."

"But it's a mom," said Clyde. "With a baby."

"I fucking see that," Johnny spoke through gritted teeth while examining a bottle of furniture polish. "I don't like the idea either, but she's also well-dressed and has nice stuff, so she can probably afford to take the hit." He looked at Clyde. "*I'm* homeless."

Jarrod tugged Clyde's shirt. "Maybe her husband's a Rockefeller or some shit, and besides, we might not get another chance."

"Exactly," said Johnny. "Now get up next to her and start something."

"Like what?" asked Clyde.

"I don't know. Improvise. We don't have time for a rehearsal."

Jarrod tapped Clyde's arm. "C'mon, man, we got this."

The pair backtracked toward the mother, who had stepped away from the cart to compare prices. When they were a few yards away, Jarrod put his foot out and tripped Clyde, who fell to his hands and knees. The box of cereal skidded across the floor. "You fucking asshole," he said, crawling to his feet.

Jarrod fought the impulse to laugh. "God, you're so clumsy!"

"I am not." Clyde shoved Jarrod, who pushed him back.

The woman stepped toward them. "Boys, boys, calm down. It was just an accident."

"Was not."

"Was too!"

As Jarrod and Clyde kept the woman distracted, Johnny slid up to the cart. He smiled at the gurgling baby while unfastening the woman's purse. Her wallet lay open. He pulled out a stack of bills, closed the purse and ducked away.

Outside, the three met up, bolted around the corner and kept running until fits of laughter made them stop. "You could've said you were gonna trip me, you dick," Clyde said between breaths.

Jarrod folded over, hands on his knees. "Then it wouldn't have looked real."

Johnny leaned on a parked car to count the money, not letting the others see his guilt.

"Wow, eighty-seven bucks. See? I told you she could afford it."

"I guess so." Clyde turned to Jarrod. "But next time, I get to trip *you*!"

They went inside a diner and slipped into a booth. A Mediterranean-looking waiter sauntered over. He wore black slacks with a starchy white shirt and apron and stood at the end of the booth, arms akimbo, his dark eyes narrowed into slits.

Jarrod turned both palms upward. "What? You think we're just clogging up a table?"

The man chewed his bottom lip.

"Don't worry. We got money."

"Fine," he barked, pulling a pad from his apron's pocket and a pen from behind his ear. "Whatchya want?"

They ordered three Cheeseburgers Deluxe with extra pickles and a round of Cokes. The waiter scribbled it down and retreated to the kitchen.

"Fucking Greeks," said Jarrod. "No sense of humor." He looked at Johnny. "You speak that language, too?"

Johnny laughed. "Nah, just a few words I picked up from a kid in grade school—please, thank you, and go fuck yourself. You know, the basics." He shifted in his seat. "So, should I be nervous about tomorrow? Like, will I stand out?"

Jarrod clicked his tongue. "I don't know what your school was like in Florida, but this place is a clusterfuck on a normal day, never mind the first day back."

"Besides," said Clyde, "with all the shit you got going on, this is the least of your worries." The food came, and he shook the ketchup bottle over his fries. "I mean, what's the worst that'll happen? You'll say your registration got lost, and they won't admit you."

"Right, like maybe because they're too full or some shit?" Jarrod chewed while he spoke. "No problem. Just walk away, and we'll figure something else out."

"What if they'll admit me, but need to see my parents?" Johnny asked.

Jarrod smirked. "Clyde's sister Tiff would probably pretend she's your mom for a dime-bag of weed."

Clyde laughed, popping a fry in his mouth. "She's done more for less."

After paying the check, Johnny divvied up the rest of the stolen cash three ways. Then they wandered around, still laughing about the supermarket caper, until Johnny stopped in front of an electronics store. "Lemme pop in here real quick."

"Why, you got another scam?" asked Jarrod.

"No, but I'm gonna need some way to get to school on time."

Johnny looked at the watches that were too cheap to be locked under glass and sat on a swivel display atop the counter. He picked out a Casio with a faux leather band and lay it across his scarred wrist. As he went to buckle the strap, Orlando's piercing glare and psychotic grin flashed in Johnny's head, causing his throat to close. He ripped it away and dropped it on the counter.

"Why don't you just get a pocket watch instead?" said Clyde, peeking over his shoulder.

"And a monocle," said Jarrod. "Maybe a top hat, too, and some hotels to slap on Marvin Gardens."

"You fucking guys." Johnny exhaled, wagging his head, and returned the watch to its display. "I'll just get that." He caught the clerk's eye and had him grab a small wind-up alarm clock from a shelf behind the counter. At the register, Johnny noticed a case with assorted knives.

He pointed to a four-inch folding Buck and had the clerk ring that up as well.

The next morning, Johnny met Clyde and Jarrod on the corner of 31st and 10th, and they led him toward IS 20. The rectangular three-story brick building took up half a block and included a recess area that was nothing but concrete surrounded by chain-link fencing.

As they made their way toward the entrance with hundreds of other kids, Johnny took inventory. Groups of students were banded together, talking and laughing, while self-conscious-looking singletons squeezed around them. They all covered a broad range of colors and ethnicities. Some wore nicely pressed clothes, while others had torn jeans and T-shirts. *No problem fitting in here.*

As the crowd tapered near the pair of double doors, Clyde and Jarrod sandwiched Johnny, hollering greetings to this kid or that, but then leaned in with their personal commentaries.

"That's Paul, he's a douche."

"Reggie over there's a twin, but his brother died in childbirth."

"Whoa, check out Megan. Her tits weren't half that big last year."

Inside, the shrill squeaking of sneakers on freshly waxed linoleum punctuated the cacophony of voices as Johnny followed his friends up the stairwell and into their homeroom. They took seats in the back. The wobbly desks, etched with obscenities and assorted doodles, were packed in tight, and almost every chair was taken.

"My classes were never this crowded in Miami."

Clyde shrugged. "Welcome to the NYC public school system."

While the room settled, the teacher, donned in a knee-length skirt, blouse and sweater vest, wrote *Mrs. Gibbs—Room 320* on the blackboard. Everyone hushed as she pulled a clipboard from her desk and began calling names alphabetically. When done, she asked if anyone hadn't been called. Johnny and another kid raised their hands. Mrs. Gibbs scribbled on some paper, walked it over, and told them to go to the administration office.

Jarrod tapped Johnny. "If we don't see you, we'll meet in the cafeteria at lunch, okay?"

The trio gave each other a nod.

While walking downstairs, Johnny turned to the kid. "How's it going?"

"This is bullshit," he barked. "The same crap happened to me last year."

"What a drag." Johnny grinned into his chest.

In the office, a handful of adults were behind a long counter, working to assist the dozen students already there. The two benches were full, so Johnny leaned on the tiled wall to wait his turn. *Just be vague and act stupid.*

After several minutes, he was waved over by a woman who looked like she should have retired two decades earlier. She was white-haired with an affected smile pinned on her deadpan face, which, due to her dowager's hump, was almost level with her cleavage. "Hello, dear, how can I help you?"

"My name wasn't on the list."

"What's your name?"

"Johnny Avalon."

"Date of birth?"

"April 1st, 1960."

She hovered over a large binder. "Are you a transfer?"

"Yes."

"Your parents sent in the application?"

"I guess."

"And you received a confirmation letter?"

"I got something saying my homeroom was in 320 with Mrs. Gibbs."

She paused to look at him, head tilted.

Was I not supposed to know that? Fuck. Johnny glanced at her lapel and smiled. "What a *beautiful* pin. Is that a ruby?"

Her face brightened as her crooked fingers touched the ornate pewter petals that surrounded the brooch's oval stone. "No, dear, it's only a garnet. It has more sentimental value than anything else." She smiled, lifting the wrinkles around her mouth to make new ones in her cheeks. "My late husband gave it to me on our forty-fifth anniversary."

Seven hundred years ago? Johnny lowered his head. "I'm so sorry, but it is very pretty."

"Thank you." Her focus returned to the application. "Bear with me. We've just got a few questions left."

Johnny answered everything as she wrote but got stuck when she asked for his social security number. "I don't know it off the top of my head, but I can get it."

"Is there a parent I can call?"

"They're both at work."

"All right. Have them fill this out and bring it to me tomorrow." She handed him the form with a class schedule. "If you want to change anything, you have two weeks, okay?"

"Yes, ma'am."

"Your homeroom teacher will hand out bus passes at the end of the day."

"I'll need one of those."

"Anything else?"

"No. You've been very helpful. Thank you."

The halls were mostly empty as Johnny walked out, reading the schedule to see where his first-period class was located. As he approached the stairwell, someone's shoulder banged into his. He turned to apologize and saw an older white kid walking by like nothing happened. He was tall and pale with a pushed-up nose, and Johnny could have sworn there was a smirk on his face. There had been plenty of room to pass, but Johnny let it go.

For the rest of the morning, Johnny bounced from class to class with the masses, keeping to himself while taking in the surroundings. He didn't see Clyde and Jarrod again until lunch.

"I take it everything's cool?" Clyde asked as they loaded up their trays in the cafeteria line.

"Piece of cake. Just like you predicted."

They took seats at the end of a long table half-full of kids. While eating, they compared schedules and found they each had a few classes in common.

"What should we do after school?" asked Jarrod.

"We could go to the record store and get some albums with that money we got," said Clyde.

65

Johnny slurped from his tiny carton of milk. "I thought we'd go to the library and do our homework."

Jarrod shrunk back. "Are you nuts? Who wants to be here longer than we have to?"

"That's what I did in Miami. The lessons are fresh, so that makes it easier, and if you get it out of the way, you can fuck off the rest of the day." He turned up a palm. "That, and I was never in a hurry to get home."

Jarrod scooped up the remnants of his sloppy joe with a plastic spork. "My strategy is wait till the last minute, stay up too late getting it done, then hand in a bunch of half-finished assignments."

Johnny laughed. "That doesn't work for me. I don't have lights. Besides, if we do it together, it'll be more fun. Then we can stash our books in a locker and not have to schlep them around when we're hanging out."

"I'll try it your way," said Clyde.

"Fine," said Jarrod.

After classes, they met in the library on the second floor, grabbed a corner table, and ran through their assignments. There weren't many since only the hard-ass teachers gave homework the first day, so Johnny pulled out the school's application. "Do you guys know your social security numbers?"

"Yeah," said Clyde. "My mother made me start memorizing it a few years ago."

Johnny wrote what Clyde rattled off but inverted the last two digits. "What should I put as my phone number?"

Jarrod held a pen to his mouth and mimicked a nasal voice. "Hey, kids, New York's hottest rock station is one-oh-one FM on your radio dial. That's right, ROCK one-oh-one. To call for your requests, dial R-O-C-K-1-0-1, or 762-5101."

Clyde laughed. "I listen to that station all the time, too. Can't forget that number, they spout it off every five minutes."

"Works for me." Johnny scribbled down the digits, then practiced signing Juan Avalon on a piece of scrap paper before penning it on the form. "All I gotta do now is hand it in tomorrow and see if they buy it."

They wandered the streets until Clyde and Jarrod had to get home for dinner. Each of them invited Johnny over, but he said that he didn't want to appear too homeless too soon. Once they parted, Johnny made his way to Washington Square to look for the Brick. As he circled the fountain, he counted the weeks. Six. And nobody had come looking for him yet.

He made a wide berth around a couple of guys tossing a frisbee before heading to the chess tables. It was so easy to forget here. Like, *really* forget, as in not even think he saw his father's face on a crowded subway or catch what looked like his mother's reflection in a store window. Nothing. In Miami, he used to think he saw his brother everywhere, even after Miguel had locked him up. It didn't take much. Any passing glance at a teen with Orlando's body type could liquefy Johnny's bowels.

With the Brick nowhere in sight, Johnny plopped down on a bench, dropping his backpack between his feet. He couldn't help acknowledging that the mere absence of that constant, underlying terror made existing so much easier. He just had to stay alert and listen to his instincts.

"Colombiano!"

Johnny smiled. "What's going on?"

"This and that," said the Brick. He sat down, eyeing Johnny in a way that was hard to read.

"Is something wrong?"

The Brick's bottom lip pursed. "No. In fact, I did a little investigating. Turns out you were right. Those men *were* out to beat me."

"No shit. Do they know how you found out?"

"No, and it's best they don't. Keeps me mysterious." He winked. "But *I* know, and I appreciate it." He put his hand on the bench near Johnny's hip. There was a folded bill under his thumb.

"You don't have to do that, Rick, I was just trying to help."

The Brick's eyes widened. "You ain't gonna leave me hanging here, are you?"

"No, sir." Johnny inched the bill under his own palm and pocketed it.

"All right then." The Brick leaned back and crossed his legs. "So, tell me, what's *your* story?"

"Me?"

"Boy, I know you got a story."

Johnny tried to act nonchalant but was no match for the seasoned dealer.

"It's all right, little brother, I don't need to know, especially if it's something I'm gonna have to testify against in court." He grinned. "All I need to know is if you got people who'll be coming 'round here looking for your ass because you're late for dinner or some shit."

"No," Johnny said. "You don't have to worry about that."

"Well then, I could probably find a little work for you if you're interested."

"I'm very interested, as long as it's after school. I don't like to miss."

"I hear you. You don't need the truant officers crawling up your ass. That's smart." He smacked Johnny on the thigh and stood. "I'll be in touch."

"Cool." Johnny watched as he strutted out of the park, then pulled the bill from his pocket. It was a fifty. He smiled and stuffed it back.

CHAPTER TEN

The next morning, before homeroom, Clyde and Jarrod followed Johnny as he stopped by the office to drop off his application. It was emptier than the day before, so they walked right up to the counter. "Excuse me," Johnny said to a man with a phone cradled between his ear and shoulder, "I was supposed to drop—"

"Thank you," he mouthed, grabbing the document and tossing it in a basket full of forms.

"What'd I tell ya?" Jarrod said on the way out. "Gotta love this shithole."

"Speaking of shitholes," Clyde said to Johnny, "When do we get to see your apartment?"

Johnny laughed. "There's nothing to see."

"So what?" said Jarrod. "Besides, I wanna meet this older woman you're fooling around with."

Johnny rolled his eyes. "Shut the fuck up."

"Let's go today after homework," said Clyde.

When they got to Johnny's building, he picked up a bottle top from the gutter and chucked it at Lily's half-open bedroom window.

She looked out and leaned over the sill. "Hey, you. Who are those guys?"

"My friends," said Johnny. "Can you come over?"

"I can for a while before my snatch of a mother gets home, but she's still pissed at me for being late the other day."

"Cool. Meet us in the hall."

She was already waiting by the time they got to the second floor, and Johnny made the introductions.

"Such a nice surprise," she said as they hiked up the stairs. "What's the occasion?"

"No occasion. We were just kicking around," said Johnny. "How's your school so far?"

"It sucks. This clique of older girls singled me out for no fucking reason, and now they harass me whenever I pass them in the hall. I have to slink between classes and use the back staircase."

"Can't you tell someone?" asked Clyde.

"Are you crazy?" said Lily. "If I snitch, it'll get worse."

"Don't you have friends to defend you?" asked Jarrod.

"The kids I knew in junior high are going to other schools. If my mother gave two shits, she could've sent me somewhere else, too, but she didn't wanna be bothered with the extra paperwork to enroll me outside my district."

When they entered the apartment, Clyde and Jarrod broke off, opening closet doors and looking at the tub where Johnny slept. "It's not *that* bad," said Jarrod. "You *could* fix it up."

Johnny laughed. "Yeah, right."

"I'm serious. You could screw a lock into the front door, so at least you'd be safe when you're inside. Then you don't have to sleep in the bathroom. Maybe get a sleeping bag and some pillows."

"You should check out the Salvation Army," said Clyde. "They have all kinds of used stuff—blankets, furniture, clothes, dishes—for cheap money. I don't know why I didn't think of it before. Maybe this weekend we can pitch in to buy you some shit."

"Damn, I'll get some shit and move in, too," said Jarrod.

"You all should," said Lily. "Then you can be my protectors." Her head cocked. "So, how are you getting money to buy stuff?"

Johnny looked between Clyde and Jarrod, but they were waiting for him to come up with an answer. "Um, I got an uncle up in the Bronx. He owns a moving company, and he'll throw us a few bucks for helping him load furniture. You know, like every now and again."

Clyde and Jarrod nodded like it sounded believable.

Lily fiddled with her hair. "Maybe next time I could help, too."

"Sure." Johnny's head bobbled. "I'll make sure to ask him."

When it came time for Clyde and Jarrod to go, Johnny walked them to the door. He stood at the threshold watching them walk away, each step punching a greater hole in Johnny's solar plexus.

"I should get going, too," Lily said from within. "I don't want to cause my mother to have another shit fit."

Johnny returned. "Right, because if I hear her trying to murder you, I don't have any way to call the cops." He forced a half-smile, and Lily did the same.

"Thanks for introducing me to your friends."

"Sure." Johnny nodded and took her hand. "Are you going to be okay at school?"

She frowned. "I don't know."

"I wish there was something I could do."

"At least you give a shit. That's more than anyone else I know."

He leaned in to kiss her, but her hair got in the way. He repositioned to try again, thinking she might pull it back, but she didn't. Instead, she gave his palm a squeeze before releasing it. "I'll see you later."

When Johnny closed the door behind her, the apartment felt more desolate than ever. Having seen it through the eyes of his two best friends made him yearn for something more. He made a pass through the kitchen with its cracked, empty counters and grimy gaps where the stove and refrigerator once stood. Even the roaches didn't come around much anymore. He circled the barren living room, then bedroom, both carpets slightly less desecrated where there had been furniture. Orlando's prison in the cellar had more stuff. The thought made him shudder, and he tried to unthink it, but the grim memories still squeezed through.

Johnny sat on the living room floor in his pajamas, listening to the record player through headphones. Orlando had started yelling and banging, and it was reverberating through the house. Johnny wished he could go out, but it was too late, so he put his head down and cranked up the volume. Before long, he felt his father stomping across the floor. He yanked the cellar door open so hard that the gust of air reached Johnny where he sat. He thought about making a break for his room, but if Miguel saw him, it might make him angrier.

Johnny heard a burst of commotion from below, but then everything went silent before his father stormed back to the kitchen. This was Johnny's opportunity to retreat. He pushed himself up but didn't realize the headphone's cord was caught on his leg. The plug disconnected from the receiver, causing music to blast through the speakers. He groped at the volume knob while fumbling for the needle, but it skipped across the vinyl, making a horrific screeching sound. He tried to shut off the power but wasn't fast enough.

An open hand smacked the table. "PUT THE BOY IN THE CELLAR!" his father yelled in Spanish.

"Papá, it was an accident," Johnny pleaded, but his mother was already dragging him across the floor by the back of his shirt. He tried to reason with her in Turkish, but she wouldn't even look at him. The latch flew back, and the door swung open. She lifted Johnny up by his armpits, plunked him onto the top step, then slammed the door and flipped the bolt.

Unlike other times, Orlando was not at the bottom of the stairs, gloating. Johnny inched down, step by step until he saw his brother in a ball on the floor with his face in his arms.

"Orlando?"

No answer.

"You okay?"

As crazy as Orlando had become, it was hard to forget the allies they had once been. Ignoring his better judgment, he put a hand on his brother's back. "Hey."

Orlando spun around and grabbed Johnny by the front of his shirt. He had a welt under one eye, and his top lip was split. Still, he leapt up, dragging Johnny around by his shirt with one hand while swinging punches with the other. His attempts were sloppy enough that Johnny could dodge most of them until what was left of Orlando's energy petered out. He released his brother and flopped on the bed.

Johnny straightened his ruffled clothes. "You want a cold cloth?"

Orlando sat up, projecting so much rage it made Johnny gulp his outgoing breath. "What the fuck is wrong with you?"

"Huh?"

"Why are you being nice to me? I just tried to beat the shit out of you."

"I—I don't—"

"You want to make me feel better?" Orlando growled. He went to the workbench to grab the pieces of rope. "Come here."

Johnny froze.

"Come. Here." He continued in a schizophrenic concoction of languages. "It'll be worse if you struggle. Gimme your hands."

Johnny was so terrified his arms felt too heavy to lift, and they trembled as he struggled to outstretch them. Orlando spared him the trouble and grabbed his wrists. He bound them in a tight knot, then pointed at his feet. Johnny sat on a ratty chair to hold his legs out, and Orlando tied them, too. He then grabbed Johnny and spun him upside down, securing his ankles to the hook chained to the rafter.

"Not upside down, please!" Johnny's blue-striped pajama top draped over his head. Orlando unbuttoned it, so it dangled from Johnny's tied hands. The impulse to fight was overwhelming, but Johnny knew it wouldn't help. He began to cry, the tears tickling his forehead before disappearing into his curly black hair. He felt the room swirl as his vision narrowed and sounds muffled into one.

The next thing Johnny knew, he was sitting on the top step of the cellar. His head was fuzzy, and he ached all over. Natural light streamed under the door. It was daytime. Why had Aylin not released him last night? Were his parents already at work? It hurt his brain to think about it, so he put his head in his folded arms.

"Hey asshole, you hungry?" Orlando said from below.

"Huh?"

"There's some cereal down here, and milk, in this little fridge."

Johnny didn't know if he could trust him, but he was hungry. As he stood, the pain in his sides almost caused him to collapse, but he bore it and crept down the stairs, feeling tiny pings in his legs and chest as well. Johnny pulled over a wobbly dining room chair as his brother portioned out bowls of cornflakes. They ate in silence. Orlando seemed less angry now. Peaceful, even. When he scooped cereal from the bowl to his mouth, he almost looked like a normal teenager.

After they ate, Orlando turned on the television to watch a game show. Johnny went to the bathroom to urinate and evaluate his wounds. The razor-knife cuts were bad, deeper than the first time, and spread out over his thighs and abdomen. There were also red, swollen welts that looked like whip marks across his ribs. He knew soaking in cool water would make him feel better.

"Can I take a bath?" Johnny called, but his brother never answered, so he filled the tub and sat in it for a long time. After patting dry with Orlando's towel, he dressed, sat on the edge of the basin and wept.

"Hey, can someone else get a turn on the crapper?" Orlando opened the door and swept his brother out.

Johnny shuffled into the room, wiping tears from his eyes. *The boxcutter.* He went to scan the workbench, which was cluttered with the tools Miguel had deemed too benign to bother getting rid of. Things like socket wrenches, levels, tape measures and paint brushes. *How did he miss the fucking boxcutter?* Johnny poked around, lifting the rumpled clothes and books Orlando had tossed there but could not find it. When footsteps sounded in the upstairs hallway, Johnny fled for the stairs.

"Javier?"

"Yes, Mama."

The bolt unlatched, and the door opened. Aylin stood in the hallway holding a plate with a sandwich and apple slices. "Out," she barked in Turkish. "And leave this for your brother."

From below, the toilet could be heard flushing. Johnny grabbed the plate, slapped it on the top step and scrambled out. Aylin locked everything up and exited as abruptly as she had arrived. Johnny stood in the hallway, baffled. Had she left work just to release him? And should he take that as some disfigured display of affection? His eye caught the headphones lying where they had fallen the night before, so he put them on the shelf, returned the album to the proper jacket, and filed it with the others.

Walking to his room, Johnny peeled off his blood-speckled pajamas and stuffed them into the hamper, then put on sweatpants and a T-shirt before curling up in bed. The rhythmic throbbing of his wounds made him try to recall what had happened. Did he faint? If so, why was he out so long, and how did he get to the top step? None of it made any sense, but it seemed less disturbing than witnessing everything Orlando had done to him.

Johnny drifted into a dreamless sleep. When he woke, it was dusk, so he sat up to orient himself. The house was quiet, other than some clanging coming from the kitchen. The sound made Johnny's stomach grumble. It was a night Miguel worked a double shift, and he should already be gone, so Johnny tiptoed across the living room. He paused to watch Aylin pull a meatloaf and roasted potatoes from the oven. She must have sensed him there because she spoke in Turkish without facing him. "Do you want me to fix you a meal?"

"Yes, please."

Aylin pulled two dishes from the cupboard, plated the food and set it on the table. Johnny went to his chair and sat down. She poured a glass of milk for him and water for herself. Aylin sat across from Johnny, forking dainty portions into her mouth, which she chewed with lips sealed tight. Johnny kept stealing glances at her as he ate. She used to be so beautiful. She still was. It was just masked by anger. Johnny sipped the milk, his feet wagging under the table. What if they left? Packed a few things and got the fuck out. Would she be happy then? How much worse did it have to get before she did something? He tapped some salt onto his meat. *Because you know he's gonna kill me, right?* Johnny's glance must have turned into a glare because it prompted Aylin to look up. He speared a potato. "This is delicious."

When they finished eating, Johnny brought the dishes to the sink, thanked his mother and went to wash up and brush his teeth. He noticed a few tiny blood spots on his T-shirt, where some cuts had leaked, so he pulled it off to scrub them in the sink. The damp shirt was slung over his arm as he went to his bedroom. Aylin passed him in the hallway. He slowed his pace, giving her plenty of opportunity to view the wounds.

"Goodnight, Javier," was all she said before continuing to the bathroom.

Johnny felt like he had been punched in the throat. His voice wafted down from his nasal passages. "Goodnight, Mama."

CHAPTER ELEVEN

For the next several months, the school's administration never questioned Johnny's paperwork. He was acing his classes and blending in with the other students. The friends continued their after-school library study group, and, as a result, Clyde and Jarrod brought their B averages up to As.

They shared the same band class, but the only instruments available were brass and woodwinds, most of which had sticky joints and keys, but they made do. And at least they were learning to read music. After repeated appeals to the instructor, he let the three kids fiddle on the meager drum set, untuned upright piano, and acoustic guitar wedged in the back of the closet while he did paperwork at the end of the day.

Fall hung around as long as possible, lulling Johnny into thinking it would not get much worse until one morning when he woke to snow blowing in every direction. He threw back the quilts and blankets he had gotten at the Salvation Army, pushed up off the bedroom floor and went to look out the bare window. "Holy shit." It was still pre-dawn as Johnny watched the fluffy white flurries oscillating in unison under the yellow glow of the streetlight, like a murmuration of starlings. "Damn. Here, it even snows *up*." The draft seeping through the sill made Johnny shiver, so he peeled away to get ready for school.

After washing, he opened the walk-in hall closet, where he kept tidy stacks of clothes he had amassed. Some were passed along from Clyde and Jarrod, and others shoplifted or purchased cheap from second-hand stores. He piled on layers for his trek to school but was ill-equipped for the brutal smack in the face when he turned onto the block. The buildings created a numbing wind tunnel that almost blew him down. He tucked his face in the collar of his jacket and jogged to the subway.

Johnny watched the blizzard intensify through the rattling classroom windows. By last period, they were completely whited out by sideways snow. In the library, after classes, Clyde and Jarrod donated a hat, scarf and gloves to Johnny, promising to raid their closets for more. They killed time, waiting for the weather to calm down, but it only grew worse.

Outside, the streets were a slippery, slushy mess, which made bracing against the elements even more treacherous. The extra clothes helped, but Johnny's sneakers were soaked by the time he got to the train. Uptown, he trudged through the courtyard, sticking to the footpaths carved into the unshoveled snow. It was already dark as he fumbled through his pockets for the front door key. As Johnny stepped into the lobby, his eye caught a large figure slumped beneath a flickering overhead light, and his heart jumped. It was so bundled up he couldn't tell the race or gender until it spoke.

"Hey, kid." The gravelly voice echoed off the lobby's tile, tickling the hairs on the back of Johnny's neck. "Spare some change?" An arm outstretched. A few calloused fingers poked through the holes in his wool glove.

"Jesus Christ," Johnny muttered, trying to normalize his breath. He spun for the stairs, his shoes squishing with every step. As he climbed, voices could be heard coming from various empty units. He softened his steps, hoping the junkies kept themselves to the lower floors.

In his apartment, Johnny did a quick sweep to make sure nobody was there, then fastened the heavy-duty hook and eye lock he had installed on the front door. He exhaled and saw his breath. Johnny kept his coat on as he went around, lighting candles and laying a hand on all the radiators. "Coldest day yet, and these things are barely working." Further compounding the issue were the old windows, which were no match for the cyclone that formed between buildings. The draft was so severe it made the candles flicker.

Johnny pulled off his wet shoes and socks, set them atop the lukewarm living room radiator, then turned on the hot water in the tub. After letting it run a bit, he stuck a hand under the flow. "No hot water either? Fuck this shit." He shut the tap and put on dry socks, but he was too cold to bother changing the rest of his clothes. Instead, he cocooned himself in his bedding and pressed against the bedroom's radiator, trying to absorb whatever scant warmth made its way to his floor. *Fucking apartment.* He tried to sleep but kept waking up shivering. He found if he rocked back and forth, it would warm him up enough to drift off again.

"Are you wearing the same shit?" Clyde asked Johnny as they walked toward the lunchroom the next day.

Jarrod tried to unflatten Johnny's hair. "Seriously. I thought you were trying *not* to look like a raggedy-ass orphan."

Johnny pushed his hand away. "It was too fucking cold in that apartment to change. I hardly slept at all."

They got their food and slid into a table before Jarrod continued. "That shit ain't right. I can't be worrying that you're freezing to death."

"Maybe I should look for someplace else."

Clyde sporked a Tater Tot and popped it in his mouth. "You know how loose my mom is about sleepovers because you guys are there all the time. But not on school nights."

"We definitely don't want to blow it with her," said Jarrod.

"I could smuggle you in, probably bribe Tiffany to keep quiet, but it's Clair and Cecily I worry about. Those girls can't keep a secret worth a shit."

Johnny squeezed tartar sauce from the paper cup onto his fish sandwich. "And if your mother found out, how could she *not* report me?"

Jarrod waved them both off. "Listen, I know my place ain't a picnic, but my parents are so fucked up all the time that I could probably feed them some line of bullshit to let you stay over. At least when it's *really* cold, like today. It's only like ten fucking degrees and still blowing like four whores." He stuffed his sandwich in his mouth and bit off a portion. "I'm calling them right after lunch."

Johnny laughed. "Thanks, brother."

After school, Jarrod brought Johnny to his high-rise on West 25th Street. The lobby was drab and characterless, with rows of buzzers on one side of the foyer, mailboxes on the other. Behind the thick glass door were twin elevators, a staircase, and housing for a fire hose that had been tagged with graffiti to read: *IN CASE OF EMERGENCY, suck my dick.*

They got in the elevator, and Jarrod pressed the button for the ninth floor. "I told them your place was being bombed for roaches, so you needed a place to stay. In case they ask any questions."

When the car opened, they followed the flame-retardant orange carpet to Jarrod's apartment. As he opened the door, Johnny had to brace against the smell. Most identifiable was a combination of cigarettes and burned food, but lingering in the background was a hint of decay, maybe even urine.

"Come on, what are you waiting for?" said Jarrod.

Johnny followed him to the living room, where his parents sat in front of a blaring TV set, Jarrod's mother on a sunken brown paisley sofa and his father on a stained baby-blue recliner. Cigarettes dangled from their lips, and iced drinks coated in condensation rested on furniture an arm's length away.

Jarrod stood between them, his arms akimbo. "I see happy hour is in full swing."

His mother cradled her butt in a half-full ashtray. "Oh, you're home."

His father craned his neck to see the talk show Jarrod was blocking.

"You remember I told you my friend Johnny was coming for dinner and sleeping over, right?"

"What time do you expect him?" asked his mother.

Jarrod rolled his eyes at Johnny and waved him closer. "He's *right here.*" Jarrod outstretched a hand. "Johnny, allow me to introduce Missy and Kurt King."

It took Missy a few thrusts to push her stout, unshapely figure off the couch. She wore a floral housecoat and slippers. Her graying hair sat in a sloppy bun atop her head, the loose strands corralled by hairpins. "Johnny, is it?" She shuffled over to Jarrod and planted a wet kiss on his cheek. He crossed his eyes at Johnny, who choked back a laugh. She surprised Johnny by doing the same to him, but he turned, and she got his ear instead. The slushy sound made him shiver. "Welcome. Make yourself at home."

"I'm sure he'll be itching to move right in after this," said Jarrod.

"Kurt, did you meet Jarrod's friend, Johnny?" said Missy.

Kurt stuck out his bottom lip and grunted. He was a big man whose belly stretched the limits of his blotchy white undershirt. He was balding, with a saggy face that bore the stubble of several days.

Missy looped an arm in Johnny's. "Did you meet my brother, George?"

"No, Mom," Jarrod said before Johnny could answer. "We literally *just* walked in the door."

A thin man with red hair appeared from the kitchen. The spider veins on his nose and cheeks were the only thing offsetting his pallor. "Howdy. I'm Uncle George." He extended his hand, and Johnny shook it. "I hope you like spaghetti. I made a whole bunch."

Johnny smiled. "Yes, sir, I sure do."

"We'll be in my room." Jarrod pulled Johnny away. "Call us when it's ready."

Jarrod had a large room with lots of natural light, but, unlike Clyde's, it lacked much personal flair other than the meager drumming equipment piled in a corner. Also, where the DeMarcos' house was cluttered but clean, the Kings' was sparse but dirty. The floors were sticky and stained, and the windows were filmy.

"Let's get this folding bed out," Jarrod said, opening the closet door. "Then you can grab a hot shower, and I'll find you some fresh clothes."

"Thanks, man." The cot was wedged in, so they had to wrestle it out. "I take it you don't have much company."

"Are you fucking kidding? Did you see how messed up they are? And it's not even dinner time." They unfolded the bed in the middle of the room. Jarrod grabbed sheets and a pillow, and they made up the mattress. "I hate being here. It's fucking embarrassing. But after hearing about your conditions…"

"Has Clyde ever stayed here?"

"He did once because he didn't believe it was that bad." Jarrod laughed. "Now he knows. But when it warms up, I ought to stay with you. It can't be any worse. We're both surrounded by drunks and junkies. The only difference is I have electricity."

Johnny grinned. "That's a pretty big difference." He walked across the room to look out the window. "Don't your folks have jobs?"

"My mom collects disability for a back injury she *claims* she got working at Woolworths ages ago. My dad *could* get a job if his drunk ass got out of bed in the morning. Sometimes his carpenter friends will pay him under the table to help them out, but ultimately, he'll get shit-canned for being late or not showing up at all."

"That's fucked up." Johnny turned to face Jarrod. "Kinda sad, too."

"Tell me about it." Jarrod sat on the bed and picked at a loose thread on his blanket. "And it's frustrating because they *could* get ahead if they weren't so satisfied with getting by. Like, when George is off the dope and allowed to crash here, he'll throw them a few bucks from his dishwashing job, and then my father won't even *try* to work." Jarrod spit out a laugh. "Unless the liquor's low."

Johnny cocked his head. "But on the bright side, it should be pretty easy to sneak me in and out."

"You know something?" Jarrod stood, the fingers of both hands snapping alternately. "It *would* be easy. I can probably milk the bombing-for-roaches story for the rest of this week, but after that, you could come over after school and just never leave. Those dimwits won't notice."

"You think?"

"One hundred percent. And, they're never awake before eleven, so we'll have plenty of time to shower and get ready for school."

"What about your uncle? He sleeps on the couch, right?"

Jarrod waved the air. "Fuck him. He won't say shit because his invitation is shaky anyway. Plus, I've covered for him when he's gone back on the smack so that motherfucker owes me."

"I'm game to try it if you are." Johnny sat on the cot and bounced a few times. "Because it beats my freezing cold apartment."

"Don't speak too soon," Jarrod smirked. "You haven't tried the food."

CHAPTER TWELVE

Over the winter, the Brick made good on his offer to throw Johnny some work, but the details remained cryptic. He was to call a phone number, where he was told a day and time to make a pickup. That occurred in the Financial District, out of a dingy building near the intersection of John and Gold Streets. At the apartment, after being identified through the peephole, the door would open as much as the security chain allowed, and a hand would pass a package to Johnny through the opening. The bundles varied in size but were always well-wrapped in brown paper and bound with twine, like meat from the butcher. A piece of paper telling Johnny the delivery location was tucked under the string.

The drop-offs varied. Some were local, others took him to different boroughs, but he welcomed the opportunity to get to know the city even better. When the task had been completed, he would return to the park, where the Brick would give him twenty bucks. Sometimes, his payment came with a bonus of weed.

It was mid-March, and Johnny had just delivered a meatloaf-sized package to an apartment on 11th Street between Avenues C and D. As he stepped out of the building, he tipped his face to the warmth of the afternoon sun. Only the last little bits of soot-covered snow remained in the darkest corners of the streets. He did it. He had survived his first winter in New York. It felt good, gave him confidence, like things might get easier from now on.

As Johnny walked past Tompkins Square Park, he noticed three boys leaning on the wrought iron fence. One he recognized from school. It was the tall blond kid with the pushed-up nose. The same one who bumped him in the hallway on the first day. He stood with a freckle-faced black kid with glasses. His frizzy hair was pulled into a ponytail. The third was white with braces and scraggly shoulder-length brown hair. Each looked about a grade ahead of Johnny. They wore ripped jeans, dirty Keds, and black jackets. Johnny caught them watching him, so he looked down and kept walking.

Pug-nose spoke out. "You're in my school, aren't you?"

"Yeah," Johnny said, not stopping.

"Come here. I need to ask you something."

Despite the churning in Johnny's gut, he paused to turn, letting his eyes sweep the surroundings. A few people were inside the park, but most looked like druggies. There was some foot and car traffic on the avenue, but that was half a block away. "What do you want?"

The three teens circled Johnny. "You live around here?" asked Ponytail.

Johnny shrugged. "What's it to you?"

"Maybe it's a lot," said the kid with braces.

Pug-nose spit on the ground. "You too good to talk to us?"

Johnny snickered. "It doesn't matter what I say because you've already decided to have a problem with me." He started to back away, but Pug-nose smacked him across the head. Johnny guessed he could outrun these kids, but that would only give them permission to fuck with him again and again. So, he balled up a fist and hit the kid square in the eye. Pug-nose let out a yelp, cradling his face with both hands. Braces sucker-punched Johnny in the side of his head. Ponytail slammed him twice in the ribs. By then, Pug-nose had recovered enough to join the others.

It was hard for Johnny to get any accurate shots in the melee, but he made a good effort, focusing on his schoolmate. If he could just get him out of the way, then he would deal with the others. After three successive punches, Johnny knocked Pug-nose to his knees, but that only invigorated his friends, whose fists started coming from every direction. As Johnny ducked, an elbow connected with his eye. He tried to block his face, but one of them yanked his hand away while the other hit him in the nose.

"Hey!" someone called out.

The punks backed away from Johnny as two kids hurried over. One was a stocky Latino with kinky brown hair, the other a muscular, dark-skinned black teen with a large afro. Johnny had seen these two hanging out together in the school lunchroom, and the black kid was in one of his classes.

It was the Latino who had spoken. "Well, well. Look at this. We have *three* guys beating up…" His head swiveled, looking around. "…*one* guy. Seriously? That's it?" He turned to his friend. "Does that seem fair to you, Mario?"

"No, man." Mario's voice was deep for his age. "That does *not* seem fair at all."

"But you know what?" The Latino walked closer, patting his chest. "I'm one—" he waved a hand toward Mario. "—you're two, and then there's this guy." He looked at Johnny.

Johnny was still catching his breath, bent over, with hands on his knees, but he forced a nod. "Now it's even." Mario outstretched both arms. "So, how 'bout it?"

"Fuck you," said Ponytail.

Mario stepped up to him. "No, motherfucker, fuck *you*." Ponytail went to shove him in the chest, but Mario punched his hands away, then put his face in Ponytail's. "You want some of this?"

"Go on, do it," Chico goaded the kid. "He ain't lost a fight yet."

Ponytail looked at his friends, whose enthusiasm for trouble appeared to be waning. He took a step back. "Yeah, it's not worth it."

"That's what I thought," said Mario. "Take your sorry asses the fuck outta here."

Pug-nose brushed himself off, sneering. "We were leaving anyway. C'mon guys."

Mario spit out a laugh. "You were leaving anyway? What kinda lame shit is that?" When the three punks started off down the block, Mario grabbed his crotch "All y'all motherfuckers can suck my *whole* dick!" He shook his head at Johnny. "Unreal. You okay, man?"

"Yeah, I'm all right."

"You don't look it," said the Latin kid. "What's your name, hermano?"

"Johnny."

"I'm Chico, and this is Mario. You're in our school, right?"

"Yeah. He's in one of my classes." Johnny pointed at Mario.

"C'mon, man, we'll get you cleaned up."

"Cool. Thanks." Johnny blotted his bloody face with his shirt. When he took a step, pain shot through his midsection, and he winced. Chico and Mario positioned themselves on either side of him for support.

"It's not far. I'm over on 5th, between A and B. My pops is the super there."

"And I'm up on 4th and C," said Mario. "You're not from this neighborhood, are you?"

"Nah," was all Johnny offered.

Chico's block was rows of five-story walk-ups. The trash piled on the curb made navigating the narrow sidewalk difficult. They stopped in front of a wide stoop and helped Johnny up the steps. Inside a glass-paned door, Chico pushed the button for 1A, which read Velasquez. The buzzer sounded, and he led them inside. The hallway's black and white tiles were cracked and chipped but otherwise spotless, and everything smelled faintly of bleach. Out back, Johnny could see a courtyard with a little garden and some patio furniture.

A stout middle-aged woman emerged from an apartment at the end of the hall. Her long black hair was twisted into a bun, and her eyes were dark and intense. She was scolding Chico in Spanish for not using his key.

"Mama, I didn't because I was helping him." Chico stepped aside so she could see Johnny. "Some kids were beating him up by the park."

She threw up her hands, reciting a string of prayers and ushered them inside. The apartment was light with an open floor plan. A spacious kitchen, with windows facing the garden, segued to the living room. The furniture was sparse, but everything matched.

"*Mamá, éste es Johnny.* Johnny, this is my mother, Lucinda."

"*Lucinda,*" he said. "*Es un placer.*"

She nodded a greeting, then had them sit at the dinner table.

Johnny's eyes followed Lucinda as she gathered bandages, ointments and herbs, muttering in Spanish.

Mario smiled at him. "Don't worry, man, she'll fix you up good. She's like a witch doctor. She's taken care of me a few times after I fell into some shit."

"Cool." He looked at Chico. "Does she speak English?"

"No, but she knows more than she lets on." Chico folded his arms on the table. "We came up from Puerto Rico eight years ago 'cause my pops couldn't get enough work down there, but my mom never wanted to come. Not speaking English is her way of rebelling, or maybe she's just embarrassed that she won't speak it good."

"Well."

"What?"

"She won't speak English *well*," Johnny smirked despite his sore face.

Chico laughed. "Man, if you weren't so beat up, I'd smack you."

Lucinda sat beside Johnny and turned him to face her. He had a split lip, a cut on his nose and one of his eyes was swelling. She cleaned his wounds with a cold cloth, then applied a disinfectant before slathering on a thick balm that smelled of alcohol, menthol and spices. She asked Johnny to lift his shirt so she could tape an ice pack to his ribs. When he did, she turned and barked at Chico and Mario to get some bags of soil from the basement and bring them to the garden.

Once Lucinda had Johnny alone, her eyes hardened. "What is your family name," she asked in Spanish.

"Avalon."

"Where are you from?"

"Washington Heights."

She scowled. "Why are you lying to me?"

Johnny held her gaze. *How the fuck does she know?* He tried to quiet his brain and listen to his gut. For some crazy reason, she didn't feel like a threat, and he was too beaten up to resist. "You're right. I'm not from New York, but I live here now."

"What is your real name?"

Johnny didn't answer.

"Who are your parents?"

"I don't have any."

"These parents you don't have, are they dead or alive?"

It was one question he could answer honestly. "I wish they were dead."

Lucinda relaxed, taking Johnny's injured face in her small hands. "Listen, I take care of my own. I will not repeat your secrets, but I need to know that they will not hurt my son or my family."

"My secrets won't hurt anyone. They will only protect me."

"If you are honest with me, I will protect you, too, because I can see that you are smart and that you and Chico will be friends for a long time." She folded her hands on the table. "Now, tell me your real name."

Johnny looked at the ceiling and swallowed hard. "Álvarez, Javier Álvarez."

"That was difficult."

"Yes. I've been trying to forget."

"And what happened to you?"

"I got jumped by three guys in the park."

"I'm not talking about today." She put her hands against the razor-knife scars on his bare torso. "What *happened* to you?"

Johnny slouched in the chair, closing his eyes before giving the abridged version of his family history and how he had been managing thus far to this woman he just met. Lucinda didn't want specifics, which was fortunate because the rough overview was hard enough.

When she had heard enough, a hand went up to stop him. "It is good you have friends, but an adult ally is also necessary." She patted his knee. "What you did, what you are *doing*, takes great strength and courage. People see that in your character, even if they don't know your story. It is why intelligent people are drawn to you, and stupid people are threatened by you. Let that be your barometer." She sat back in her chair. "Don't worry, you can trust me."

Johnny believed her. "Thank you."

"Are you going to school tomorrow?"

"I want to, but will it be a problem showing up like this?" His hand circled his face.

"That school?" Lucinda laughed. "They wouldn't notice if you showed up with an axe wedged in your back." She grabbed a napkin and wrote down a phone number. "But here, just in case somebody asks to speak to your parents. Who am I pretending to be?"

Johnny smiled. "Maria Avalon, and we live at 550 180th Street, apartment 6F."

She scribbled it down. "You will have dinner with us and stay the night." Her tone allowed for no argument.

"Yes, ma'am."

"Come, lie down." Lucinda led Johnny to the couch and propped him up with pillows and ice packs. She handed him a damp sack that smelled of lavender and lemon. "Hold that on your eye." She went to the kitchen and returned with a cup of warm liquid. "You need to drink this."

"What is it?" He sniffed its pungent aroma.

"Don't worry what it is, just drink it."

He took a large gulp and almost gagged, but she wagged a hand at him to finish. The rest went down easier once his taste buds were numbed by the initial shock.

Lucinda smiled. "Rest. I'll wake you when dinner is ready."

Johnny slid down, tipped his head back, and lay the fragrant sack on his eye. She expected him to sleep? In a strange house with a bunch of people he didn't know? But as he listened to Lucinda puttering around the kitchen, he forced his eyes closed. The throbbing parts of his body only hummed now, allowing him to relax. Hushed voices and people walking in and out filled the apartment, but Johnny found the noise comforting.

When he woke, Chico was standing over him. "Are you alive?"

"I think so."

"You've been out for an hour."

"Shit, really?"

"It's dinnertime. Can you get up?"

The pain and stiffness were all too familiar. The nurturing atmosphere was not. The latter made it easier to press through as Johnny stood. Chico walked him to the kitchen table, where people were already seated. Platters of delicious-smelling food were steaming in the center.

Chico made the introductions. "This is Johnny, he goes to my school. He had a little accident today, so that's why he looks like this."

The faces around the table smiled at the understatement as Johnny sat.

Chico whipped out a finger. "That's my pops, Luis, my older sister, Rosita, and my even *older* sister, Raquel." Chico went to sit opposite his father.

Luis's round face beamed. "Welcome. Nice to meet you." He was tall and muscular with a protruding belly. A horseshoe of brown hair wrapped around the back of his head. He wore a white undershirt, red suspenders and grease-stained Dickies. His bold-framed glasses had an earpiece held together by electrician's tape. "We heard about what happened, but you need to eat. My wife's food is medicinal!" He scooped up a large portion of yellow rice with onion and peppers and plopped it on Johnny's plate. "Just ask this one. He's here almost every night." He turned to Mario. "You *do* have a home, don't you?"

As Lucinda forked crispy fried chicken legs and cooked greens onto everyone's plates, Mario leaned across the table to Johnny. "Don't listen to him. This family loves me. Especially Rosita." He turned to her and winked.

Rosita scrunched her face. "Ew, gross. I'm trying to eat." She was short, like her mother, but curvier. Raquel was tall and solid, like Luis.

After dinner, the three boys lingered at the table, getting to know each other until Lucinda sent Mario home so Chico could do his homework and Johnny could rest. On the way to his room, Chico patted Johnny's shoulder. "You should shower tonight. That bathroom's pretty busy in the morning with those girls trying to get ready at the same time. I'll get you a towel and a clean shirt."

"Thanks, man."

In the bathroom, Johnny turned on the water and peeled off his clothes. Before pulling back the shower curtain, he caught a look in the mirror. The three punks had gotten in some good punches, but they could've done a lot more damage had they been better fighters. All in all, Johnny didn't think he fared too badly. He was pissed off about having been jumped, no doubt, but at least it was a manageable anger that didn't come attached to a bunch of complicated feelings. *Besides, I will get even.*

CHAPTER THIRTEEN

Johnny woke to the clamoring of pots and pans. He peeled off the blanket and sat up. The act was less painful than expected. Mario had been right about that witch doctor shit. Lucinda saw him and left her breakfast prep. She took his chin and turned his face from side to side.

Johnny smirked. "I bet I look like nothing happened."

"Not exactly, but there is some improvement from yesterday." She smiled. "Come, breakfast is ready."

The rest of the family filtered into the kitchen. "Check you out, hermano," said Chico. "Now you look like you only fought *one* motherfucker!"

Luis ruffled Chico's hair. "You and that cursing." He grabbed a pot that had been percolating on the stove. "Would you like some coffee, Johnny?"

"Sure. I'm down for anything Lucinda makes."

"Me, too." Luis patted his belly with his free hand, then poured a cup and set it in front of Johnny.

Lucinda came around with a pan, dishing out portions of scrambled eggs with tomato, green peppers and cheese. On the table was a basket of biscuits and a bowl of assorted fruit. Johnny relished every bite. When he was done, Lucinda caught his eye. "Good luck today."

"Thank you." Johnny smiled. "For everything."

Mario was waiting for Chico and Johnny on the corner. He circled Johnny, looking him up and down. "See? I told you that voodoo shit works."

"No doubt," said Johnny. "But what's her deal? She's pretty intense."

Chico led the way toward the bus stop. "She's just got a good intuition about people, and she'll call them out on what she sees. My pops won't rent to anyone without going through her first."

"She liked you," said Mario. "That's saying a lot."

On the school block, Johnny spotted Clyde and Jarrod leaning against a parked car. "C'mon, I want you to meet my friends."

As they neared, Jarrod pushed off the car, throwing his hands in the air. "Clyde, you seeing this shit? Unbelievable. He fucking replaced us!"

Johnny laughed. "Shut up, idiot."

"Looks like he got his ass kicked in the process," said Clyde, stepping closer. "What the fuck *happened* to you?"

"I got jumped yesterday, but these guys helped me out. Mario and Chico, this is Jarrod and Clyde."

Mario's brows knitted. "Clyde? What the fuck kinda name is that?"

Clyde shrugged. "I don't know. I'm named after my grandfather."

"That's old school. What's your last name?"

"DeMarco."

"Are you Italian?"

"Yeah."

"How do you get Clyde with DeMarco? That don't fit. You should be named Vito or Luigi."

"Or, perhaps..." Clyde grinned, "Mario?"

"Hey, *I'm* named after Mario Lanza, my grandma's favorite singer, with the last name of Washington, as in descended from our founding father, you dig?"

Chico smacked Mario's arm. "And I'm a distant cousin of Ponce de Leon."

"Ponce de who?"

"Exactly."

The others snickered at the exchange.

Mario jutted his chin at Jarrod. "What about you? What's *your* last name?"

Jarrod's spine straightened. "King."

Mario coughed out a laugh. "Aw, snap, *nobody* messes with the King!" He put out his hand, and Jarrod slapped him five.

The bell rang, and they went to their respective classrooms but reconvened for lunch. As the five of them marched through the cafeteria, other kids yielded to their presence. They loaded their trays with food and commandeered a table in the back. As they ate, Johnny provided details of the assault.

"I've seen that kid around," said Jarrod. "Pale eighth-grader, always drawing shit on his ripped jeans."

"Me, too," said Clyde. "Loner, kinda dorky and weird."

"Yeah, that guy," said Johnny. "Keep a lookout because I can't have him starting anything with me here." He turned to Chico and Mario. "My parents are strict when it comes to school."

"Tell me about it," said Chico. "You met my mom. If I ever got suspended, she might poison my ass." He laughed.

"Don't worry about that kid," said Mario. "Without his friends, he ain't shit."

Chico slurped some milk from the mini carton. "What are you guys doing later? We should hang."

Jarrod and Clyde looked at each other, then Johnny.

Johnny turned both palms to the ceiling. "What?" Then he sighed. "Oh, I get it." He looked at Chico and Mario. "We usually do homework in the library after school."

Mario wagged his head so hard his afro wobbled. "Say what?"

"Let me get this straight," said Chico. "You stay at school *after* school is over?"

Jarrod threw a thumb Johnny's way. "It was his idea."

"But," said Clyde, "teaming up does make the work easier and more fun. And once it's done, it's done. You can leave your books in the locker and be free till the next day."

Chico and Mario gave it a thought, then nodded in unison. "We'll try it," said Mario.

Johnny smiled. "Cool. It won't take long, then we can do something after. But at some point, I'm gonna need to cut out and swing by Washington Square. I run some errands for this guy. I was supposed to check in with him yesterday, but *that* never happened."

"Errands?" Chico said, smirking.

Johnny's stomach clenched. "What?"

Mario coughed out a laugh. "Anybody who uses the words 'errands' and 'Washington Square' in the same sentence ain't talking 'bout no motherfucking shopping list." He put a hand on Johnny's shoulder. "But whatever you're into, my brother, it's cool with us."

"Yeah, man," said Chico. "Do whatever you got to do."

CHAPTER FOURTEEN

Johnny found the Brick on a bench, sitting with a few regulars, and walked over.

"Whoa, Colombiano, check out that shiner." He shook his head and grinned. "Damn, boy, I told you to stop messing with those married women!" His friends chuckled.

Johnny grabbed his crotch. "Yeah, but she was *so* worth it."

"What a little smartass." He laughed. "You better not be fucking with *my* wife!"

"I guess you'll know tonight when she starts screaming my name." He switched to a falsetto. "Oh, Colombiano, give it to me, yeah, ooh, ah!"

Everyone cracked up.

"You little motherfucker!" The Brick turned to his friends. "You see why I like this kid? He ain't afraid to give me no shit! Gimme five, brother." He held out his hand, examining Johnny's face as they traded slaps. "You all right?"

"Yeah. I'm fine."

The Brick stood up. "Walk with me a minute." He set off into the park, and Johnny followed.

"Everything go okay with that drop yesterday?"

"Yeah, piece of cake."

The Brick dipped his head to look at Johnny over the rim of his shades. "Don't be lying to me, boy."

"I'm not. I swear. I ran into some punks who didn't like how I looked."

"It wasn't over that package?"

"No. It was afterward."

The Brick folded his arms. "Do I need to worry about you?"

"No, Rick. I can take care of myself." He grinned. "You should see the other three guys."

"Three?" He slapped his knee. "No shit, Colombiano, I guess you *are* all that."

Once they got to a side street, the Brick took something from his pocket, then put a foot on a parked car's bumper, pretending to tie one of his white Capezios. As he did, he motioned for Johnny to take the offering. His eyes widened when he saw a baggie with several joints and a folded one-hundred-dollar bill, but he remained cool and slid the items into his pants pocket.

They circled the block and headed back toward the benches.

"I might have some bigger things for you if you're interested."

"I'm definitely interested."

"There'd be more risk."

"I need money. I can handle the risk."

The Brick hissed through his teeth. "You don't *need*, boy, you *want*. When people need, they get desperate and sloppy. There's no room for that here."

Johnny nodded.

"I see that you can handle a lot of shit. And you got big balls for a little kid. Don't think I haven't noticed that you keep calling me Rick, neither. You know I reserve that name for my close friends, right?"

"I know that."

"Okay, just checking." He paused before the entrance to the park and took Johnny's face in his hand. "You need me to get anyone for doing this to you?"

"No, man, I've got it, but thanks."

"You sure?"

"I'm sure."

"I'll bet you are, kid." The Brick grinned as they continued toward his friends. "It must be true what they say on the street. Don't fuck with the Colombians."

95

Johnny laughed. "You know it."

Climbing the stairs to his apartment, Johnny paused on the third-floor landing. Hushed voices and flickering candlelight were coming from one of the vacant units. *Junkies.* Before he could sprint up the next flight, he recognized a laugh. "Lily? Fuck." Johnny pivoted on the step and crept down the hallway, past a few legit apartments, to the half-open door of the vacant one. He couldn't see much beyond the entryway, so he pushed the door open wider. The light from the hallway illuminated the barren living room. A woman Johnny recognized from the neighborhood sat on the floor, swirling a piece of cotton around a tarnished spoon with a syringe. Lily was beside her, a sheet of tinfoil in one hand and a paper funnel in the other. She looked up when he entered.

"Johnny? Shit. What are you doing here?"

He stepped inside. "I heard your voice and wanted to make sure you were all right."

Lily turned to the woman, who looked even older and ashier up close. "Aw, isn't that sweet? Stacy, this is my friend Johnny."

She better not say anything to this skanky bitch about me. "Stacy, yeah, hi. I think I've seen you around."

Stacy acknowledged him with a nod accompanied by a hum.

Johnny slid his hands into his pockets and looked at Lily's glassy eyes. "What's going on?"

She held out the funnel. "Wanna try a hit?"

"Not really." Stacy cradled the syringe in her teeth to tie off an arm. When she saw Johnny watching, she shot him a look and he snapped his attention back to Lily. "I thought maybe you'd come hang out with me."

"You mean," Lily batted her eyes, "like a date?"

Stacy giggled before sinking the needle into her vein.

"Whatever you want to call it. Just come."

"One more hit."

"Okay. One."

Lily flicked a lighter under the foil and inhaled the stream of smoke coming from the brown substance. Johnny watched her head tip back as she swooned. For once, she looked kind of peaceful.

"Sure you don't want some?" she asked after returning from her head spin.

Johnny sighed. "No. C'mon."

As Stacy fell into a nod, Johnny extended a hand to Lily, then supported her as they stumbled to the sixth floor. His bruised ribs ached under the additional weight. Inside the apartment, he set her down on his pile of quilts, lit some candles, and got a can of juice from the kitchen. He sat beside her and made her drink.

As Lily sipped, she noticed his black eye. "Did you get mugged again?"

"Kind of. It's nothing."

She looked at the floor. "You're mad, aren't you?"

Johnny bit his lip. "Why are you hanging out with *her*?"

"Who the fuck else is there? You're never around."

"So using smack is *my* fault?"

"I didn't say that."

They both looked down at the apple juice can, which Lily was rotating with her fingers. "You don't tell these people that I stay up here, do you?"

Lily's face scrunched, insulted. "No."

"Because I got shit here, and even though it's not valuable, I don't need people fucking with it."

"Jesus, I'm not—"

"And if the cops come around, my parents will find out I'm camping up here, and then I'll have to deal with all of that." He exhaled and leaned back against the wall. "Why are you even doing that shit anyway?"

She sniffled up some snot and wiped an eye. "It makes me feel better, forget that everything sucks."

"Are you even sixteen?"

"Yeah. My birthday was a month ago. And guess what?" She threw up her hands. "Nobody cared about that either."

"Why don't you just have some beer or smoke a joint?"

"I'm not shooting the stuff, so what's the big deal?"

Jesus Christ. This fucking girl. "Don't you care about getting your shit together?"

97

"Why?"

Because your *shit is gonna compromise* my *shit.* "So you can get a job and move someplace nicer." He faced her again. "I thought things were getting better at school."

"Only because I stopped going."

"You quit school? For what? To spend more time getting wasted?" Johnny's eyes searched the ceiling. "How can you just give up that easily? You're not even gonna *try* and fight for yourself?"

Lily's brows furrowed. "Fuck you. You don't know a goddamn thing about it. Big deal, your family argues a lot, so you hide out in this apartment. Boo-hoo." She rolled her eyes. "You have no idea what it's like to feel trapped, stuck in some goddamn shithole, where no one listens to you or cares about what happens to you."

Johnny covered his face with both hands. *Really, bitch?* His home life made hers look like a fucking fairytale. Maybe if she spent less time feeling sorry for herself, she could do something about it. When Johnny uncovered his eyes, Lily was looking at him with her head cocked. *Don't. Just let it go. I'm not blowing my cover over some stupid bullshit.* "You're right," his voice croaked. "I *don't* understand everything you're going through, but I *do* care."

"Thank you." She smiled, the high seeming to have washed away everything that was said. "Do you mind if I crash here? I can't go home like this."

"Of course." Johnny flattened out the quilts, and Lily scooted down. He shook out the blanket and covered them with it, then peeled off his jeans. Lily did the same and curled to face the wall. Johnny lay on his back, listening to her breathing grow heavier. When it turned to soft snoring, he rolled over and fell asleep, too.

When Johnny woke, Lily was stepping over him. He rolled onto his back, blinking at the dawn's light that filtered through the bare bedroom windows. He listened as she puttered in the bathroom. After a few minutes, she emerged naked and crawled under the covers. Johnny froze, unsure what to do, until she leaned over to kiss his neck and chest. His hands found the warm skin of her buttocks. She straddled him, and they kissed, her tongue swirling around his.

Johnny still harbored anger toward Lily, but it all kept getting eclipsed by desire. When he swelled beneath her, she pulled off his briefs and guided him inside. It was the most extreme pleasure he had experienced, and he pushed into her. Johnny watched Lily's face as she tipped back her head and moaned. She looked almost as content as she had after smoking the dope.

As they rocked in unison, conflicting thoughts swam in Johnny's head. It felt wrong that she had climbed on him without any discussion, and he felt guilty for enjoying it. He also knew he should not be getting any closer to this girl, yet he couldn't stop. The sensation was too exhilarating, and he erupted inside of her. Johnny gasped, surprised at the ferocity and duration of the ejaculation, which was much more intense than masturbating. Lily seemed to take pride in his release, which inspired her to grind against him enough to bring herself to orgasm. After, she climbed off and lay beside him, looking into his face. He looked back, fingering her hair.

"You know I'm kind of in love with you, right?" she said.

"I guess so." *Me and whoever pays you any attention.*

"I know you don't love me back, but I'm all right with that." She shrugged. "I mean, just because we fucked doesn't mean it has to change anything."

"Lily, I like you," was all Johnny could manage. He wrapped both arms around her to avoid the discomfort of looking her in the eye. "I like you," he repeated into her hair.

When the embrace became awkward, Lily got up and dressed. "I better get home before my mother calls the cops."

"I should get ready for school anyway." Johnny threw on his briefs and walked her to the door. He kissed her. "I'll see you around?" He grimaced because it sounded so trite, but Lily didn't seem to notice.

"Yeah, see ya." She walked into the hallway without looking back.

CHAPTER FIFTEEN

Saturday was gray and windy, so the five friends hung out at Clyde's all afternoon. They smoked a joint, put a Led Zeppelin album on the turntable, then sat around the kitchen table playing cards. The game was interrupted when Tiffany came home from work with an armful of groceries. She wore a red miniskirt with black tights, white go-go boots, and a cut-off sweatshirt. Her bleach-blonde hair was teased up high.

She plopped the bags on the counter. "Are we running a fucking foster home around here?" Her eyes swept the new faces at the table. "Just what we need, more stray dogs for your dimwitted litter." Her chin jutted toward Johnny. "And why is that one all beat up?"

Mario jumped up to offer his chair. "Have a seat, sugar. Clearly, you've had a hard day." He ushered her over. "Sit your fine ass down. We'll put them groceries away."

Tiffany turned to Clyde while pointing a thumb Mario's way. "Who the fuck's this?"

Before Clyde could answer, Mario bowed. "Allow me to introduce myself. I'm Mario Washington, and this here is Chico Velasquez."

Chico gave her a nod. "How do you do?"

Jarrod and Johnny smirked at each other, and Tiffany squinted to look into their eyes. "You little fuckers are stoned, aren't you?"

"There is a reasonable probability that we may have partaken in certain illicit endeavors," said Mario. "However, I'm sure we could make a contribution to your own personal mental wellness." He glanced at Johnny. "Ain't that right, my brother?"

"I'd be delighted to share with you." Johnny smiled at Tiffany and winked.

"Ew!" She recoiled. "That's just creepy." But then she leaned across the table and wagged her fingers at him. "Hand it over, Joe Frazier."

Johnny pulled a joint from the jacket on the back of his chair and tossed it to her. Chico struck a match, and Tiffany took a few puffs. She passed the joint to Mario. "So, what *is* this—" Tiffany waved a hand at the group around the table, "—some remedial starter gang?"

"Might be," said Jarrod.

"You ought to call yourselves the Mangey Strays." Tiffany pointed at Johnny's black eye. "Except *this* dog got beat."

"Don't worry," said Chico. "There's gonna be an all-out war on the assholes who beat him."

"That's right." Johnny took a hit and passed to Clyde. "Then we'll be the Dogs of War."

"Great," Tiffany sneered, "because nothing's scarier than a gang of stoned, prepubescent dorks." She laughed. "Good luck with *that*!"

They sat around the table, razzing and bantering until Tiffany realized how late it was. "Are you losers planning on hanging out here all night because the girls will be home soon, and I need to start dinner."

Mario's head popped up. "There's more girls coming?"

Clyde rolled his eyes. "Gross!"

"It's all right," said Chico. "He hits on my sisters all the time. But we gotta get going anyway."

Clyde looked between Johnny and Jarrod. "You two are staying over, right?"

"I am," said Johnny.

"I can't tonight," said Jarrod. "My dad *actually* has some job to do tomorrow, early, and he asked me to help him."

"Cool, but find us when you get done. We'll be at the park."

Johnny's eyes hurt as he blinked them into focus. They were as dry and gritty as his mouth. His neck was stiff, and his head pounded. The room was familiar—Clyde's—but the perspective was all wrong.

"You okay now?"

Johnny tipped his head toward Clyde's voice. He sat several feet away, cross-legged on the floor with a blanket draped over his shoulders. Johnny was on the floor, too, pressed into the corner by the closet. He straightened out the tension in his spine. "What happened?"

"I don't know. I think you were sleepwalking or having a bad dream or some shit." Clyde scooted closer. "Something woke me up around one this morning, and I saw you sitting there, in that corner."

Johnny squinted at the light peeking through the blinds. "I've been here all night? What was I doing?"

"Hugging your knees, rocking back and forth, muttering some shit I couldn't understand. I tried talking to you, but it was like you didn't see me. Like you didn't know I was there until I tried to touch you. Then you shoved me. Hard."

"Fuck. Are you okay?"

"Yeah. It just surprised me. I kept my distance after that, but I still felt like I shouldn't leave you alone." Clyde stretched. "Has this happened before?"

Johnny slid onto his stomach, hiding his face in his folded arms. "Yeah. It used to happen a lot in Miami."

"No shit. What is it?"

"I don't fucking know, okay?"

"Look, I'm not judging you. I'm just trying to figure it out."

"I know." Johnny rolled onto his back. "But it pisses me off. I finally get away from my family, but this part still happens. I wish I could erase everything about my life with them."

Clyde picked at his socks. "After my father ran off, my mother took us all to a family therapist because she was worried how it might fuck us up. I remember that lady telling us to face all the shitty feelings instead of trying to pretend nothing happened, even if it's uncomfortable because if you bottle that shit up, it only gets worse in the long run." He looked at Johnny. "Maybe if you thought about it more, instead of trying to forget, you could stop these episodes."

"But what do you do when you *have* no memories, like a lot of shit is blocked out?"

"I don't know." Clyde pouted. "We only went four times before my mother couldn't afford it anymore." He sighed. "So, you never remember anything about being in that state?"

"No." Johnny covered his eyes with a forearm. "Usually, I just come to with a bunch of bad feelings."

"Like, bad how?"

"Mostly the feeling of being trapped, scared."

"That makes sense because you've got all those scars from being locked in the basement with your brother."

"And sometimes it's like I can't breathe."

"Like you're being suffocated?"

The words hit Johnny hard, and he sat upright.

"Shit, I didn't mean to upset you."

"No. It fits." Johnny's voice weakened. "I think my brother tried to suffocate me."

"Whoa. That's seriously fucked up."

Johnny waved the air. "I—I can't do this anymore."

"It's all right. I understand." Clyde took a long breath. "How often have these episodes happened in New York?"

"Only a few times, in my apartment, but I was embarrassed to mention it."

"You need to get over that shit. What if it happens at school or out in the streets? We have to be able to cover for you."

"You're right. Jarrod needs to know, but I want you to tell him because it's too hard for me."

"I get it, and I will." Clyde tried to comfort Johnny with a smile. "And don't worry. We'll figure this out."

CHAPTER SIXTEEN

The walk to Washington Square was quiet. Both Johnny and Clyde were cranky from lack of sleep, and the events of the night lingered between them. It was hard enough for Johnny to deal with the feelings caused by these episodes, but Clyde, having witnessed one, added a layer of shame. He kept thinking through the previous day, hunting for something that might have been a trigger, but there was nothing. Miami had never entered his mind. But that was even more fucked up because it meant it was random.

As they entered the park, Chico and Mario were standing by the fountain. Mario crossed his arms. "Who died?"

"For real," said Chico. "Why do you two look so serious?"

"We're just tired," said Johnny. "Stayed up *way* too late shooting the shit. You know how it is." He forced a laugh, then looked at Clyde.

"Way too late," Clyde parroted.

When Jarrod arrived a while later, he was scowling.

"You, too?" barked Mario. "You motherfuckers are like three turds in a punchbowl!"

"I swear," said Jarrod. "That's the last time I try to help that drunk son of a bitch."

"What happened?" asked Clyde.

"All we had to do was clean this construction site, the first floor of a building they're gonna convert into offices or some shit. Easy money." Jarrod stormed a circle around the others, arms waving. "First off, getting that fat useless fuck up at six a.m. just about required smelling salts and a hoist. But,

104

whatever, we get there. On time even. And I'm all sweeping here, tossing trash there, until I look around and realize he's nowhere to be found."

The others couldn't help laughing.

"I'm peeking under bathroom stalls, in closets, everywhere, until I see this blue tarp sprawled out on the floor, and I'm like, what the fuck is that?" Jarrod put a hand to his ear. "Is that snoring? So, I get closer, and it was! That asshole was passed the fuck out under the tarp. Can you believe that shit?"

"What'd you do?" Johnny asked.

"I grabbed a piece of plywood and a marker and wrote FATHER OF THE YEAR with an arrow. I propped it up by the tarp, then fucking left, so when the contractor guy comes back at lunch to check on us, that's what he'll find."

Chico clapped his hands. "That's harsh, man."

"Serves him right," said Mario. "Good for you."

Jarrod rolled his eyes. "But now I won't get paid."

They migrated to the playground near the arch. A woman sat reading a book on a bench while two kids laughed on the swings nearby. In a shady corner, a young couple talked and cuddled. The group headed for the monkey bars.

"Hey, Johnny," said Chico, climbing up the rungs. "When do we get to take care of those assholes who fucked you up?"

"Now you're talking." Johnny grinned. "That'll lighten up the mood around here."

"We should jump that pug-nosed douche in the hallway next time we see him," said Jarrod.

"No," said Clyde. "We're not fighting at school."

Mario clicked his tongue. "So, what *should* we do?"

Johnny draped over one of the bars. "Stare him down. Let him know that we see him. Meanwhile, we'll do some research, scope out where he lives, hangs out. But when the time comes, I want to fight him."

"Fuck that!" said Chico. "We should *all* kick his ass."

Johnny straightened up. "I won't fight like a pussy."

"I hate to state the obvious," Clyde hung his knees over a bar to swing upside down, "but he's older and bigger."

Johnny grinned at him. "But I'm crazier." Energized, he grabbed a high bar to do a few pull-ups. It made his bruised ribs ache, but the pain invigorated him to do even more.

"Hey," said Jarrod. "Do I get to pound one of them and pretend it's my father?"

"As long as I get the freckle-faced motherfucker with the ponytail," said Mario.

Johnny nodded. "I'm okay with that."

The five friends wandered the city for the rest of the day before each headed home. But this time, when Johnny heard voices in the vacant third-floor unit, he ignored them. He locked himself in his apartment, stripped to his underclothes, and lay on his quilts.

Even though he was exhausted, Johnny's mind kept spinning. What if Clyde was right? Maybe if he stopped pushing away the parts he *could* remember, the holes would fill in themselves.

When he walked in the door, Johnny's parents were at their usual places at the kitchen table. He didn't bother to greet them, only slid into his room and closed the door. He could hear that Orlando was restless and rustling around the cellar. He wasn't at the point of infuriating Miguel, but it was close. Johnny sat on his bed, hugging his knees as he rocked back and forth. He hoped things would calm down, but he was familiar enough with the patterns to know that they rarely did.

Before long, Orlando was at the top of the stairs yelling profanities in multiple languages and pounding on the door. Johnny heard his father bang back, threatening to beat him, but that only riled Orlando more. Then Miguel's open hand smacked the wall. "AYLIN! PUT THE BOY IN THE CELLAR!" he yelled in Spanish.

"What?" Johnny said aloud. The other times he'd been sent to the cellar was because he'd angered his parents—albeit for something trivial. This, however, was totally unfair. He jumped up to block the door, but Aylin was already halfway inside. "I didn't do anything!" Johnny yelled in Turkish.

Aylin came at him, but he pushed her away. She chased him around his room, able to grab an arm, but he fought back. She was not used to such disobedience, so he was able to sprint into the hallway, but his father was there to block him.

"Papá, I didn't *do* anything! You can't send me down there if I didn't do anything!"

Miguel refused to acknowledge Johnny. He only glared at Aylin as she grabbed her boy from behind. Orlando had gotten quiet with anticipation as Johnny kicked and thrashed, but his mother's arms were wrapped around him. Miguel unlatched the door as she dragged him to the stairwell. Orlando had stepped back and was waiting midway on the stairs.

Johnny turned to his father. "At least look at me, you fucking asshole!" Aylin fought to shove him through, but Johnny braced a foot against the doorway. "LOOK AT WHAT YOU'RE DOING TO ME!"

Miguel stood like a palace guard, waiting for his wife to complete the task so he could close the door. Aylin gave one big thrust, dropping Johnny just inside the threshold. He scrambled to pull himself back in, but she kicked him hard and he tumbled down some stairs. Orlando stepped out of his way as the door slammed, the bolt clicking into place.

Johnny crawled the rest of the way down and lay in a ball on the floor. Orlando circled him. "Now, *this* is some kind of punishment! I guess old Dad is getting too lazy to come down here and beat me himself. Either that or he's too scared, so he sends *you* to shut me up?" He laughed. "You must be pretty sore from that fall." Orlando poked Johnny with his socked feet. "Don't be such a spoilsport. Think of the fun we could have down here!" He went to the workbench to grab some pieces of rope.

Johnny clenched his fists in front of his face. How dare his parents toss him down here for no reason. If they were going to do this every time Orlando got restless, that changed everything. That meant there was no order to this madness.

When Orlando came closer, Johnny jumped up, punching and kicking with all his might. He hit his brother several times, but Orlando was able to overpower him and threw Johnny on the bed. He knelt on him, tying his arms behind his back, then bound his feet. Johnny struggled, but the rope was tight, so he rolled onto the floor with a thud. Orlando dragged Johnny by his feet. The carpet moved under his weight, exposing the concrete floor. There were tiny cracks in it that resembled a road map, and he allowed it to draw all of his attention. Johnny's peripheral senses narrowed, sounds muffled together and everything faded to black.

CHAPTER SEVENTEEN

Johnny's hand swatted the alarm clock while his heavy head remained anchored to the pillow. It would have been so easy to nod back off, but as groggy as he was, he knew that would be dangerous. *I was supposed to be filling in the holes. Instead, I passed the fuck out.* Behind his crusty eyes, he conjured up an image of the basement, but the memory would not restart. "C'mon. I can do this." His brain forced Orlando into the picture. *You were dragging me across the floor. Then what?* Orlando pointed a finger at him and said, *You better get your ass up, or you're gonna be late.*

"Fuck this." Johnny threw back the covers and jumped up to shower.

At school, the five friends slapped hands all around, then camped out on a parked car half a block from the entrance. Their eyes combed the throngs of students making their way into the building. It was almost first bell, and the crowds were thinning when Chico perked up. "Here he comes."

All heads turned toward the skinny, pug-nosed kid as he ascended up the block. His faded green hoodie was pulled up, but not enough to cover the yellowed bruises on his face. Johnny smiled, admiring his work.

The teen marched closer, focused on the ground, but it was hard not to sense the rabid glare coming from the curb. He looked up and halted. His body braced a second, waiting for them to come at him, but they didn't. Instead, they smiled and waved. He flipped a middle finger, then tightened his hood and hurried inside.

"See?" said Johnny. "We didn't have to do shit, but now he'll be thinking about us all day."

Jarrod laughed. "That was fun. Let's do it again this afternoon!" And they did. They also stared him down the next morning, then spoke to classmates who revealed his name was Shawn Watkins. Clyde followed him after school and discovered he lived on East 15th Street. Another time, when Johnny was tailing him, Shawn left home to go to a high-rise on East 23rd. Johnny wondered if that was where one of his punk buddies lived.

Friday, after their study session, the five friends compared notes.

"Who should we get first?" asked Jarrod.

"I'm having too much fun watching Shawn sweat," said Johnny. "If we get his friends first, he'll know he's next."

"Let's check out that building on 23rd," said Chico. "See if we catch one of them."

Everyone was game, so they stuffed their books in lockers and headed across town. The building was a post-war high-rise, surrounded by some restaurants, bars and electronics stores. They camped out a few doors down and smoked cigarettes that Mario had swiped from one of his sisters. The tobacco was an adjustment from the weed they were used to, but they choked through the taste.

As dusk neared, they were about to call it quits when Mario saw the brown-haired kid with braces come out of the lobby. They all ducked behind a parked car to watch as he walked west. As soon as he turned the corner, they sprung out to follow him. Just as they began to close the gap, he turned into a supermarket.

Mario snapped his fingers. "We should've nabbed him sooner."

"No problem," said Johnny. "We'll just wait."

They stood off to the side of the automatic door. A short while later, he emerged carrying a brown paper bag. All five circled him as he walked.

"Hey, how's it going?" said Johnny.

The kid clutched the bag tighter, looking at the surrounding faces.

"What's the matter, gringo," said Chico. "Don't you remember him? Think hard." He took the bag from his grip. "Here, let me hold this for you."

Mario grinned in the boy's face. "Not as much fun being on the other side, is it?"

The teen scanned the area for help before being ushered away from the busy store.

"What's your name?" Johnny asked.

"Eric."

"You know we have to get even, right, Eric?"

"I suppose." The color drained from Eric's face. "But it wasn't my idea."

"I actually believe you," said Johnny. "It was Shawn's, wasn't it?"

"Yeah."

"I figured. What's your other friend's name?"

"Gordon."

"Where's he live?"

"Same building as me."

Mario coughed out a laugh. "Bonus!"

Johnny held up a hand to curb Mario's excitement, then turned back to Eric. "So, here's the deal. Because I'm a gentleman, you only have to fight one of us. But after *that*, you're gonna call Gordon and tell him to come out, okay?"

Eric swallowed hard. "Okay."

"Perfect." Johnny gave Jarrod a nod. "He's all yours."

Jarrod stepped up to Eric. He looked so nervous it almost didn't seem worth it. "I'll give you the first shot. You want to hit me?"

Eric's limp arms dangled at his sides. "Not really."

Jarrod bobbed around a bit. "C'mon, let's go. They won't jump in. I promise."

Eric didn't move.

"Hit him, Eric," said Chico, thumbing through the bag of groceries. "If you don't, your mom is gonna be late cooking dinner." He pulled out a box of pasta and grinned. "Oooh, and it looks like we're having *spaghetti*!"

"Last chance," said Jarrod. The others yielded space while keeping eyes out for rubberneckers. When Eric didn't budge, Jarrod hauled back and socked him in the cheek. The kid's head rolled to the side, but once he resigned to defending himself, Eric connected some punches with Jarrod's jaw and forehead. That fueled Jarrod to abandon whatever sympathy he had for Eric and start swinging with more ferocity. He slammed Eric in the ribs and stomach, then punched him in the mouth.

"Stop." Eric doubled over, covering his bloody face. "Enough."

Jarrod shook out his hand, the braces almost doing as much damage to his knuckles as Eric's lips. Johnny gripped his shoulder. "You good, man?"

"Yeah, I'm good," said Jarrod.

Johnny looked at Eric. "You gonna be all right?"

"Yeah," Eric grunted.

"Great. Let's go call your buddy."

They walked to a phone booth on the corner. Mario uncradled the receiver and handed it to Eric. "Tell him to meet you over there, on 20th and First." Mario pointed to a block that looked more deserted. "Say you gotta talk to him about something private."

Eric wiped his face with his sleeve, and Clyde handed him a dime.

"If you fuck this up, you'll be sorry," said Chico.

Eric nodded, then dropped the coin into the slot. His tone sounded authentic as he asked Gordon to meet him. When he hung up, he looked at the others. "He's on his way. Can I go now?"

"Not yet," said Mario, guiding him across the street. "We gotta make sure you don't snitch before we get a piece of him."

Dusk's orange hues settled over the city as the group of kids walked away from the heavier avenue traffic. Johnny stopped at a stoop and gestured for Eric to sit, then tapped Clyde. "Make sure he doesn't run. The rest of us need to duck out so we don't scare that guy off."

Clyde nodded and sat beside Eric. Chico set down the groceries, then went around the corner with Johnny. Mario and Jarrod pressed into a nearby doorway. After a few minutes, Gordon appeared, and Eric waved. "Over here."

Gordon's palms turned toward the sky. "What the fuck was so important?" He strode over, eyeing Clyde. "And who's that?" Then he looked closer at Eric's face. "What the hell happened to you?"

Eric remained quiet as Mario and Jarrod emerged from their post, then Johnny and Chico. When Gordon spotted them, he bolted into the street. Mario darted after him, lurching to grab the back of his parka. He spun Gordon toward the sidewalk, the centrifugal force flinging him into a parked car. Gordon flopped over the hood. His glasses flew off and landed at Chico's feet.

Mario pulled Gordon off the car and began hitting him, but Gordon was a lot scrappier than Eric had been. He threw up his forearms to divert the incoming blows while thrashing with his knees and feet. A sneaker connected with Mario's shin, making him wince. Gordon seized the opportunity and punched him square on the nose. Mario didn't have as much weight to his advantage and began skirting from left to right, getting in a jab here and a smack there while Gordon kept swinging. He got Mario in the ear and forehead a few times, hard enough to make him stumble, but with each hit, Gordon looked more fatigued.

A taxi rolled down the street and honked. Both fighters halted to look up. The driver's stubbly face leaned out the window, the nub of a cigar wedged in the corner of his mouth. "Get da fuck outta da street, why dontcha!" He beeped again. "Fuckin' idiots!"

Mario and Gordon stepped aside to let him pass before squaring off again, but the break in momentum further sapped their energy. Gordon looked like his fists were too heavy to hold up as the pair circled each other, breathing hard. Mario's tongue tasted the blood dripping over his lips before stealing a glance at his brothers at the curb. He burst forward, swinging with both fists, using all the strength he could muster to connect with Gordon's face.

When Gordon cradled his head with his arms and dropped to his knees, Mario threw up his hands. "We're done here."

Chico went to Gordon. "You all right, hermano?" He offered up the glasses.

Gordon straightened to sit on his heels, then snatched the glasses from Chico's hand. Blood trickled from his nose and mouth. Chico's arm remained extended to help Gordon up, but he swatted it away. "Fuck you." He spat a red gob onto the sidewalk before standing on his own.

Johnny stepped in front of Gordon and looked him in the eye. "You want to be an asshole? Fine. But you know we could've done you like you did me, right?"

Gordon tried to match Johnny's gaze despite his taut lips and quivering chin.

"It won't be so fair the next time if you rat us out." Johnny looked back and forth between Gordon and Eric. "You catching my drift?"

Eric nodded. "I get it."

"Yeah. Whatever." Gordon rolled his eyes.

"Then it's settled," said Johnny. "You're free to go." He made a shooing gesture, and Gordon backed away.

Clyde handed the groceries to Eric. "Here, aren't you going with him?"

Eric took the bag but remained seated.

"Seriously, Eric?" Gordon turned to walk off alone. "Then fuck you, too!"

Chico folded his arms. "That was an interesting turn of events."

"Not really," said Eric. "He and Shawn have been getting on my nerves for a while now." He turned to Johnny. "What we did to you was shitty. I don't blame you for coming after us."

Johnny nodded. "It takes balls to say that."

Once Gordon had rounded the corner, Eric stepped off the stoop and shuffled away.

"Mario, let me look at your nose," said Johnny. "Is it broken?"

"I'm fine," said Mario. "It already stopped bleeding." He wiggled it.

"You guys ought to get cleaned up," said Clyde. "My house is closest, and my mother won't be home yet."

"Good plan," said Johnny. "I'm splurging for a taxi."

They filed into the DeMarcos' and slumped around the kitchen table. Tiffany was at the sink washing dishes and spun around. "What the fuck kind of shit are you mutts into now?"

"They had a little fight," said Clyde.

"Again?" She rolled her eyes. "With each other?"

"No, with some other kids. Don't we have something to clean them up with?"

"What do I look like, a fucking nursemaid?"

"Jesus. Nice bedside manner!" Clyde went to get some washcloths.

Johnny leaned into the others. "She ain't no Lucinda, that's for sure."

"Listen," Tiffany looked around the table. "I'm not getting involved in your Canines of Calamity bullshit." Clyde returned with soaked cloths and handed them to Mario and Jarrod. Tiffany lit a Newport as they dabbed their faces. "Fucking Puppies of Peril."

"*Mira, puta, somos los Perros de Guerra,*" Chico snorted.

"What's the Mexican kid ranting about?" she asked.

Johnny grinned. "He's Puerto Rican, by the way, and he *said* we're the Dogs of War." He paused. "That, and he called you a whore." They all laughed, even Tiffany.

"Dogs of War," she parroted. "The Retarded Rovers is more like it!" She rolled her eyes, then turned to Clyde. "If you're in for the night, I'm going out."

"Yeah, I'm in."

"Cool, but Clyde, I wouldn't let Mom see your friends looking like that. It'll make her worry, and she's got enough shit on her plate."

"I hear you."

"We need to get going anyway," said Chico, getting up with Mario. "But we'll see you *dogs* tomorrow."

Johnny laughed. "Yeah, see you dogs."

CHAPTER EIGHTEEN

On Monday morning, the gang waited by the school's entrance but never saw Shawn. They didn't see him the next day either, nor did they pass him in the hallways. They were starting to wonder if he had dropped out just to avoid his payback. But Friday, while exiting the cafeteria, he appeared. "Which one of you am I supposed to fight?"

Johnny stepped forward. "That would be me."

"Where and when? I wanna get this shit over with."

Johnny stroked his chin. "Maybe I'm not in the mood just yet."

"Whatever." Shawn stood, arms crossed, rolling his eyes. He was trying to project indifference, but his gawkiness made it comical.

Johnny smirked. "All right. Meet us outside after classes."

"Fine." He stormed away.

At the end of the day, Shawn was waiting out front as promised. Though his darting eyes suggested fear, his jaw was locked in determination. Johnny had to respect that and gave him a nod. "Let's get away from the school."

Shawn shrugged and followed the others as they took off down the block. They walked under the West Side Highway to an empty lot, where the wind from the Hudson River blew litter around in little cyclones.

Johnny stopped to spread his arms. "You good with this?"

"Why not?" Shawn shook the backpack off his shoulder and tossed it to the ground.

The others stood aside as Johnny squared off, lifting his fists, but it was pointless. Shawn charged at him like a bull, head-butting Johnny in the stomach and grabbing around his waist. Johnny was forced backward but managed to stay standing as he beat on the kid's back to make him let go. They spun around the lot until Johnny was able to twist free.

When Shawn straightened up, Johnny landed two punches to his cheek. Shawn backed up, then rushed forward to attempt another tackle. As he barreled closer, Johnny ducked to the side and got him in a chokehold. He held tight as Shawn bucked and reared, but when Johnny felt the kid trying to elbow his groin, he turned his hips to the side. That freed Shawn's hand enough to find Johnny's inner thigh. He pinched the soft flesh beneath Johnny's pants and twisted his fingers.

"Motherfucker!" Johnny shoved him away.

Shawn straightened up and lurched again, this time clawing at Johnny's clothes and hair until he latched onto a clump of black curls.

"Jesus! Who the fuck taught you to fight, your sister?" Johnny's head jerked back, but he still managed to smack Shawn's hand away and punch him in the face.

To keep from getting hit, Shawn grabbed both of Johnny's wrists. His long fingers and arms thwarted any attempts for Johnny to kick him or shake free. The pair pushed and pulled, but the more they struggled, the tighter Shawn gripped.

"Really, asshole? *This* is your strategy?" Sweat dripped down Johnny's face, and his teeth gnashed in frustration. He turned to his friends, who looked just as annoyed. They were shaking fists at Shawn and yelling comments, but their voices had merged with the sound of traffic. When Johnny turned back to Shawn, his peripheral vision had narrowed. All he could focus on were the hands clenched around his wrists.

"This motherfucker's got some serious kung-fu grip!" said Mario.

"No shit," said Chico. "It ain't normal."

Clyde shrugged. "Gotta give the guy credit for doing what he can to save himself."

Jarrod shook his head. "We should break them up, start a new round."

The four of them followed as the fighters drifted around the lot in some hostile, spasmodic ballroom dance. Shawn's face was contorted, his

117

fingers clamped on like his life depended on it. But then Johnny stopped and went limp. Shawn also paused, mouth agape, panting, but kept hold of Johnny's wrists, just in case.

"Johnny? You okay, man?" asked Chico.

When he didn't answer, Clyde scooted closer. Johnny's eyes were burning into Shawn's, with pupils so dilated they looked black.

"You okay?" Chico repeated.

Johnny's balled-up fingers opened to find Shawn's forearms. They grabbed hold to yank him closer. Johnny then rocked back on his heels, tucked his chin and launched upward at a forty-five-degree angle, slamming Shawn in the face with the crown of his forehead.

The others winced as blood sprayed everywhere. Shawn let out a yell, releasing Johnny to cover his nose. Once loose, Johnny lunged at Shawn, punching recklessly, over and over, until Shawn collapsed backward onto the ground. Johnny pounced on Shawn continuing to pummel him, even after his arms flopped to the side.

Johnny's friends rushed to pull him off, but he whipped around to fight them too. Clyde held out his hands. "It's all right, Johnny, calm down."

"Yeah, man, you got him," said Mario. "That's enough for now."

Chico reached out for Johnny's shoulders. "C'mon homie, let's walk it off."

"No!" Clyde's eyes widened. "Don't touch him!"

Chico turned around. "What the fuck? Why not?"

"I—I don't know—just don't!"

Jarrod and Mario knelt beside Shawn. Both of his lips were split, his nose looked broken, one eye had a massive cut, and blood trickled from his left ear.

"Is he breathing?" Mario asked.

Jarrod leaned closer. "I can't tell. It's too loud around here." He patted the kid's cheek to see if that would wake him. They looked at each other across Shawn's mangled body. "Fuck."

Clyde stood in front of Johnny. "C'mon man, it's all right. Everything's gonna be okay. Just stay with me."

"Clyde, what the fuck?" said Chico. "What's wrong with him?"

Clyde sighed. "Sometimes he has flashbacks and stuff. It helps if I talk to him."

"Flashbacks? Was he in Vietnam?" Chico waved the air. "No. He looks like he's in shock. You need to shake him out of that shit."

"NO!" Clyde stuck a finger at Chico. "Do *not* touch him!"

Chico backed away, hands up. "Jesus. *You* handle it then." He went to Shawn instead. "Man, he don't look good. Should we call an ambulance?"

"I don't know." Jarrod's eyes swept the area. "There's no phones around here. Maybe we should get him up."

"It's worth a try," said Mario.

They laced their fingers under Shawn's armpits and hoisted him to standing. He started to sputter and flail, but they would not let go. Jarrod and Mario walked him until he was able to take some steps on his own.

Several yards away, Johnny paced back and forth, muttering a string of incomprehensible sentences. Clyde stayed close, trying to snap him out of it.

Chico rifled through Shawn's backpack. "Where's this kid live again?"

"Somewhere on the Eastside," said Jarrod.

Chico pulled out a single dollar bill and a few coins. "He ain't got enough for a cab home."

"He needs to go to a hospital," said Mario. "There's one on 59th Street. I'm sure we could find him a few bucks."

"Johnny's always got cash," said Jarrod.

"He's not able to give it up right now," said Clyde.

"I'm okay," Shawn mumbled. "I just want to go home."

"Yeah, well, a cabbie's gonna take one look at your ass and have a different idea about that," said Mario. "Let's scrape up some dough and get the fuck out of here."

They dug into their pockets and were able to pool together just over five dollars. Mario collected the money and handed it to Shawn, who was finally able to stand unassisted. He couldn't see out of his left eye, but he managed to put the cash in his pocket. Chico passed Shawn his backpack. "You sure you're gonna be all right?"

"I'm sure." Shawn looked at Johnny, who was still pacing. "But *that* kid is fucking crazy."

They watched him teeter off. Across the street, he flagged a taxi. When the cab drove toward the hospital, they breathed a sigh of relief but also knew the police would be called.

"Can you talk to him and make him walk at the same time?" Mario asked Clyde.

"I've never tried."

"Well, you need to try it *now*," said Chico. "We gotta get the fuck out of here."

"Johnny, man, if you can hear me, we need to move."

The others formed a horseshoe around Johnny and managed to urge him forward without threatening his space. They zigzagged up and down the less populated blocks of the Lower Westside to keep his blood-soaked clothes from raising concern. Walking was already starting to calm him down. His muttering slowed, and he seemed less panicked. Chico and Mario were concerned but accepted Clyde's decision to let Johnny explain it when he came around.

Near 14th Street, Johnny swerved off and sat on a loading dock. Clyde folded forward to look in his face. "Are you back?"

"Huh?" Johnny's head tipped up to look at Clyde, but then he noticed his clothes and tattered knuckles. "Fuck. It happened again."

Clyde sighed. "Yeah."

"Did you tell them?" Johnny thumbed toward Chico and Mario.

"No. I was waiting for you to."

"What did I do?"

Mario hissed. "Yo, man, you nearly killed that motherfucker."

"Yeah," said Jarrod. "We had to pull you off him."

Chico nodded. "He went to the hospital."

Johnny looked at Clyde. "But what *happened*?"

"He wouldn't fight you," said Clyde. "He just wanted to wrestle, and we knew you were getting frustrated."

"I remember *that* part."

"Then he grabbed your hands to keep from getting hit and wouldn't let go. It was nuts."

Johnny rubbed the red blotches circling his scarred wrists. "You mean he held me here?"

"Yeah. That's when you lost it, channeled some Tasmanian devil shit." Clyde wagged his head. "You flicked him off like a booger and started wailing on the dude."

"How long have I been… away?"

"Almost an hour."

Johnny looked at the others. "Sorry."

"Fuck that, don't be sorry," said Chico. "We just wanna make sure you're okay."

Johnny lay his head in his palms. "Sometimes I—I get these episodes. I think they're triggered by shit that happened a while back."

Chico pursed his bottom lip. "Hermano, that must be some serious shit."

Johnny swiped his face and pushed off the dock. "I can't talk about it right now. Clyde can fill you in while we walk."

Clyde shrunk back. "You want me to tell them *everything?*"

"Yeah, everything. We're a gang now, right? We're all in this together."

Chico grinned. "*Sí, muchachos. ¡Los Perros de Guerra, juntos por siempre!*"

"Exactly!" Jarrod patted Chico's back. "Whatever the fuck *he* said!"

Johnny smiled. "He said, 'the Dogs of War, together forever.'"

CHAPTER NINETEEN

The gang spent the next few weeks guarded. They checked the newspapers for stories about a kid being brutalized in a fight and listened if anyone around school was talking about Shawn, but there was nothing and no sign of him anywhere.

"What if he hasn't tattled because he's in a coma?" Jarrod said while they all smoked cigarettes by the fountain in Washington Square.

"He's right," said Chico. "He could've dropped dead in the emergency room. Instead of reading the news, we *should* be checking the obituaries."

Mario flicked his butt across the park. "Yo, what if you knocked him in the head so hard, he got some of that amnesia shit? And now he can't remember who hit him."

Jarrod snapped his fingers. "Maybe he's been back to school for a while, but they had to do so much plastic surgery that we don't recognize him."

Clyde rolled his eyes, "Jesus! Johnny doesn't need to hear all this shit."

Mario raised a brow at Johnny. "Are we bothering you?"

Johnny smirked. "Not at all." He took a deep drag of his Marlboro. "Truth is, it's hard to feel bad about shit you don't remember. But still, whatever *did* happen, Shawn deserved it. That just as easily could've been me lying there after those three jumped me, so fuck him. Fuck all of them."

"Them boys didn't get anything they didn't ask for," said Mario.

"That's for sure." Jarrod snapped his fingers. "Hey, I almost forgot, tomorrow's my birthday. My parents told me to invite my friends over for a stupid party or some shit. It's in the afternoon before they get too blotto. I know it's gonna be lame *and* suck, so don't make me go by myself. We'll eat some cake, then go do something else, okay?"

"Of course, we'll go," said Clyde.

"Will there be booze and strippers?" asked Mario.

Jarrod clicked his tongue. "There's always *booze.*"

Johnny pinched Jarrod's cheek. "Aw, our little boy is becoming a teenager."

"Fuck you." Jarrod swiped at Johnny, who ducked. The two sparred for a bit, then sat together to watch the park traffic. They saw one of the Brick's joint-slingers slipping some product to a businessman in an expensive suit. Chico tapped Johnny. "You think you'll ever get that job?"

"I wouldn't want it. Too high profile, too much risk." He picked at the fabric of his sneaker, which was starting to detach from the sole. "The Brick did mention he might have more work, but he didn't say what, and I'm gonna need extra money soon."

Clyde perked up. "Now that the weather's warming up, we ought to get our instruments down here and start playing."

"You're right," said Jarrod. "What have we got to lose? Let's pick a bunch of songs and start practicing."

Johnny looked at Mario and Chico. "You guys play anything?"

"I play tenor sax in band," said Mario.

"Are you any good?"

Mario laughed. "Are any of us *good?*"

Clyde and Johnny both glared at Jarrod.

Jarrod threw up his hands. "I play pots and pans, for fuck's sake."

"But you play the shit out of them," said Johnny, and they all laughed. "How about you, Chico?"

"Nah, I take acting as my performing art." Chico grinned. "It's where all the chicks are."

"Then you should MC and collect the money," said Jarrod.

"What type of stuff you wanna play?" asked Clyde.

"Anything but that shitty marching band crap," said Mario. "How about some funk and soul?"

"I'm down with that and some rock and roll," said Johnny. "We can jam at Clyde's, throw together a set." The others whooped and clapped at the prospect.

The next day, on the way to the Kings', Chico sidled up to Jarrod. "Hermano, now we get to see how *you* live!"

Jarrod sighed. "Disappointment guaranteed."

"On the bright side," said Johnny, "we might get groped by Jarrod's mom."

"Yeah, maybe some tongue and an ass pat," said Clyde.

Mario's eyes widened. "Really? Is she fine?"

Johnny smirked. "*So* fine!"

"Ew. Gross!" Jarrod stormed ahead to unlock the building's main door, then led the way to the elevator, where his friends made slurping kisses at him. Jarrod wretched at them. "I swear, I'll throw up all over you."

When they entered the apartment, Missy was in a housecoat and apron, pulling a pan of cupcakes from the oven. The empty Duncan Hines box lay on the counter. Kurt was watching a bowling tournament from his recliner, wearing sweatpants and a tank top. A few wrapped gifts sat near the kitchen table.

Missy set the pan down. "My birthday boy is here." She removed an oven mitt, then shuffled over to wrap her flabby arms around Jarrod. She kissed him on the cheek. "My sweet baby."

"Mom, you're embarrassing me." He slid from her embrace. "Here, meet my friends. You remember Johnny and Clyde..."

They both nodded an acknowledgment while slinking out of reach.

"...and this is Chico and Mario."

Johnny shoved Chico toward Missy, whose broad smile exposed a row of nicotine-stained teeth. "It's so nice to meet you." She reached for Chico's cheeks and pulled him in for a kiss that landed between his chin and bottom lip.

His body stiffened. "Hi, Mrs. King," he managed through a grimace. "Thanks for inviting us."

"Our pleasure."

Chico tried to step away, but she pulled him in for a hug. Johnny and Clyde laughed at his face scrunched between her head and shoulder. When she let go, he glared at them, wiping his chin on his sleeve.

Before Missy had the chance to greet Mario, he threw his arms open, then bent down to envelope her stubby body. He squeezed tight, rocking her back and forth. "Mrs. King, *so* nice to *finally* meet you. Jarrod talks about you *all* the time." He then planted a big kiss on her lips.

Missy seemed stunned and delighted. "Well," she brushed her apron, "I better get back to the kitchen."

"Good plan," said Jarrod. "Call us when everything's ready."

As the gang filed through the living room, Johnny paused. "Hey, Mr. King, how's it going?" But Kurt only grunted and sipped his drink.

Once they had retreated to Jarrod's room, he shuddered. "I fucking hate it here. Sorry you had to come."

"Don't apologize," said Johnny. "We agreed that we wouldn't hide our shit anymore."

"Yeah," said Clyde. "We support each other no matter what."

Mario stuffed his hands in his pockets and bowed his head. "While we're being all honest and whatnot, I have a confession to make."

"What is it?" asked Jarrod.

"When I hugged your mother, I got chub."

"You fucking asshole!" Jarrod smacked his arm.

"I swear." Mario ducked, laughing. The others cracked up, too. "I felt it move!"

"You're so full of shit."

"I'm gonna think about her later. In the shower."

Jarrod smiled. "You fucking guys."

When Missy called, they rushed to the kitchen. On the table was a bowl of supermarket-brand chips and ranch dip. A dozen sloppily frosted cupcakes sat on a serving plate in the center. There weren't enough chairs, so Kurt and Missy stood at the counter, allowing the kids to sit at the table and pick at the food. After mixing a fresh drink and lighting a cigarette, Missy passed Jarrod a few gifts. "Here, dear. From me."

Jarrod tore off the paper to find a hooded sweatshirt and a six-pack of socks. "How imaginative," he muttered, stuffing a cupcake into his mouth.

125

Missy passed him an envelope. "This is from Uncle George. He couldn't be here because he had a job out of town."

Jarrod leaned into the table. "That's code for 'He's back in rehab.'" Inside, there was a ten-dollar bill folded up in hospital stationery. Jarrod read the scrawled message aloud. "'Wishing my favorite nephew a happy fourteenth birthday.'" Jarrod slapped the letter on the table. "Really? He doesn't fucking know I'm *thirteen*?"

Kurt coughed out a phlegmy laugh and muttered, "Idiot." Missy shot him a scowl.

Jarrod slipped the cash in his pocket and looked at his father, whose normally soured face beamed. "What?"

Kurt bent down to pass Jarrod the biggest gift. The Kings must have run out of birthday wrapping because only the center of the box was covered, and that was as wide as the roll of paper.

Jarrod ignored his father's goofy expression and stood to take the present. He held it up, gauging the weight, turning it left and right, then gave it a shake. The contents rattled, and a smile appeared on his face. "Could it be?" He looked at his friends' expectant faces. "Maybe a snare and a high-hat?" He set the box on his chair and ripped off the paper, then pulled open the flaps to look inside. Jarrod's face fell. "What *is* this?"

"What do you mean?" said Kurt. "It's a baseball bat and glove set."

"You shopped for it, or you found it in someone's trash?"

Kurt scowled. "Of course, I shopped for it. Every boy likes to play baseball."

Johnny saw the rage welling up in Jarrod, so he tapped his knee under the table and motioned for him to let it go.

Jarrod held Johnny's gaze a moment but then looked up with a forced smile. "Sure. You're right, Dad. Thanks." He pushed away from the table. "C'mon, guys, let's go outside and bat some balls around."

Kurt grabbed a cupcake and returned to his recliner with a drink while the kids put on their jackets. "Thanks for the nice party, Mrs. King," said Mario, leaning in for a hug.

"You're welcome, dear." She hugged him back. "Jarrod, come give me a kiss goodbye."

Jarrod blinked hard and walked over. He tried to offer his cheek, but she planted one on his mouth anyway.

As soon as the apartment door shut, Jarrod stormed around the hallway. "Are you fucking kidding me?" He shoved a bat into Johnny's hands. "Ever since I was in diapers, I've been banging forks and spoons around the house. You know, the first thing I ever bought after saving up my allowance? A pair of drumsticks. I was seven. But what do those clueless motherfuckers get me? Socks and a fucking *baseball bat*? I'd feel better if he'd said he found the damn thing in the gutter." When they got to the elevator, Jarrod punched the button so hard the wall shook.

"We could hit the ball into people's windshields if that'll make you feel better," Chico said as they rode down to the lobby.

"I have something to make the game more interesting," said Mario with a grin. He opened his jacket and flashed a pint of vodka from an inside pocket.

Jarrod's face brightened. "When'd you nab that?"

"When your mother was in there tonguing you guys. They had so much booze on that counter they'll never notice."

CHAPTER TWENTY

Johnny and Jarrod followed the flow of students out of Homeroom when they saw Clyde elbowing his way upstream.

"You're late," said Johnny.

"I know, but—"

Jarrod waved a hand. "Go check in. We'll wait."

"Later." Clyde pulled them against the wall. "You gotta hear this."

"What?" asked Johnny.

"I just saw him."

"Who?"

"Shawn."

Johnny felt his stomach flip. "Where?"

Clyde looked around, then hushed his voice. "I slept through my alarm, so by the time I got to the school block, hardly anyone was outside. I was rushing, trying to make Homeroom, when I almost ran into this kid and his parents heading for the door. I was just about to blow by them when I realized it was *him*."

"Did he see you?" asked Jarrod.

"No. I backed way the fuck up, then ran here to find you guys."

Johnny bit his lip. "Where'd they go?"

"I don't know," said Clyde. "What do you think it means?"

"I think it's pretty fucking obvious what it means." Jarrod cupped Johnny's shoulders. "It means *you* need to get outta here."

Johnny shrunk back. "I'm not gonna run and hide."

"Yes, you are!" Jarrod shook him. "If you get nabbed, it's over."

128

Johnny smacked off Jarrod's hands. "Slow down, both of you. Something doesn't make sense." He turned to Clyde. "Were there any cops on the block?"

Clyde's head wagged. "No."

"If I beat him as bad as you said, people would've demanded an explanation, right? At least his parents, anyway." Johnny rubbed the scars on his wrists. "Unless they're as negligent as *my* parents."

"You think he made something up?" asked Jarrod.

"He must have—claimed he got mugged or some shit—because it's been over a month, and nobody's come sniffing around."

"As far as we know," said Clyde.

"Please. It's not like I've been hiding. And the school has my address." A smirk appeared on Johnny's face. "I don't think he told."

Jarrod hacked out a disgruntled cough. "You're willing to bank your freedom on that?"

"What do you want me to do, drop out? Live like a fugitive?"

"No," said Clyde. "But we do need to be careful, keep our eyes peeled and warn you if anything seems funky, so you can book it if you need to."

Jarrod patted his chest. "And if that motherfucker *does* sic anyone on you, I'll say *I* beat him up. Let 'em haul *my* ass to juvie."

"Me too," said Clyde. "But for now, we better warn Chico and Mario."

After fifth period, Johnny and Mario were huddled outside their science class, reviewing a handout their teacher had given them. The hallway swelled with students, the cacophony of voices making it difficult to concentrate. Johnny felt a tap and looked up. He saw Mario's eyes focused down the hall and traced his gaze to the swarm of kids bobbing toward them. Shawn's head floated above most of them despite his attempt to slouch.

As Shawn drew closer, Johnny squinted to examine his face. There was a depression on his lower lip and a bump on the bridge of his nose. But those flaws were minor compared to his left eye. The entire socket was askew. A scar stunted the growth of hair on part of his brow, and the pupil drifted to the outside.

"Fuck me," Johnny said under his breath. "*I* did that?"

Mario was about to answer when Shawn saw them. His gate faltered for a moment, and he clutched his books tighter to his chest. But then he straightened his spine and marched forward, facing the pair full-on as he went by. Johnny acknowledged him with a nod.

"That was awkward," Mario said after he passed.

Johnny exhaled. "No shit."

"Was he looking at me or you?"

"Both."

"At the same time? That's a skill." Mario huffed. "He oughta thank you."

Johnny grimaced. "That's not funny."

"At least we only gotta see him for another two months. He graduates in June, right?"

"Yeah."

"You hope." Mario smirked. "All that head trauma will probably hold him back a grade."

Johnny grinned. "Now *that's* funny."

CHAPTER TWENTY-ONE

The school year ended without incident. The gang made a point of ignoring Shawn, and he did the same. Johnny attributed his silence—and Gordon and Eric's—to the honorable way he had chosen to exact revenge. It turned Johnny's pangs of guilt into righteousness and further bonded him to his band of brothers.

The crew followed through on their decision to rehearse some songs for the park. Johnny splurged on a battery-powered Casio keyboard, which he tried to figure out while providing some tentative vocals. Clyde's guitar playing was decent for his age, but he struggled to keep up with the fingering. Few of the songs called for a saxophone, and Mario's ability was limited, but he would still crowbar in some hilariously bad solos anyway. Jarrod, however, had a good sense of rhythm, and his incorporation of buckets, with the snare and hi-hat, was crowd-drawing.

They were disorganized and off-key but stuck with it. Chico made up for their greenness by playing a great emcee. He was funny, flirtatious and had a knack for goading people into giving them money without it seeming too much like a robbery.

Sometimes, they would spend their tips on excursions to Coney Island, the Bronx Zoo or Rockaway Beach. Other times, they would loaf around the streets all day. That summer, they met a few other kids compatible enough to join their gang. JJ Thompson was a small-framed white boy with thick blond shoulder-length hair. Despite being a year younger than the others, he was just as quick-witted and had a mischievous spirit.

Tito Juarez was a tall seventeen-year-old from El Salvador with light-brown wavy hair and green eyes. He was quiet, withdrawn and couldn't speak much English, but liked listening to the band jam. When Johnny and Chico struck up a conversation with him in Spanish, it was revealed that he played bongos, so they let him sit in, which solidified their percussion section even more.

Johnny split his nights between Clyde's and the squat on 180th Street. When he was uptown, he tried not to bump into Lily, but would sometimes find her asleep in his blankets. Her excuse was always that her mother had thrown her out, and she had no place else to go. Johnny believed it because whenever he saw her, she was some degree of fucked up. She was still smoking heroin and drinking, which she supported doing odd jobs.

Whenever Lily was there, she would come on to Johnny, and her offers of sex were hard to resist. By the third or fourth time, he even stopped feeling conflicted about it.

Johnny continued working for the Brick through eighth grade. He delivered the small packages but sometimes was summoned to swap out a gym bag from a luggage locker at Port Authority or Grand Central. During those runs, he would be escorted by Joe Jackson, the Brick's nephew and driver. Joe was dark-complected with a short-cropped afro, muscular and handsome. He would shuttle Johnny to and fro in a 1968 black Cadillac Fleetwood or a blue 1970 Olds Ninety-Eight. Johnny thought Joe looked a little too young to be driving and asked him about it during one of their excursions. Joe handed over a New York State driver's license that said he was eighteen, but Johnny was still not convinced.

Johnny liked Joe because he was professional, prompt and laid-back, which made him easy to be around. The runs to the lockers were also more lucrative. They paid fifty bucks and a bonus bag of weed. Between the Brick's money and his share of the band's tips, Johnny was accumulating a lot of cash. He was storing most of it in Clyde's closet, in the pockets of an old coat, but even those were filling up.

"I think you need to open a savings account," Clyde suggested one weekend when the now seven members of the Dogs of War were sprawled out in his living room.

"How do you do that?" Johnny asked.

"I think kids can get one if a parent cosigns. I bet Tiffany would help me."

"That'd be cool."

Tiffany arrived home from work a while later laden with groceries. She glanced at the troop before plunking the bags on the kitchen counter, then doubled back to the living room. She whipped out a finger to take a head count. "Jesus fucking Christ, you idiots multiply like cockroaches! We're up to *seven* now?"

They all giggled except Tito, who remained deadpan.

She glared at Clyde. "Can't you and the Furious Fleabags ever hang out at someone *else's* house?"

"We're the Dogs of War," said Jarrod.

"The Dogs of Woe is more like it." She jutted her chin between JJ and Tito. "Who the fuck are these two?"

Clyde made the introductions, and JJ smiled and waved, but Tito sat slack-jawed, staring at her big hair and colorful makeup.

"What's wrong with this one? Was he debarked?" Tiffany moved closer to Tito. "Do-you-speak-Eng-lish?"

"I wouldn't do that if I were you," said Chico. "It's the quiet ones you gotta look out for."

"You don't say." She folded her arms.

"It's true," said Mario. "He once snapped a man's neck once for telling him the wrong time."

"And suffocated an infant on the subway for crying," Johnny added, straight-faced.

Mario smirked. "He once bit off a man's tongue for whispering during a movie."

Tiffany rolled her eyes. "Shut the fuck up!"

Tito stood up and walked to the bathroom.

"Seriously," she whispered after he'd gone. "Is he okay?"

"Yeah," said Clyde. "He's fine. He's just quiet."

133

CHAPTER TWENTY-TWO

July 25, 1974, was Johnny's fourteenth birthday, but he refused to let the gang fuss over him. It had been two years since he left Miami, and the milestone brought up a lot of mixed emotions, none of which he felt like sorting out amid his brothers. He was happy for the distraction they provided. When it got late, however, Johnny declined the standing invitation to sleep at Clyde's. He used the excuse that he hadn't checked his mailbox uptown in a while. It was lame, and he knew it, but nobody pressed him about the decision.

Once in his apartment, Johnny checked around for Lily. Relieved she was not there, he locked the door and lit a few candles. He took a shower, dried off and stood in front of the mirror. His thin, athletic build was filling out. The muscles in his arms and chest had become more defined, and he was taller. There were changes in his face, too. His rounded cheeks were becoming angular, making him look less cute and more rugged. Johnny was curious to keep up with his pubescence, but it pained him to see shades of his parents reflected back. *At least I don't look like Orlando.*

Johnny carried the candles to the bedroom. He lay on the quilts and tried to read one of Lily's books. After scanning the same sentence several times, he put it down and stared at the ceiling.

It was just before six when Johnny walked through the door. The aroma of steak filled the house, but Aylin had not cooked that in ages. The vibe was off, too. It seemed less dismal.

Johnny went to peek in the kitchen. Miguel was at the table reading the newspaper, and Aylin stood at the stove frying T-bones. On the counter was a homemade layer cake with fancy swirls of chocolate frosting. Sitting on a decorative floral platter, it looked like the cover of a cooking magazine. *Am I in the right house?*

Miguel glanced over his paper. *"Javier, feliz cumpleaños."*

Johnny cocked his head. Did his father really just wish him a happy birthday? "Gracias, Papá."

Aylin turned to him and smiled. "I'm making your favorite," she said in Turkish. "Steak and French fries, with cake for dessert. It's almost ready, so wash up and sit down."

Displays of affection were so rare. It was hard to stifle his excitement, but scrutiny was still warranted. Johnny crept over to the sink, slowing as he passed the cake. He inhaled a whiff of the buttery frosting and resisted the urge to swipe a finger in it. He went to the basin instead. As he lathered his hands, he noticed something on the window sill. It was an amber prescription bottle, like from a pharmacy, but without a label. *What the fuck are those?* Was that why his parents were so cheerful?

He shook off the thought and went to sit down. Aylin poured him a glass of milk, then returned to the stove to portion out their dinners. Johnny was so excited about the change in his parents that he wanted to tell them about how he and his friends met a group of other kids playing baseball in some big lot and how he scored *two* home runs! Instead, he stuffed his exuberance and enjoyed his meal.

When Johnny wanted some salt, he didn't dare ruin things by asking for it, so he reached across the table. Midway, his arm clipped his glass of milk. It tipped over onto the table, spreading a sea of white around the plates like an incoming tide. Johnny felt the blood drain from his body as both parents jumped back from their chairs. He scrambled to mop up what he could with napkins.

"¡Estúpido hijo de puta!" Miguel's open hand smacked the wet table, spattering milk everywhere.

"And after all the trouble I went to?" Aylin yelled in Turkish.

Johnny ran to grab a roll of paper towels from the counter, splitting apologies between languages. When he returned to the table, Miguel swiped them from his hand. *"¡PONGA EL NIÑO EN EL SÓTANO!"*

Aylin dug her nails into Johnny's upper arm and dragged him to the hallway.

"But it was just an accident!"

She unlatched the cellar door.

"All right already!" Johnny said in English. "And don't push me down the fucking stairs this time." It was the first time he refused to speak Turkish to her—a small act of rebellion. Aylin scowled, opening the door, and he marched into the stairwell. The bolt slid shut behind him. Johnny descended a few paces to see what Orlando was doing. It looked like he had been sleeping until all the commotion started. "What's going on?" he mumbled.

"I guess I fucked up again."

"Hmm."

Johnny watched Orlando push himself to a sitting position at the edge of the bed. He was slumped over and not displaying his normal lunacy. *Holy shit, the pills. My parents are drugging him!*

Orlando slogged off to the bathroom to splash some water on his face. "What'd you do now?" he asked through the open door.

"I spilled something."

"Damn, that motherfucker is really intolerant."

"Tell me about it."

When Orlando emerged, his evil grin had returned. He ran a hand through his brother's black curls. He grabbed a clump of hair and yanked Johnny's head back. He was eighteen now, and almost a foot taller, but Johnny stood his ground. He vowed not to show any fear this time and not to black out. Orlando closed his other hand around Johnny's throat until he gasped, then let go to peruse the workbench.

Orlando returned with a piece of rope and tied his brother's hands in front. Johnny was compliant. When he struggled, the ropes were only made tighter anyway. Orlando found a black plastic garbage bag. It was wrinkled like it had been used. Something about the sight of it made Johnny shudder. When Orlando held up a white nylon belt, Johnny pieced together why he sometimes emerged from blackouts with a red ring around his neck.

Stay strong, stay present, he told himself. As Orlando approached, Johnny ducked, but there was not much room to run. Orlando attempted a half-assed lunge, then began ranting in mixed languages, but

136

his psychosis lacked its usual intensity. Johnny bobbed and weaved until Orlando mustered a big spurt of energy and grabbed the back of his shirt.

Once caught, Johnny stopped resisting. There was no point. Orlando pushed him to his knees and wrestled the bag over his head. He brushed the excess air out of it before wrapping the belt around his brother's neck.

You've been preparing for this. Johnny took one last breath as the belt tightened. *Stay strong, stay present, stay strong, stay present, stay...*

Johnny rolled over to blow out the candles. *So goddamn frustrating.* He balled up his pillow and stuffed it under his head. Why couldn't he just remember that one time? He pressed his eyes shut. The scene was so vivid. He could feel the plastic bag on his face, smell the polyethylene, but then nothing until coming to and seeing Orlando face down in a puddle of blood. The box cutter and some pieces of rope were on the floor nearby. A three-foot section of chain lay across the workbench. For once, something good happened down there, and he couldn't fucking remember.

Johnny manufactured some scenarios to see if they fit but couldn't stop them from turning cartoonish. One had him wielding the chain at Orlando like Bruce Lee. Another resembled a fight from a Batman comic, complete with onomatopoeia in starburst bubbles.

Fuck this shit. Johnny rolled over, letting his thoughts fast forward through what he did remember: Aylin releasing him. Waiting until she and Miguel were sound asleep. Packing his knapsack with some clothes and all of his savings. Then, creeping to the kitchen, where Aylin kept her purse, and pocketing all of her cash.

And the motherfuckers had the nerve to leave out a piece of cake? Johnny sat up and ran his fingers through his hair. "Like that would make up for throwing me down there on my birthday." He could picture the cake at his place on the immaculate table, a fork centered on a perfectly folded napkin. "With a card!" Johnny hurled his pillow across the room. "How the fuck do you do that to your own kid and then give him a card? That's some pathological bullshit right there."

Johnny got up to rifle through some pockets for his cigarettes. He lit one and looked out the bedroom window, remembering there had been a five-dollar bill inside the card. *What an insult.* He had kept the money, then ripped up the card without reading it and tossed the pieces in the air. The plate he flipped upside down, pressing on the back until cake and frosting squished out around the sides. "I should've trashed that whole fucking house." He took a long drag of his Marlboro, holding the nicotine in his lungs until it hurt. When he exhaled, a portion of his anger discharged with the smoke.

CHAPTER TWENTY-THREE

It was a hot mid-August night. The gang had been hanging out in Greenwich Village with several new recruits, but when it got late and the last of them made off for home, Johnny was still wired. Instead of going to his apartment, he stayed out to wander the city. Heading downtown on MacDougal Street, he approached a kiosk that sold falafels and gyros. Several small tables offered sidewalk seating, only one of which was occupied by two men rapt in conversation. One man was slight in stature and wore a greasy apron over his undershirt. The other was in a teal polyester polo that stretched around his beefy frame. The big guy seemed familiar, but his back was turned.

As Johnny got closer, he recognized that they were speaking Turkish, and his heart jumped. It was the boss man who had tried to rip off the Brick. Johnny's pace slowed as he debated turning around or crossing the street. But that was almost two years ago. And the man had never seen him anyway. *At least, I don't think so.* The curiosity to hear what they were so intent about overruled the risk, so he turned inside to peruse the menu board. The guy with the apron got up from the table. "What you want?" he barked in a thick accent. "We close soon."

Johnny ordered a gyro and a coke, then stood at the counter while the man shaved meat into the pita bread, added sauce and veggies and wrapped it in paper. He set it on the counter with a coke from the dispenser, took Johnny's money and returned to his friend.

Johnny moseyed to a table several yards away and ate with his back turned. Even though the men were using some unfamiliar Turkish slang, he could tell they were talking about a shipment and kept using the word *pure*. When the cook cleared his throat and muttered something about Johnny's presence, the big man dismissed it, saying, "Fuck him. He's just a stupid kid. He can't understand us." But to appease him, he hushed his voice even more.

Johnny stopped chewing to hear better but still had to strain, so he balled up a napkin and rolled it off the table. Leaning over to pick it up, he cocked an ear and caught the word *heroin* and how it needed to move quickly because the Feds were sniffing around. Johnny straightened up and slurped his soda. When their discussion switched to which strip clubs had the sluttiest girls, he cleared his table and left.

He had to find the Brick, tell him what he heard.

Johnny went to the park and entered near the man's usual haunt, but there wasn't a single chess piece to be found. Instead, the tables were littered with trash and empty booze bottles. One had a guy draped over it; his arms splayed like he had dropped from a tree. Vomit trickled off the edge. On a bench nearby, a pair of calloused feet in tattered socks poked out from under a blanket of newspaper. Another table was surrounded by three men. Two slouched on the bench with their feet on the rim. The third sat on the inlaid board, lighting a joint.

"You lost, young'un?" said one, stubbing his cigarette on the granite.

"He must be, coming here at this hour," said another.

Johnny gave them a nod. "I'm good, but thanks for looking out." The comment seemed satisfactory, and they resumed passing the joint.

During the day, the dealers were a minor annoyance, flitting around, listing their products, but now the darkened path was more like a receiving line.

"I got what you're looking for here, boy, Ludes, Black Beauties, Darvon..."

"Nah, man. Over here, I'll get your mind right with some Window Pane, mesc, blotter..."

"What you need is some primo flake, son. I'll hook you up with a taste. No extra charge."

Some even followed Johnny for a few paces with their competing sales pitches. And these guys were full-grown, street-hardened men. Nothing like the Brick's young joint-slingers, all of whom were conspicuously absent. Nevertheless, Johnny knew how infuriating being ignored could be, so he looked each pusher in the eye as he declined, thanking them for their offer. To his surprise, it worked. They fluttered away like moths to a dimming light.

Johnny stepped into the more well-lit area surrounding the fountain, but even that had a seedier vibe. The buskers had been replaced by panhandlers and lunatics. One guy stood fixated on a tree, tracing the outline of the leaves with his finger while speaking pig Latin. Johnny grimaced. *Whatever he's on, I'll ass-pay.*

A haggard woman with a bicycle's inner tube tied around her head wheeled a laundry cart full of empty cans. She was barefoot, wearing a jog bra stretched almost to invisibility and a tattered pair of pajama bottoms. She was yelling into the wind about how John F. Kennedy faked his own death to run an underage sex brothel out of the back of a Pizza shop.

Johnny hooked a left to exit under the arch. *No wonder the Brick stays away after dark.*

CHAPTER TWENTY-FOUR

It was midmorning when Johnny returned to the park and found the Brick. When he told him what was overheard the previous night, the man scratched his chin. "Pure, huh? You sure he said that?"

"I'm sure."

"Hmm, I ain't been dealing too much with Mustafa since that last incident. Just a little here and there since he *did* apologize for that fat fuck trying to rip me off. But it doesn't make me feel good that they're still working together."

"I definitely heard them say the name Mustafa a few times." Johnny waited while the Brick digested the information.

"There's a lot of heat out there right now, which would explain needing to move it quick, and on the cheap."

"Uh-huh," Johnny agreed—about what, he had no idea.

"I mean, if it's pure, it's worth looking into. I could probably rustle up enough cash to get a decent chunk." He pondered some more. "Let me scope it out. You gonna be around later?"

"Yeah. My crew is meeting me here with the gear. We'll be around most of the day, jamming."

He smacked Johnny's thigh and stood up. "Thanks for looking out, Colombiano."

A few hours later, the band was near the Sullivan Street entrance, playing *Lola* by the Kinks. One of the Brick's soldiers caught Johnny's eye and gestured for him to go to the chess tables. When the song was done, he found the Brick sitting alone with all the pieces set up.

"Is *this* how it's gonna be?" Johnny said, sitting across from him. "You're gonna make me kick your ass in chess just so you can get a word with me?"

The Brick coughed out a laugh. "Motherfucker, *please*. I'll beat you so bad they won't even recognize your dental records. I dare you to get one pawn."

"One pawn? My bishop will have your queen bent over and moaning in three moves."

"Shit, boy, you're either high or crazy." The Brick snickered. "But that's what I like about you, Colombiano, you got balls."

As they started playing, the Brick picked off Johnny's pieces with ease but took his time so they could talk. "I looked into that thing, and you were right. There appears to be a very sweet opportunity."

"Yeah?"

"But it might be best if I stay a little more detached—in the background, if you know what I mean."

"Not really."

"Given past history with those business people and all, I wouldn't want any tempers to flare. Least of all, mine…"

Johnny stared at the board, nodding, as the Brick continued to make some lengthy cryptic point about alliances, protocol and etiquette versus risk.

"…I guess what I'm trying to say is, you want in?"

Johnny's head snapped up. "Say what?"

"You heard. You've done right by me, and I think you've earned the chance to prove yourself, make a little something extra, maybe in the area of five Gs."

Johnny tried to contain his excitement. "Sure."

"I think I can get an associate to set up a buy, but you'd make the transaction. That way, it stays anonymous. I don't want to talk about it here, but if you're interested, I'll get with you another time."

"I'm interested, Rick."

"All right then," he said, gliding his queen across the board and taking Johnny's rook. "Checkmate."

Johnny stared at the board, baffled, but then leaned back, smirking. "I *let* you win."

"Get the fuck out of here!" They both had a good laugh before Johnny went to rejoin his friends.

Two days later, the Dogs of War were sitting by the Garibaldi statue when the Brick walked by without stopping. "Colombiano, *ven aca.*"

Johnny jumped up and trotted after him. They went out the east side of the park and across the street, where Joe was waiting in the Cadillac. The Brick motioned for him to get in the back seat, then slipped in front and turned around. "Are you ready? Because it's going down." He waved a hand, and Joe pulled out.

"Right now?"

"No. Ten o'clock tonight. You're gonna pick up two kilos of product from Mustafa's men. I don't know which ones. I couldn't get that info."

Johnny's brows furrowed. "Okay, I guess…"

"He doesn't know who's making the buy, but he knows it's legit because he was given a reference from a reliable source. Either way, I don't trust that motherfucker, so you need to be careful."

Doesn't sound like I have much choice. "I will."

"You might want to bring some of those friends of yours along for backup."

Good plan. "I can do that."

"There's an old pier on the west side. We're gonna drive by now, scope it out." He turned to watch the road. "Look, if shit goes down or something doesn't feel right, you need to take the money and get the fuck out of there, okay?"

"I will."

"Because I'm trusting you to hold a *lot* of money."

"How much?"

"A fucking lot, okay—like a hundred grand."

Johnny felt the bottom drop out of his stomach.

"If you need something extra, to protect the money, I can hook you up."

"What do you mean?"

"I could lend you a piece. You ever shoot a gun before?"

Before Orlando was *too* crazy, Johnny remembered Miguel had given them pellet guns for Christmas. A pretty stupid idea, now that Johnny thought about it, but the man was never vying for Father of the Year. The boys would take the rifles to a vacant lot and find stuff to use as targets. Johnny always had better aim, which really pissed off Orlando to the point of him getting violent, so Johnny started missing intentionally. He would aim for something beyond the target, thus increasing the degree of difficulty and honing his skills even more. Johnny would feel satisfied while his brother laughed at him for being inept.

"Yeah. I've fired a gun."

The Brick pursed his bottom lip. "I got a .38 I could lend you in case some shit goes down. Someone your size can't get in too much trouble with a piece like that."

"I've shot bigger," he said.

"Who the fuck do you think you are, Dirty Harry?"

"Who's that?"

"Boy, you're lucky I don't just give you a slingshot."

"I'm pretty good with one of those, too."

The Brick caught his nephew stifling laughter behind the wheel. "Joey, remind me why I do business with this motherfucker again."

The car turned south on the West Side Highway. Johnny gazed out the window at the dilapidated piers hanging over the Hudson as his heels tapped the floor mat. Bravado and luck had been saving his ass so far, but nothing trumped experience, and he would soon face people with way more of it than him. *I guess if Rick trusts me to handle shit...* He took a deep breath to slow his heart. He would have to remember to stay calm and alert.

When Joe slowed down near Canal Street, Johnny relaxed a bit more. He had wandered this neighborhood plenty of times and was relieved the transaction would happen someplace familiar.

"That's the one, there." The Brick rolled down his window as Joe pulled off the highway.

The Caddy crept toward a wooden structure the size of an airplane hangar. In front were two enormous sliding doors, rusted out and graffiti-covered. One was open partway, wide enough to fit a car.

"You want me to drive in?" Joe asked.

The Brick threw up a hand. "Oh, *hell* no! The shit looks sketchy enough from here." He leaned out his window, and Johnny did the same.

Through the opening, they could see that half of the structure had been gutted by fire. Daylight poured through the charred skeletal remains of the roof. The floor's planks looked loose and had sections missing. Litter and discarded clothing flapped in the wind, blowing through the gaps.

"I'm meeting them in there?" Johnny asked.

"That's the word."

"Shouldn't I go inside to scope it out?"

"It's not a bad idea, but do it on your own time. I can't be seen around here." The Brick wrested his eyes away and tapped Joe's arm. "Come on. Let's go."

As they merged back onto the road, the Brick pulled an unpaid parking ticket from the glovebox and began to scribble on it. He turned toward the back seat. "When the deal is done, call this number, and I'll pick up the goods."

Johnny stuffed the paper in his back pocket. "How will I know I'm not getting gypped?"

"Two kilos equal about four and a half pounds. Pick it up, feel it, look at it. If it's wrapped in anything other than plastic, peel that shit back, make sure it ain't a prop."

Johnny nodded.

"Joey's gonna meet you on Washington, between Canal and Spring, at nine o'clock with the money and a gun. That should give you enough time to get situated."

"Got it."

"As soon as you're done, call that number."

"Okay."

Back at the park, Johnny slid out of the car. Only Clyde, Jarrod, Chico, Mario and JJ were found horsing around by the fountain. "Where'd everyone go?"

They circled around. "The others got bored of waiting," said Chico.

"And we didn't know how long you'd be," said Clyde, "so we let them go."

Jarrod turned his palms to the sky. "What the fuck happened?"

Johnny looked around. "Not here."

"Where, then?"

"Let's walk." Johnny explained everything as he led them back downtown. He needed to get a closer look at that wharf structure while it was still light so they could concoct a plan.

"A plan?" said Mario. "You have no fucking idea what's going down. How do you plan for that?"

"I'm hoping they come in, swap bags and leave. But in case shit gets sloppy, you guys are my backup."

"Yo, so we're *all* gonna die. That's the plan," said Mario.

"Hermano," Chico smirked, "when the cops ask us to identify your body, which name should we give them?"

"That's right!" Jarrod laughed. "We'll have to have two funerals. One for Johnny Avalon and one for Javier Alv—"

Johnny spun around. "Can you motherfuckers focus for five goddamn seconds?" He raked the curls from his face with clawed fingers. "This shit is serious, but I think we can pull it off if we prepare."

"But the Brick didn't give you many details," said Clyde.

Johnny resumed walking, and the others followed. "But he also wouldn't give me a bag full of his money if he thought it was a suicide mission."

"I guess you're right."

Johnny stopped and pointed. "C'mon. That's it there."

The six of them waited for a break in the traffic before jogging across to the riverside. They went through the sliding door and fanned out to explore the building. Warped boards creaked and shifted under their feet as the Hudson River lapped the pilings below. It was open space, but on the south side, where the fire had hit the hardest, it looked like there had been a separate room, though only a single blackened wall remained. To the north were sections of metal scaffolding and an aluminum door. JJ opened it, and the wind almost yanked the knob out of his hands. Still, he went out to investigate the perimeter.

"While I'm waiting for them, you guys should be hidden," said Johnny. "I don't want them to feel intimidated."

"Really?" said Clyde. "A bunch of seasoned, most likely armed, drug dealers are gonna be intimidated by six teenagers?"

Jarrod turned to him. "You're sounding as cynical as your sister."

"Hey, down there," a voice called from above. The others looked up to see JJ's face through the roof's frayed opening.

"Holy shit," yelled Mario. "That does *not* look safe!"

"There's a ladder on the side of the building," said JJ. "The roof feels pretty stable if you stay along the rafters. I have a great view from here, inside and out. I can see who's coming, all of that!"

"That's right, homie," said Chico. "*And* you'll see your head explode as you fall on it from thirty fucking feet."

"If JJ's okay being up there, we should let him," said Johnny. "We might need all the advantages we can get."

"What's our plan?" asked Clyde.

Johnny paced. "You guys should come early, by maybe half an hour, and find places to hide. JJ on the roof, Mario and Chico could lean some boards against the scaffolding and hide behind that." Johnny looked at Jarrod and Clyde. "You guys can hang on the other side of that burned wall. If any shit goes down, you can jump out to distract them, and we'll all run."

"Except for JJ, who'll be stuck on the roof getting shot at," said Chico.

"They'll never know I'm up here," said JJ. "I'll just wait it out and meet up with you later."

"Should we call the rest of the crew?" asked Chico.

Johnny thought a moment. "I don't think so. There're not enough places to hide, and it might be too distracting."

"True." Mario nodded. "But we'll need a place to rendezvous in case gotta scatter."

"How about the Canal Street subway station, the IRT?" Jarrod suggested, and everyone agreed.

They all hung out for the next few hours until the crew went to take their places in the hangar. Johnny split off to wait for Joe on Washington Street. The block, consisting of nothing but warehouses and offices, was desolate after business hours.

The blue Oldsmobile pulled up at nine. Joe rolled down his window and handed out a small duffel bag. "The piece is in there with the cash.

It's pretty straightforward. Cock, aim, shoot. And the sights are accurate. I've practiced with it before. As long as you keep your hands steady, it'll do the rest."

Johnny tried to feign apathy.

"Hopefully, you won't need it, but whatever goes down, protect the money." Joe gave Johnny a tight-lipped smile. "Be careful. I'll see you when it's over."

"You definitely will." The two locked hands.

After Joe had driven off, Johnny unzipped the bag. The gun sat atop stacks of bound hundred-dollar bills. It was a Smith and Wesson .38 Special. He picked it up, felt its weight and made sure it was loaded. Then he stuffed it in the waistband of his jeans and untucked his shirt.

It was hot and humid as he walked to the pier, but the breeze off the water made it more bearable. Johnny slinked over to the building and ducked inside. The only light came from where the silver half-moon streamed through the hole in the roof. He made three low-toned whistles to alert the crew he was there. They stepped out from their designated corners to acknowledge him. JJ returned a whistle from above. When they went back into position, each was camouflaged by darkness.

Johnny picked a spot to stand, his figure bisected by the moon's glow, the duffel bag between his feet. There was a disturbing familiarity about waiting in the dark. The desperation to predict the unpredictable. He felt his internal organs constrict with anxiety and put his hand on the .38 for reassurance. It had been a while since he fired those pellet guns, so he closed his eyes to rehearse. He visualized the lot, a pitted Campbell's soup can atop a rusty barrel. He felt his finger on the trigger, pulled and pictured hitting the can dead center. The fantasy relaxed him until he heard a car. Its muffler had a low rumble, like a boat.

Johnny looked up. "JJ, are they alone?"

"So far."

Headlights approached, then stopped at the entryway. Johnny stood his ground, squinting through the glare to make out who was inside. Was he supposed to go over or wait for someone to come out? As he debated, the car began a slow roll through the sliding door. Floor planks bowed and swayed under its weight, and Johnny held his breath. In all the gang's planning, they never imagined anyone would be stupid enough to drive on such a precarious foundation. The vehicle crept past, and Johnny repositioned to keep it in sight. It was a dark green 60s Mustang. Exhaust fumes filled the air as the driver made a three-point turn, flooding the back of the building with light. Johnny worried his brothers would be spotted but had to trust they were ducking tighter behind their posts. The Mustang stopped in the center of the hangar, about two car lengths from where Johnny stood, shifted into park and cut the headlights. That put him midway between it and the exit—something he considered a lucky break.

The trunk popped, and both doors opened. Interior lights illuminated the area. Two men climbed out and stood on each side of the car. The driver was tall and olive-skinned, with a mustache. His beer belly pressed against his white tank top. Johnny thought there was something a little dopey about that one. The passenger was white, red-haired, with big sideburns. His sleeveless denim shirt was half unbuttoned. The stern expression on his face made him seem like the brains of the operation. He didn't see any weapons but knew they could have one tucked in their pants just like he did.

"Who the hell are you?" asked the one with the mutton chops.

"I'm here for the swap."

He looked at his partner across the car and shook his head. "Kostas, are you seeing this shit? It's a fucking kid."

"Yup, I see it," said Kostas.

The sluggish cadence of his voice confirmed Johnny's suspicions, but he couldn't take it for granted. Intelligence was not a prerequisite for good aim.

"Who you work for, kid?"

"No one."

"He looks too young to be a narc," said Kostas.

"Can we just do this? I've got the money."

The redhead walked around his open door to lean on the front fender. "Is that it, in the bag?"

"Yeah. It's all there."

"Lemme see."

"Where's the dope?"

"In the back."

Johnny saw Mario crane his neck out from behind the scaffolding to peek inside the trunk. He shrugged and nodded, which let Johnny know there was something in there. Whether or not it was the drugs was anyone's guess.

"Give me the shit, and I'll give you the money," said Johnny.

The man sighed, rolling his eyes. "Look, kid, I don't know how *you* conduct business in that little schoolyard of yours, but here in the *adult* world, we look at the money first, count it, make sure it ain't fake. But if you don't want to play with the big dogs…" He pushed off the fender to return to the passenger seat.

Shit. "Wait."

The man turned around. Johnny picked up the bag and tossed it. It landed halfway between them. Mutton Chops walked over to grab it, then set it on the hood. He opened the zipper and flipped through a few stacks of bills before looking at his partner. "I'm impressed. Kid must've saved a bunch of allowance."

"You want me to get the shit?" Kostas aimed a thumb in the direction of the trunk.

The redhead stroked his chin, a sneer appearing on his face. "You know something? Fuck him. What's he gonna do, tell his mommy that we stiffed him?"

No way, motherfucker. Do not make me do this. Johnny reached behind him for the gun.

The guy snatched the money off the hood and headed back toward his seat. His driver didn't realize that was a cue to leave and kept standing there, so he smacked the roof of the car. "Hey, numb-nuts, let's go!"

"Don't you fucking dare!" Johnny held out the .38 with both hands and cocked it, locking his elbows to steady his grip.

Mutton Chops looked up, grinning. "Oh yeah, tough guy?" He stepped away from the car door, the bag handles still clutched in one fist. "Show me what you got, you little shit!" The other hand fumbled to lift his shirt for a revolver tucked behind his belt buckle.

Whatever words were being said, Johnny did not comprehend. All he could focus on was the man's forehead bookended between two sideburns. He grounded his feet to center his balance and squeezed the trigger. A loud *pop* echoed in the darkness as the gun lurched back in Johnny's hands. The force was more than he expected, and he had to scramble to get repositioned, but it wasn't necessary. Mutton Chops dropped where he stood, the bag of money falling beside him.

Kostas rushed out from his seat to look over the hood. "Fuck. Jack! Are you okay?"

Johnny stood, aiming the gun between the two men. He didn't know if the driver was armed or if he had only stunned Jack, who might jump up any second.

Kostas tried to walk around the car to help his partner, but Johnny stepped closer. "Don't even fucking try. I'll drop you, too!"

The man halted, threw up his hands and backed off.

Johnny noticed his brothers peeking out from their posts. He signaled to Mario, who yanked a small hardshell suitcase out of the trunk, then slipped back into the shadows.

"Get in that car and go. Now!" Johnny wagged the gun at Kostas, who retreated behind the wheel. He yanked his door shut and threw the shifter into drive. Tires screeched as the Mustang lurched forward toward the hangar's half-open slider, but the trunk and the passenger door were still open. The entryway could not accommodate the extra width. As the car sped through, its swinging door cracked shut with a force great enough to shake the building.

Johnny sprinted to watch the taillights disappear down the avenue, the trunk's hatch bobbing up and down with every dip and pothole. When he turned back, the others were rushing toward him, Mario with the suitcase and Jarrod with the Brick's bag of money.

Johnny shoved the gun back into his waistband. "C'mon, we gotta get the fuck out of here!"

"Is he dead?" asked Chico.

"I don't fucking know," said Jarrod. "I just grabbed the bag."

"And we're not going back to check," said Johnny. "We need to boogie, like now!"

CHAPTER TWENTY-FIVE

Johnny and the others jogged across town. Once they felt they were far enough away, they slowed to a walk.

"What's gonna happen now?" asked Clyde.

"I don't think *shit's* gonna happen," said Mario. "That dumb-ass motherfucker still thinks he's got the drugs!"

"Shit's gonna happen, all right," said Chico, "when he shows up to that Mustafa hombre empty-handed."

"Think of the story he'll have to make up," said Jarrod, "No one's gonna believe the truth."

"That's right." JJ exaggerated his strut. "Two *adults*, in the very *adult* world of drug dealing, just got shafted by a schoolyard juvey! Take *that*, motherfuckers!"

Johnny waved the air. "But what if that Jack guy isn't dead?"

"Where'd you pop him?" asked Jarrod.

"I aimed for his head, but it was dark."

Mario slapped Johnny's shoulder. "Yo, you the *man*, brother!"

Johnny brushed him off.

"When that car door hit the slider, the roof shook," said JJ. "I thought it was curtains for me!"

"I thought the whole place would collapse," said Chico.

"Maybe it still will," said Clyde. "Next time a seagull lands on it."

"I hope so," said Jarrod. "Get rid of the evidence."

At City Hall Park, Johnny looked around. Despite the late hour, pedestrians were still using it as a cut-through. "Let's check that case before I call the Brick, but there's too many eyes here."

The gang headed under the Brooklyn Bridge, where there were little more than parked cars and rats. They stopped on a side street. The few businesses on the block were locked behind security grates. The hollow hum of traffic reverberated from above. Johnny took the suitcase from Mario and set it on a bulkhead. He flipped the two brass clasps and lifted the top as his brothers circled around. Inside was a layer of bubble wrap. JJ reached in to pop one of the bubbles. Johnny smacked his hand as the others stifled grins. Beneath the packing were two bricks of white powder wrapped in plastic.

"How do you know it's legit?" asked Clyde.

"I don't. But if it isn't, at least I didn't pay for it."

"You're giving the money back?" asked Jarrod.

"Of course. I'm telling the Brick exactly how it went down." Johnny shut the case. "He's gotta know because he does business with those people. Besides, I'm not gonna steal from someone who gave me a break."

"I was just asking."

Johnny looked around the circle. Nobody disagreed, but Chico was pouting. "It's just, we ain't never gonna touch a hundred thousand dollars again," he said. "Before you call him, lemme hold it. Ten seconds, tops."

Johnny smiled. "We'll be holding more than that soon enough. Be patient." He spotted a phone booth on the next block. "I'll be right back."

Jarrod held up the bag of cash and shook it. "You need a dime?" The crew laughed as he trotted off.

When the Oldsmobile appeared, Johnny signaled for his brothers to hang back, then scurried between parked cars to stand at the driver's side. Joe rolled down the window. The Brick was beside him and looked upset.

"What the fuck is this?" he barked, leaning over his nephew. "Why you got *two* bags?"

"Some shit went down."

"What shit?"

"When they saw how young I was, they thought they could play me."

"Yeah?"

"It wasn't my fault. I did everything just like you said."

The Brick spun in his seat, looking around the deserted block before tapping Joe's arm. "Take those."

Johnny handed the bags through the window, and Joe passed them to the Brick. As the man rifled through the contents muttering expletives, Johnny leaned on a parked car to await his fate. Joe looked at him and smiled. When Johnny smiled back, it seemed to release the tension he had been holding in all day, and he started to giggle into his fist. That made Joe do likewise.

"What's so motherfucking funny?" The Brick shoved the bags between his feet and glared at Johnny. "Boy, put your goddamn head in this car and tell me exactly what the fuck happened here."

Johnny obeyed and ran through everything from beginning to end—names, descriptions and all that was said. The Brick calmed down after the first few sentences and lit a Newport.

"...so, I don't see how we could get made," Johnny concluded. "I never said who I was, and, like, those guys are gonna be in so much shit with Mustafa—"

"Whoa, whoa," the Brick threw up a hand. "Just facts. I don't need none of your *expert projections*. We ain't holding a motherfucking discussion group, you dig?" He cracked his window to flick the ash off his cigarette, then took a long drag. "I gotta think about this, put my antennas up, see what the word is around the way."

Johnny watched and waited as the Brick gazed out the windshield, percolating the information.

"But for now?" A tiny curl appeared on the man's lips. "It sure does feel good to get even with that shady motherfucker." He patted both bags and looked at Johnny. "You done good, Colombiano."

Johnny exhaled. "You want your piece back?"

"Fuck no! You shot a man. My suggestion is you drop that thing off the bridge, but that's up to you." He clenched the Newport in the corner of his lips. "You got big pockets?"

"I don't know, why?"

The Brick picked through the money bag and passed Joe some stacks to hand out his window. "That's your pay, plus a little bonus."

"Thanks." When the stacks kept coming, he reiterated. "Shit, thanks!"

CHAPTER TWENTY-SIX

The original three climbed the stairs to Clyde's apartment.

"Will Diana yell at you for being late?" asked Johnny.

"His mother's too nice to yell," said Jarrod.

"True," said Clyde. "And she works so much she passes out as soon as she gets home."

Once in Clyde's room, he and Jarrod made up the couch and foam mattress while Johnny hid the money and gun in the closet. They lay in the dim light from a reading lamp, exhausted but too wired to sleep.

"That was a lot," said Johnny.

"No doubt." Jarrod propped up on an elbow. "So? What does it feel like?"

"What?"

"Killing a guy."

"I don't know if I killed him."

"That fucker was *not* moving."

Clyde sat up to hush them. "Jesus. Aren't you guys even a little freaked out over what happened?"

Johnny thought about it. "I was until we got a few blocks away, and I realized nobody was coming for us. And then, when I saw how impressed the Brick was to get the drugs *and* his money back…"

Clyde rubbed his face. "But you killed a guy."

"None of us know that." Johnny sat cross-legged. "It was dark."

"So you keep saying, but come on. Why else would he just drop?"

Johnny pinched his temples. "Look, maybe I like not knowing. Maybe that's how I keep from feeling bad. But even if I *did* kill him, I still don't care. Maybe that's fucked up, and I shouldn't admit it, but he didn't have to try and screw me."

"I just think that if I shot a guy, even a bad guy, I'd feel something," said Clyde.

Johnny grinned. "That's just because you're a much nicer person than I am."

"And you have a better home life," added Jarrod.

Clyde groaned. "I'm not some fucking tight-ass, you know. I get that there wasn't much choice." He swung his feet to the floor. "If you lost the Brick's money, he'd be coming after *you* with a gun. So, yeah, you had to do something." He looked at Johnny. "What I'm more worried about is if it's gonna set off one of your episodes."

"Why would you think that?"

"Because you flipped out over a fistfight. Tonight, you shot a guy."

"That was different. Shawn grabbed my wrists. We know that's a trigger."

"The truth is, we don't know shit. It happened in the middle of the night, after a *normal* day."

"I think you're overreacting," said Jarrod.

Clyde scowled at him. "Am I? Really? Because now he has a gun." When nobody said anything, Clyde turned back to Johnny. "You don't see yourself when you're like that. You're completely gone. None of us know what you're capable of."

Jarrod's lips pursed. "I guess it *is* a consideration."

"Fuck." Johnny swiped his flushed face with both hands. "I hate that you guys worry about this shit." He looked at Clyde. "And you're not a tight-ass. It's good that you're the voice of reason. The gang needs that. Even if sometimes I don't want to hear it." Johnny fiddled with the corner of his blanket. "I stashed the shit in the pockets of one of your old winter coats. I'm gonna go pee now. While I'm gone, you can hide the gun somewhere different. Will that help you sleep better?"

Clyde smiled. "It might."

157

It was late morning when the trio woke. They took turns washing and dressing, but Clyde still looked exhausted.

"You didn't sleep well, did you?" asked Johnny.

"Not really."

"But see?" Johnny outstretched his arms. "I'm fine." He grinned. "Know what'll cheer you up?"

"What?"

"Counting the money."

Jarrod's face lit up. "Fuck yeah."

"Will anyone walk in?"

Clyde shook his head. "My mother's at work, Tiff hasn't come home yet, and the other two wouldn't dare."

"Cool." Johnny pawed through the closet and tossed several stacks of bills on Clyde's bed. They each took one and counted it twice.

"Damn," Jarrod whispered.

"Holy shit," said Clyde.

Johnny split his gaze between them both. "There's twenty thousand dollars here."

"What're we gonna do with it?" asked Clyde. "I can't deposit that in my savings account without someone getting suspicious, can I?"

"I don't know."

"And what if my mother goes on a cleaning binge and starts throwing out my old clothes?"

"Well, we gotta put it somewhere for now."

Johnny pocketed two hundred dollars while Clyde looked at some board games stacked on his closet's top shelf. Twister had the largest box, so he took it down, folded the bills inside the game's spotted plastic mat and replaced the cover. It bowed out but was less noticeable after piling a few jigsaw puzzles on top.

"I bet you could deposit a few grand at a time," said Jarrod. "If anyone asks, just say it's a gift from your grandparents for your college fund."

Johnny nodded. "Use different tellers. If they start eyeing you, back off a bit." He sat on the bed. "I want to lay low today, keep an eye on the news to see if they're reporting anything about that guy."

Clyde and Jarrod agreed.

"But let's also check in with the rest of the gang. We should meet tomorrow, go over what went down, and tell them about our money."

"What do you mean *our* money?" said Clyde. "That's *your* money."

"How do you figure?"

"The Brick hired you for that job. We were just backup."

"You're right, but I sure as shit wouldn't have gotten that suitcase out of the trunk by myself. And if he starts giving me jobs that require more risk, you guys will have to work harder to protect me, right?"

"I guess," said Clyde. "We're also making decent scratch with the music thing. Since the gang keeps growing, there's more people to help us carry our shit around. Should we pool that money, too?"

"Yeah. But we can still use it to buy better gear and lessons because that helps us make more money as a whole." Johnny laid back. "Maybe one day we'll make enough to get a place. That's what I need most of all."

"I hear you," said Jarrod. "I can't wait to get away from my folks."

Johnny smiled. "It'll all come together one day. We just gotta be patient."

CHAPTER TWENTY-SEVEN

When all sixteen members of the Dogs of War arrived in Washington Square Park, Johnny ushered them to a grassy spot off the footpath. As they sat in a circle, he had to tamp down the eager glares of the ones who had witnessed the drug deal.

"I'm gonna get to that, but we need to cover other business first." Johnny turned to Rafael Barrientos, a recently recruited Dominican. He was a handsome teen with a chiseled body. "You're going into your second year at Roosevelt High, right?"

"Yeah."

"In a few weeks, a bunch of us are starting ninth grade there. I want to know what to expect and if my forged papers might be an issue."

"That school?" Rafael clicked his tongue. "Fuck no. They're too busy breaking up fights to worry about paperwork." He looked around the circle. "I won't lie. It's rough."

"I was there last year, too," said Patrick Ryan, a tall, scrappy-looking white kid. "There's a lot of delinquents, and they *love* to fuck with the new kids. I got a pass 'cause my older brother looked out for me, but he's in juvey now for robbing a guy."

Mario waved them both off. "If we flaunt our gang status, they'll leave us alone."

Johnny shook his head. "If we do that, it'll draw too much attention, and that's risky for me. We need to find a balance, display enough unity to keep the troublemakers away without alerting the adults."

"Like we're *los Perros de Guerra*, but incognito," said Alex Martínez. He and his younger brother Andre had also joined that summer.

"Exactly. We already proved we'll deal with anyone who fucks with us. We just don't have to broadcast it." Johnny turned to Tito. "On another topic, our high school graduate over here has moved in with his cousins *and* is working as a mechanic at their garage in the Bronx. Ain't that right?"

Tito shrugged, looking down at the grass.

"Because he's a man of so few words," Johnny continued, "I'll just go ahead and announce that his cousins have offered to loan him a car from their lot every now and again, which will keep us from having to hump our instruments back and forth."

Murmurs of relief came from the circle.

"All right already," Chico interrupted. "We'll watch each other's backs, Tito got a job, blah, blah, blah. Now get to the part where you *spanked* those two motherfuckers the other night!"

Johnny laughed, then ran through what went down, ending the meeting by disclosing how much cash was made. The crew erupted with back slaps and handshakes all around, then headed to the fountain's south side so the band could set up. They had been playing for over an hour when the Brick was spotted marching toward them. His stern expression caused Johnny's hands to freeze on the Casio keyboard, releasing a prolonged bad chord.

Clyde winced. "What the fuck?"

The Brick halted in front of them, wagging a finger at Johnny. "Colombiano, come with me." He eyed the bandmates. "And you cats are gonna need to find someone to sit in 'cause he'll be hung up a while, you dig?"

Johnny jumped up. "Like, how long?"

"A few hours at least—half a day."

"Is everything all right?"

"Come on, we gotta go," he said, walking away. The crew looked concerned.

"It's okay," Johnny told them. "If you're still here, I'll see you when I get back." He jogged to catch up, and they headed toward the street, where Joe was idling in the Cadillac. The Brick opened the rear door for Johnny, then climbed in beside him. He tapped his nephew on the shoulder, and the car took off.

Johnny tried to get a read on the Brick's vibe, but he remained quiet, perched forward to look out the windshield. It wasn't until they entered the Holland Tunnel that he reclined and threw his arm over the backrest. "Johnny, I know you told me what went down the other night, but I'd like to hear more details about that guy getting shot."

He never calls me Johnny. He tried to swallow despite the dryness in his throat. "I told you everything."

"I know you did." The Brick stroked his goatee. "And from what I hear on the street, you told it true."

"They're talking about me on the street?"

"Nobody's talking about *you*. They're talking about the guy found in that building."

"I told you I shot him. I had to. He was gonna rip me off." Johnny raked his fingers down his face. "I killed him?"

"Yeah." The Brick's tone softened. "Was that your first time?"

Johnny recalled Orlando face down on the cellar floor. "I'm not sure."

The Brick recoiled. "How do you *not know*?"

"I hit someone in the head with a chain once. But I never found out what happened to him."

"Well, son, the head's a pretty hard object. They call me Rick the Brick for a reason. Odds are he probably survived."

That doesn't make me feel better.

"So, I gotta know, when the shit went down, where were you standing, and where was he? You said he asked to see the money, and you threw him the bag."

"Was it wrong to hand over the money first?"

"Look, I'm just curious about the details." He offered half a smile. "How close were you to the guy?"

"Not close. Couple of car lengths?"

"He came at you, and you shot him?"

"No. He wanted to drive off with the money. That's when I shot him."

"One shot?"

"Yeah."

"That fast?"

"Yes."

"No hesitation."

"No."

"How far away were you again?"

"I don't know—a ways."

"Can you show me?"

"Sure."

"Joey, stop at that rest area."

Joe pulled off the New Jersey Turnpike. He picked a spot away from other cars and shifted into park.

"Get out," the Brick said to Johnny, then did the same. "Go stand where you were standing, and I'll be the other guy." He opened the front passenger door and waited.

Johnny backed up until he was almost thirty feet from the bumper, then waved a hand. "You need to step over a bit."

The Brick walked in front of the door.

"Not closer, just out to the side."

The Brick stepped back. "Here?"

"Yeah. That's it."

"You're sure?"

"Yes."

"Okay, let's go." They both hopped back in, and Joe continued south on the highway. "You shot randomly, or you aimed?"

"I aimed. Jesus, I *told* you I used to shoot, didn't I?" Johnny groaned. "What's with all the questions?"

The Brick looked at him, beaming an emotion Johnny found hard to read. He then put a hand on Johnny's shoulder and started to laugh.

Johnny looked at Joe in the rearview mirror, but he just tucked his smirking face into his chest.

"Boy, you hit that motherfucker dead square in the center of the head. It was so clean the cops ain't even looking at it as a drug deal. They're saying it might've been a professional hit." He squeezed Johnny's shoulder even harder. "Colombiano, man, you're the shit, and you don't even know it."

Johnny exhaled for what felt like the first time since getting in the car. He sat back to look out the window. It was pride. That was what he didn't recognize. The Brick was proud of him. Johnny smiled, drinking in the feeling as long as he could. "So, should I worry about Mustafa coming after me? Because the driver knows what I look like."

"That's the fucked-up thing, little brother, I don't think he will. It'd be way too dangerous for that man to go to a guy like Mustafa empty-handed and try to claim he got jacked by some kid. The same kid who shot his partner?" The Brick swiped a hand over his head. "If that cat's got any brains, he'll run like a motherfucker, because if *I'm* Mustafa, I'm thinking *he's* suspect number one." The Brick coughed out a laugh. "Nevertheless, I'm still keeping my ears wide open."

Joe exited the turnpike to take a few side roads. "Where are we going?" Johnny asked but then saw the sign as they turned into a gravel parking lot. It read Barnes Rifle and Pistol Club.

"Right here," said the Brick. "I need to see this shit with my own eyes."

They all exited the Caddy. Johnny had never seen Joe outside of a car before and was surprised by how tall and muscular he was. His clothes, much like his uncle's, looked expensive and tasteful. The Brick pulled a duffel bag from the trunk, then passed a few metal cases to Joe before heading to the entrance.

At the counter was a short, heavy-set man with a white mustache who resembled an albino walrus. He greeted the Brick with a soul-brother handshake. An employee from the back emerged and did the same.

"I see you got your nephew again," said the Walrus, nodding at Joe. "And somebody new?" He eyed Johnny.

"My sister's stepson," said the Brick. "I told her I'd get him out of her hair for a few hours." He winked at the boys, then went to find an empty stall at the end of the corridor. Joe handed out ear protectors, then clipped on the paper target. It outlined a man from the waist up, with a big bull's eye in the chest and a smaller one in the head.

The Brick loaded a Colt 45 M1911, limbered up and took aim. He looked comfortable as he emptied the magazine, then reloaded and fired another round while Johnny and Joe watched. When he was done, he checked the target. Most of the bullets hit within the body outline, with a few inside the chest circles.

He passed the gun to Joe, who seemed more cautious. When he missed his first two shots, the Brick spoke up. "Remember to breath, Joey, fire on the exhale, and try a wider stance." His tone was patient and paternal, something Johnny was not expecting, and it worked. Joe's next several shots were much closer to the bull's-eye.

The Brick hung a new target for Johnny and reloaded the gun. "You gonna be all right with this? It's got more kick than that .38."

"I think so." Johnny took the piece. He liked how the metal felt in his hands, the weight of it, the confidence it induced. He turned toward the target, looking at the circles within circles. The muted gunfire of the other shooters seeped through Johnny's earmuffs as he raised the pistol and squeezed the trigger. The bullet clipped the paper. "Shit." He glimpsed at the Brick to see if he planned to offer some instruction, but the man only folded his arms.

Johnny implemented the pointers Joe had been given while concentrating on the flat, basic figure at the end of the lane. *I need more incentive.* He envisioned the redhead from the drug deal, but knowing he had killed him in real life halted Johnny's breath, and he lowered the gun.

"You gonna be all right?" asked the Brick.

Johnny repositioned. "Yeah." He closed his eyes. *Think of somebody else.* When he opened them again, he was surprised to see his father standing there, jaw clenched, hands balled into fists. Before his brain could consent to the fantasy, his finger was already pulling the trigger, again and again, even after the clip was empty. When he turned around, Joe and the Brick were both slack-jawed. "What's the matter?"

"Joey, pull that motherfucking thing up here." The Brick looked at Johnny. "What are you, an idiot savant of shooting?"

Johnny didn't understand, but it sounded funny, so he snickered.

They examined the target together. Except for the first shot, all of the bullets hit very close to the center of the head.

"You know," said the Brick, pulling an older model Remington pistol out of the case, "if you adjusted your grip a bit, you'd get better consistency." He stood behind Johnny to frame him as Joe set up a fresh target. After a few rounds with that gun, they practiced with a Smith and Wesson .357 magnum and finally a PPK 9mm. Johnny absorbed the Brick's suggestions and made good progress until he began to tire.

The Brick sat in front for the ride home, allowing Johnny to sprawl out in the back seat. He pulled a pack of Marlboros from his jeans pocket and lit one.

The Brick spun around. "Make yourself at home. Should I grab you a forty for the ride?"

Johnny grinned. "That'd be great."

He cocked his head at Joe. "You believe this kid?"

Joe grinned into his fist.

"Actually, I could use a beer, too."

Joe pulled off at a strip mall package store before the highway, and the Brick went inside.

"You know he really likes you," said Joe.

"I kinda get that." Johnny smiled. "I got a shitload of respect for the man and want to do right by him."

"He knows that. Don't worry."

"What about you?" Johnny leaned forward to lay his arms over the backrest. "What's your story?"

"I don't get along with my parents, so my uncle stepped in. He and I have been pretty tight since I was about ten."

"How old *are* you? Your license says eighteen, but I'm not buying it."

Joe grinned. "I'm sixteen."

"How the fuck…"

Before Johnny could finish, the Brick returned with two bottles of Colt 45, an apple juice and a pack of Newports. He flipped the tops on the beers, put one between his legs and handed the other to Johnny. He gave the juice to Joe and lit a cigarette for himself. Johnny sipped the cold beer. It tasted bitter, but the carbonation was refreshing, and the alcohol made his head buzz.

Once they were cruising again, the Brick gazed out the windshield. "I've got more work for you if you want, in addition to those small deliveries. It'd be pickups, but not like that last one. My regular suppliers, people I've done business with for years."

"Really?" Johnny's stomach fluttered with fear and excitement. He swallowed it down with a gulp of malt liquor.

"From what I've seen, you can handle it, and you come with your own posse." He tapped his cigarette in the console's ashtray. "I got a guy doing my runs now, but I know he's skimming off the product for personal use. Not enough to pop a cap in him, but it's starting to frost my ass." He turned to face Johnny. "You need a clear head to do this shit safely, and junkies are nothing but a liability."

Johnny nodded like he knew what he was agreeing with.

"You'd have to travel to Connecticut and Pennsylvania, but Joey can't drive you. He's too easily traced to me, and if anything happens, I'll go away a long time. If *your* crew gets busted, it'd be a few weeks in juvie, you dig?"

Johnny nodded.

"It'll fetch a few grand per run, if you can get a ride."

"One of my boys drives and has access to a few cars."

The Brick sat back in his seat. "Cool."

Johnny bit his lip, suspecting these intimate moments wouldn't come often. "So, um, do you know where I could get a fake ID?"

The Brick laughed. "What do you need, *Johnny*, a birth certificate? Driver's license?" He turned around with raised eyebrows. "If that's even your real name."

Johnny hesitated.

"I knew it!" The Brick slapped his knee. "You got a fucking story and a half, don't you?"

"I—it's just—"

"No." The Brick held up a hand. "I don't *want* to know, as long as you're straight with me about all the other shit."

"You know I am. I *have* been."

"Indeed." The Brick smiled. "Most people would've just given me those drugs and never said shit about the money."

Johnny leaned forward. "You'll hook me up then?"

"I got a girl who works at the DMV. How old *are* you anyway?"

"Fourteen."

"Good Lord." The Brick rolled his eyes so hard his head followed. "If you live to be eighteen, you'll have the world by the balls." He drained his beer. "Look, don't go crazy and say you're twenty-one or nothing. It needs to be believable because this ain't no fake. She'll give you a real learner's permit, so just say you're sixteen. In the meantime, learn to drive."

"Thanks, Rick."

Joe stopped across the street from the park, and the Brick turned to Johnny. "It'll be a few weeks before I'll need you to do a run, but I'll get with you about the other things, okay?"

"Cool."

"We should do this again, Colombiano. I'm curious to see how you'd handle a rifle." He held out his hand, and Johnny slapped him five. "I'll catch you on the flip side, little brother."

CHAPTER TWENTY-EIGHT

When Johnny got back to the park, it was late afternoon. The gang was still there, but no one was jamming. The instruments had been piled to the side of the path, and most of the brothers were milling around in subgroups. They all got up to greet Johnny except Tito, who was on a bench across the park with a beautiful dark-haired woman. The two were so wrapped in conversation he hadn't noticed Johnny's return. She was about thirty, nicely dressed with tasteful makeup. Their eyes were locked, their gestures animated.

"Where'd the Brick take you?" asked Clyde. "Is everything okay?"

"Yeah. It's all fine." Johnny jutted his chin toward Tito. "Who the fuck's that?"

"Beats me," said Rafael. "But they've been at it for an hour."

Johnny strained to look closer. "Are his lips actually moving?"

"Apparently," said Mario. "He hasn't said that many words since we met him. But whatever it is, she's into it."

"Who knew he had an expression other than deadpan?" said Jarrod.

"And that woman is *smokin'*." Rafael hissed.

The stares penetrated Tito's concentration, and he looked up. He excused himself to the woman and went to his brothers.

"There's some serious gang loyalty," said Jarrod. "He left her for *us*?"

"Look at you." Johnny gaped at Tito.

Tito cocked his head. "What?"

"Who's the chick?"

"Nobody."

169

"You and *Nobody* sure looked chummy."

"She is nice. And interesting."

"But *we* can barely get a word out of you," said Clyde.

"Her name is Margaret." Tito rolled a pebble with the toe of his sneaker. "She's an escort."

"Oh *snap!*" said JJ. "You were chatting up a hooker?"

"An escort."

"What's the difference?"

Mario slapped JJ's back. "The difference is, your broke ass can't afford her."

"Was she trying to sell you something?"

Tito frowned. "No. We were talking about things."

Johnny shook his head. "You're quite an enigma."

Tito squinted at Johnny. "A what?"

"An enigma." Johnny laughed. "It means a puzzling motherfucker." The corner of Tito's mouth curled up a tiny bit, and it felt like a victory.

Johnny ran through his day with the Brick while the gang gathered the instruments. They walked to where Tito had parked the dented Pontiac Catalina his cousins lent him. Most of the gear fit into the trunk. Clyde and Jarrod sat with the rest in the back seat. Tito and Johnny slipped into the front, telling the others they'd hook up tomorrow.

Johnny cocked an elbow out his window. "Think you could borrow a car sometime and show me how to drive?"

Jarrod leaned forward. "He sure as shit ain't gonna *tell* you."

"Anyone who wants to learn, I will teach." Tito's eyes never strayed from the road. "Except Jarrod."

"Oh shit!" Clyde spit out a laugh, then punched Jarrod in the arm. "He told *you.*"

Johnny turned around. "I wouldn't fuck with Tito. He might be creepy quiet, but that's just because he's always calculating." He put a hand on Tito's shoulder. "Ain't that right, my brother?"

Tito grunted.

When they got to Clyde's building, he, Johnny and Jarrod unloaded the car and schlepped the gear upstairs. Inside the apartment, they were surprised to find Diana in the kitchen cooking spaghetti and meatballs.

She had a green salad on the table, and the aroma of garlic bread filled the house.

"You're home?" Clyde dropped what he was carrying and went to hug her.

She squeezed him while kissing the top of his head. "The elderly man I care for in the evenings had to go to the hospital, so I get a few nights off to spend with my children." She pulled back to look at Clyde and got teary-eyed. "You're not my little boy anymore, are you? You're growing up so fast." She cradled his face in her hands. "Look how handsome you are."

Clyde turned his reddening face from his friends. "Is it okay if the guys stay over?"

"Don't they always?" She raised an eyebrow at Johnny and Jarrod. "But you two *do* have homes, right?"

"We do, but we don't like them," said Jarrod.

"If you were my sons, I'd want you home every day."

"That's why we're here and not there. I don't think the drunks at my house even notice I'm gone. They're probably having a dinner conversation with a dishrag right now, thinking it's me."

"And my parents might've already changed the locks," Johnny added.

"I'm sure you're both exaggerating, but you're always welcome here. I'll set some extra places. I'm sorry, it is only spaghetti. The flip side of being home is I don't get paid, so money will be tight this week."

"Don't worry, Diana, we love spaghetti," said Johnny.

"Okay, go wash up, and I'll call you when it's ready."

They brought the instruments to Clyde's room and closed the door. "We need to give her money for groceries," said Johnny. "We eat here all the time."

"I know," said Jarrod. "A couple hundred, at least."

Clyde sat at his desk. "Won't she get suspicious?"

"Give her the tips from playing." Johnny dug in his pockets. "I got another thirty bucks."

Clyde counted the cash from the day. It came to $54.00. He had another $110.00 stashed in an envelope from their previous earnings. "All of it?"

"Yeah," said Johnny. "We gotta take care of her."

Clyde stacked the bills together and looked at Johnny. "You said this was gang money, right?"

"Yes."

"Then doesn't the gang have to vote on what happens with it?"

Johnny flopped onto the couch and massaged his temples. The events of the last few days were catching up to him. "It *is* gang money, but the gang is not a democracy. I'm down for hearing everyone's suggestions on how we spend it, but I have the ultimate say."

"I get it," said Clyde. "I was just asking."

Jarrod started to pace, a grin growing bigger with each step. "So, now that we're splitting the tips from playing with the guys who don't play, what would you *ultimately say* about buying some new instruments?" He stopped. "Better gear, better tips, right?"

Johnny stroked the corners of his mouth as he thought about it, then laughed. "That's a brilliant idea."

Jarrod cocked his head. "You're fucking with me, aren't you."

"I don't think he is," said Clyde. "But won't that cause a problem with other members, like because you're spending a lot on us but not them?"

"It shouldn't," said Johnny. "I think it sets an example that there's money available for anyone who has ideas that benefit the gang as a whole." He leaned forward. "And since you brought it up, I'm not making any decisions without you two. The three of us started this gang, and we need a clear chain of command." Johnny split his gaze between Clyde and Jarrod. "If I get killed tomorrow, who's stepping up to run shit?"

Clyde pointed to Jarrod. "He is."

Johnny eyed Jarrod. "You good with that?"

"Yeah, man, I'll be VP as long as Clyde's right behind me."

Clyde nodded. "I'm good with third in command."

"Okay then," said Johnny. "That's the rank. Do we all vote that Clyde's mother should get the one hundred and ninety-four dollars?"

They both nodded.

"And do we all vote to get some new gear?"

"Definitely," said Clyde.

"Absolutely!" said Jarrod.

"Great." Johnny slapped his knee. "Meeting adjourned."

CHAPTER TWENTY-NINE

It was Labor Day weekend, and several gang members stood outside Music World on 48th Street. While waiting for the others, they smoked cigarettes and suggested new songs for the band to play. A horn tooted, and they looked up to see a white, dinged-up Dodge van approaching. On each side was a large stencil of an upside-down rat with its eyes x'd out and lettering that read EZ Exterminating. On the hood was a cockroach depicted similarly. Tito pulled into a loading zone and activated the four-way flashers.

Mario slapped his forehead. "What the fuck is that?"

"How fitting," said JJ. "The creepy, quiet serial killer is driving an exterminator's van!"

"I'll bet the exterminator's body is in the back," said Chico.

"It was." Rafael slid out of the passenger's seat, grinning. "But we dumped it to make room for the new gear."

"Hurry up, then," said Johnny as more brothers climbed out of the sliding side door. "Let's go buy some new shit!"

The large group paraded into the store, talking and laughing as they fanned out. Some employees in matching red Polo shirts turned to look. A handful of customers did likewise. A few slinked toward the door.

Johnny and Clyde went straight for the electric guitars hanging from the ceiling in every brand and color. Acoustics were displayed on floor stands.

"This might be the happiest I've ever been," said Clyde, fixated on a Gibson Les Paul. It was blue with silver flakes.

"I should get a guitar, too," said Johnny, "now that you've been showing me how to play." He touched the tuning pegs on a Yamaha. "We need acoustics for the street, but you should definitely get an electric for home."

"Are you serious?"

"Why not? We can afford it."

"Can I help you?" A tall clerk glowered behind them.

"Sure," said Clyde. "I wanna try that Gibson."

The man folded his arms. "This isn't a toy store, you know."

"Yeah. I know."

The clerk's lips tightened before reaching for the guitar. Johnny rolled his eyes at Clyde and turned to go look around. Mario was by the woodwinds, comparing saxophone prices, and Tito was patting on congas and bongos. Some other brothers were thumbing through sheet music. A guy with a white shirt and a pencil behind his ear rushed from a back room to have a hushed consultation with the woman at the counter. As their eyes took inventory of the gang, a drum solo rang out. Johnny turned to see Jarrod behind a Ludwig five-piece, a grin plastered on his face. Despite his lack of instruction and proper equipment, Jarrod had natural talent. Several crew members, along with some remaining customers, gathered around to watch him wail.

The white-shirted manager came over, waving his arms. "What's going on here?"

Jarrod stood up from behind the kit. "I'll take it!"

"Excuse me?"

"Pack me up one just like this." Jarrod looked at Johnny. "Is that OK?"

Johnny nodded. "Whatever you want."

The tall clerk shadowed Tito and Mario as they carried over their selected instruments. "And we'll get these," said Mario.

The manager's eyes fluttered spasmodically. "And you plan to pay for everything... *how?*"

"Cash," said Johnny. "You want to see?" He pulled a stack of bills from his pocket.

The two men squinted at each other as more brothers circled around. The manager then signaled the cashier, who reached under the counter to pick up a phone receiver.

"Is there a problem?" asked Johnny, "because we *could* go spend this money at the place down the block."

"Yeah," said Jarrod. "We worked hard all summer to save this money."

Maurice Steinberg, a white recruit with kinky hair and wire-framed glasses, stepped forward. "In fact, that hard work received numerous commendations from our church."

Some gang members stifled laughter.

Mario stood beside Maurice. "Our congregation was *so* impressed that they took up a collection to pay for new instruments."

"And if we come back empty-handed," said Clyde, "the pastor will be very disappointed."

Alex put his palms together and looked toward the ceiling. "Please, God, don't let us disappoint him."

The manager waved at the cashier to put the phone down. "All right. Fine. Just make it quick."

When everything was packed up and paid for, the gang thanked the staff and carted it outside. The van was roomy, with three rows of seats and plenty of storage space, but it still took some finagling to make everything fit.

Once they were rolling, Johnny asked Tito, "What's the deal with this rig?"

"My cousin's had it for repairs," he mumbled. "But the owner hasn't paid the bill, so they're holding it."

"If he doesn't pay, ask if they want to sell it."

"You'd buy this thing?" said Jarrod.

"Why not? It's perfect."

"We could turn those dead rats into dogs," said Mario, "Then people will know the Dogs of War are coming to exterminate their ass!"

Johnny laughed. "I think it's great camouflage the way it is." He turned to Tito. "Ask how much they'll take for it."

Tito nodded. "Where to?"

"The park," said Johnny. "Earn back some of what we just spent."

Washington Square was already crowded by the time they set up by the arch. They warmed up with a few slower numbers, *If* by Bread and

Blackbird by the Beatles, but the church talk at the music store inspired an attempt at *Spirit in the Sky*, by Norman Greenbaum. They didn't know all the lyrics, but they improvised, with other gang members joining in to add background vocals. They were having so much fun that passersby stopped to sing along, too, and the tips poured in.

After a few hours, they took a break and sent new recruits, Mikey Mahoney and Oscar De Jesus, to Blimpie's for a sandwich run.

"Hey, Tito," said Johnny, gesturing across the park. "Isn't that your lady friend?"

"Mm-hm. Margaret."

She sat on a granite bench wearing a revealing floral-patterned dress and sandals. Her black hair was up in a bun, but a few strands dangled loosely around her face. They both stared as she nibbled on the rim of an ice cream cone.

Johnny nudged Tito. "Aren't you going to say hello?"

"I don't know."

"If you don't, I'm going to."

While Tito and Johnny debated, Margaret noticed them and waved. They waved back. She finished eating and got up. Both were captivated by her curvaceous figure as she sashayed toward them. "Hi. It's Tito, right?"

"Yes," he said.

"I'm Johnny." He extended a hand.

"Margaret. Nice to meet you." She shook back. "I see your band playing in the park a lot, and it sounds like you're really improving."

"Thanks. We've been practicing." Johnny clapped Tito on the back. "So, you two know each other?"

Margaret smiled. "Sort of. We struck up a conversation the other day and just kept talking." She glanced at Tito, and he looked at the ground.

"Talking?" Johnny cocked his head. "With *this* guy?"

"Yes. He knows *so* much about politics, astronomy and South American history. But you guys are friends, so you probably knew that."

"I did *not* know that, Margaret." Johnny gaped at Tito. "But then again, he *is* quite an enigma."

"Enigma," Tito parroted. "That means puzzling motherfucker."

Johnny and Margaret broke out laughing. Even Tito smiled.

"Colombiano, *¿cómo estás?*" The Brick sauntered over, holding out a hand for Johnny to slap while giving Tito a nod. "And Margaret, how's your fine self today?" He wrapped an arm around her waist and kissed her on the cheek.

She kissed back. "I'm great, B. Enjoying the beautiful day and listening to these talented musicians."

"I'm gonna have to get these cats a recording contract one day." The Brick eyed the equipment. "I see you got yourselves some new gear. *Tips* must be pretty good." He winked at Johnny.

Johnny nodded. "*Really* good."

The Brick put a hand on Johnny's shoulder. "Look out for this one, Margaret. He'll charm the pants off a nun."

She grinned. "I didn't know they wore pants."

"Smartass." Laughing, he kissed her again. "You all take it easy, now." He nodded at Johnny and Tito before strutting across the park.

"You know him?" Johnny asked Margaret.

"We go way back." Margaret brushed the fabric of her dress. "I've got to go, too, but it was nice talking to you."

"You, also, Margaret. I hope we see you again soon."

"Yeah," said Tito.

They both watched her walk away. "What is it with you?" said Johnny. "You only talk when you're alone with her? Like Mr. Ed."

"Mister who?"

Johnny wagged his head. "Never mind."

CHAPTER THIRTY

The gang squeezed as much as they could out of the holiday weekend. They jammed and cavorted in Washington Square during the day and patrolled the city at night, sometimes riding the subway for hours, swinging on commuter poles and tagging *Dogs of War* on the cars. They even explored the dark, rat-infested tunnels, where they had to flatten themselves behind steel girders when a train came whizzing by. But Johnny's mood grew gloomier as it came to a close. School was about to start. That meant curfews for most of his crew and fewer sleepovers. Shorter days, shittier weather and more time in his depressing squat.

It was Sunday night when they found themselves in Battery Park. Some members sparred in the grass before they all headed up South Street and through the Seaport. During the day, the fish market was bustling with business, but at night, the only vestige of commerce was the smell, which was apparently too pungent for even the bums and homeless.

When Johnny inhaled the thick aroma of salt and fish guts, a wave of nostalgia merged with his depression. *Miami.* Back home, he couldn't wait for summer to end and school to start. For one, it was blazing hot, and Florida schools had air conditioning. There was also plenty to keep him busy and distract him from his family. He was liked by his teachers and had lots of friends to act normal with. Johnny started to think about those old-school chums and neighborhood pals and how they had helped keep his shit together when things were crazy at home. *And they had no idea.* He had hidden everything from them. But how long would that have lasted? Eyes had already started lingering on his scars, and looks turned skeptical when he claimed the bruises were from sports. Again.

As the gang neared the Brooklyn Bridge, Johnny looked at the brothers around him. He could be honest with these guys, which only made them more loyal and more eager to protect him, yet he still felt uneasy. *Mostly honest.*

Despite being so late, the day's heat and humidity lingered. Johnny pointed to the bridge. "Come on, let's go across. It'll be cooler."

The crew walked onto the ten-foot-wide wooden promenade above the thoroughfare. The constant rumble of traffic reverberated from below. At the first stanchion, the path widened around the massive stone tower, and the gang stopped to linger. Some draped over the steel barriers to look at the East River.

"Who wants to go up there?" JJ pointed toward the stanchion.

"How do you do that?" asked Jarrod. "Can you get inside?"

"There's a little door," said Mario, pointing up the side of an arch. "But it's too high."

"We could climb the cables," said JJ.

"I know you like climbing shit," said Jarrod, "But that's just nuts."

"You ain't getting me up there, monkey boy," said Chico. "I'm afraid of heights."

"Hell no," said Leon Waits, a black fourteen-year-old with short dreads. "There's only one thing that scares me more than falling, and that's drowning."

Johnny looked at the looming granite structure, its web of cables descending from above. The sense of danger eclipsed his melancholy. "I'll go."

JJ beamed. "Really?"

"If anyone sees, you could get busted," said Clyde. "Is it worth the risk?"

"Yeah, it is," Johnny said, perking up. "But we won't get caught. You guys will be the distraction. Hang around down here and look like you're up to no good. All eyes will be on you, and no one will notice us."

"And don't stare," said JJ. "If people see you gawking, they're gonna want to know what you're looking at."

Johnny slapped JJ on the shoulder. "Let's go!"

The pair had to walk back to the Manhattan side, where the cables that ran from tower to deck were low enough to access. The main cable was over a foot wide, and JJ climbed on first with Johnny behind. They grabbed hold of the two thinner cables, which ran shoulder height, and started pulling themselves toward the top. The wires swayed as they climbed, so they synchronized their steps to minimize the motion.

At the top, Johnny and JJ crouched to catch their breath. They listened for a warning whistle from below, but there was nothing. The only sounds were the hum of the city and the hollow whirring of tires speeding across the bridge. They stood up and gazed in all directions. Johnny looked across the blackness of the East River that bisected Brooklyn and Manhattan, the impressive architecture on each side, the billions of lights and miles of traffic. The perspective made him feel powerful and insignificant at the same time.

Johnny walked to the edge, letting the toes of his sneakers dangle over the side. He looked down. The height was dizzying, but the moonlight sparkling off the water was spectacular. He stretched open his arms and wondered what it would be like to jump, what the sensation of air swirling around his body would feel like as he fell, how long it would take to hit the water. The fantasy was exhilarating because he suspected that in the moments just before every bone and organ in his body was shattered from the impact, he would finally be free. Free from his crazy episodes. Free from rage, always lurking just below the surface. And free from the shame of things still unconfessed.

"Dude, you're scaring me," said JJ. "We should go."

Johnny lowered his arms. "Okay, yeah."

He backed away, and the two returned to the main cable, taking one final moment to drink in the view. Going down was harder to do quickly. There was no focus point other than the ground, and looking down challenged their balance, so they took their time. When they got to the walkway, the rest of the gang ran over to meet them.

"We should get going," said Jarrod. "It's almost midnight."

"That was cool," JJ said as they walked back toward Lower Manhattan.

"Is that the highest you've ever climbed?" asked Leon.

"Hell yeah, but now I gotta top it, maybe scale the World Trade Center."

"You're like a tiny-ass albino Spiderman," said Chico. "What about you, Johnny? How was it?"

Johnny smiled. *It was like knowing there's a backup plan.*

By the time the original three got to Clyde's, they were tired and sweaty. The dirt of the city was ground into their skin, but none had the energy to shower. Johnny pulled the foam mattress from the closet as Jarrod flopped on the couch, and Clyde crawled into his bed. Still wired from the day, they lay in the dim light of a reading lamp.

"When you and JJ were on the bridge, I could swear it looked like you were gonna jump," Jarrod said to Johnny.

Johnny took a moment to rearranged his pillow. "I thought about it."

"Shut up, you didn't," said Clyde.

He propped on one elbow. "I just tried to imagine what it would feel like. You don't think I'd do it, do you?"

"I guess not." Clyde sat up. "But you do have a bit of a death wish."

"What do you mean?"

"Sometimes, when we've been in dangerous situations, you get…" Clyde searched the ceiling, "…calm. Like, instead of being nervous, you look relaxed, like you don't worry about dying."

Johnny considered it. "I guess, in those moments, I kinda *do* feel like I don't care, like I have nothing to lose."

"But that shit comes from your family," said Jarrod.

"Probably. But your family's a mess, too. You never think about getting them to stop haunting you?"

"I'm not *haunted* by my family." Jarrod clucked his tongue. "I see those drunks every day. Being haunted by them wouldn't be half as scary as those assholes alive!"

"So? You've never thought about it?" Johnny asked.

"Killing myself? I guess I've thought about it. Everybody's thought about it, right?" Jarrod picked at a snarl in his tousled hair. "But not seriously. And not now that I have you guys. Who wants to miss this shit?"

Johnny looked at Clyde. "What about you?"

"I could never do that to my mom."

"Well," Johnny wagged a hand. "I'm not serious about it either."

"I guess we need to add that to the list," said Clyde.

"What list?" Johnny asked.

"Yeah, what list?" said Jarrod.

"The list of requirements for gang membership." Clyde counted on his fingers. "We gotta lie about your identity, keep you away from cops and the Department of Social Services, protect the public when you're flipped and trying to murder people with your bare hands, and..." he flicked both wrists "...now we have to keep you from killing yourself."

"Sounds good." Johnny grinned. "Aren't I worth it?"

"So worth it," said Jarrod.

"I guess you *are* worth it," said Clyde. "Especially since I have thousands of dollars stuffed in my closet."

CHAPTER THIRTY-ONE

Roosevelt High School occupied most of the block between West 19th and 20th Streets in a residential neighborhood. The brown-brick structure had a small open-air courtyard near the entrance, which might have been a nice place for kids to congregate, but the decorative trees had died long ago, and most of the benches were broken and graffiti-covered.

The main floor consisted of long hallways lined with aging yellowed tile, reminiscent of a subway or public toilet. Concrete stairwells led to other floors filled with classrooms, each one indistinguishable from the next, except for a small, often askew, number plaque above each door.

The school lived up to its abominable reputation. The student population was large, many of them delinquents. Fights broke out in the street and the lunchroom and kids often got randomly punched or pushed as they traveled between classes. Little was done about it due to chronic understaffing.

Johnny's transcripts were sent over from IS 20, along with a thousand others, and his forged application never raised an eyebrow. He and his crew continued the tradition of doing homework in the library after school. They liked getting it out of the way so they could goof off the rest of the day, but it also provided an opportunity to discuss gang business and potential recruits.

During the first week, Johnny and a few of his brothers were in the lunch line when they spotted Eric Hanson, the kid Jarrod had fought a year earlier. "Damn," said Johnny. "I almost didn't recognize you. Your braces are off, and you cut that scraggly hair." He extended a hand.

Eric shook it, grinning. "I know it, right?" He gave a nod to the surrounding crew. "I made a few changes since I saw you last, like dumping those bed-wetting shit stains I used to call friends."

Johnny laughed. "They don't go here?"

"No. Thank God. I still see Gordon occasionally because we live in the same building, but that's it."

"You ever hear anything about how that Shawn kid is doing?" Jarrod asked.

"Not lately, but I saw him a few weeks after all of you beat him, and he did *not* look good."

"We didn't *all* beat him," said Chico. "That fight was one-on-one, just like with you."

"Get the fuck out of here. One person did that? Who?"

The others turned to Johnny, but he looked at his shoes. It was hard to gloat about something he didn't remember.

Jarrod shook Johnny's shoulder. "All I can tell you is you don't want to fuck with *this* guy."

"I guess not," said Eric. "I was scared shitless the day you came at me, but after it happened and I survived, I thought you guys were pretty cool about it."

"That's a bold thing to say," said Johnny. "You're all right with me."

It was the last weekend in September. The Dogs of War were in Washington Square, busking before the weather made it prohibitive. There was some foot traffic, but not like the summer, and tips were reflected likewise.

The Brick walked over between songs. "Colombiano, you got a minute?"

"Sure. We're just serenading the pigeons anyway."

They stepped away from the others. "You're taking a half-day one week from Monday."

"What do you mean?"

"Which school do you go to?"

"Roosevelt."

"Joey will pick you up at noon, take you to the DMV. Don't be late."

"Should I bring anything?"

"Yeah." The Brick grinned. "Everything you need for your new identity, wig, fake mustache, whatever. And five hundred dollars."

"No problem."

"And Joe will have directions for a pickup," he lifted an eyebrow, "if you can handle it. You'll need to travel."

"I can handle whatever you throw at me. We just bought a van. It's not as pimpin' as your rides, but it'll do."

"You're one serious piece of work." He clapped Johnny on the back. "See you later, rock star."

The bandmates were toying with the idea of packing up when ten guys, donned in a combination of jeans, cutoff shirts and biker boots, entered the park. Johnny set his guitar down to track their path. The others stopped playing, too.

One of the men veered over. He was in his mid-twenties, with stringy blond hair and a chipped front tooth. He peeked at the smattering of cash in the guitar case. The rest of his group sidled up to him and eyed the gear.

"You faggots take requests?" he said. Some of his comrades snickered.

The surrounding Dog brothers stepped closer, but Johnny stood expressionless, sizing up the men. A handful had matching tattoos with the word *Scorpions* scripted below an image of the predatory arachnid. But the drawing was amateurish. Johnny squinted at one of the guys' arms. It looked like it said *Scorpi*-ans.

Chipped Tooth pressed his fists into his hips. "What are you, a bunch of fucking mutes?"

"I got a request," said a dark-haired guy, also twenty-something, with a rolled-up bandana tied around his head. "Can I hold that guitar?" He pointed to Clyde's new acoustic.

Chipped Tooth tapped the guitar case with his boot, causing the bills and coins to jiggle inside its red velvet interior. "You dorks should pay *us* to listen to your shit. How 'bout you gimme five dollars?"

Johnny's fingers fiddled the folded knife in his pocket. "How 'bout I don't."

"Ha!" Chipped Tooth backhanded Bandana in the chest. "We got us a comedian."

"Can you spell that?" Johnny mumbled, stifling a smirk.

"What'd you say?"

"Nothing."

Jarrod got up behind his drums while Clyde put down his guitar. Mario, Rafael and Tito, the biggest of the crew, moved toward the front line. Some pedestrians began making a wider berth around the two groups. Others stopped to watch from a distance.

"Fuck these chumps," said Bandana.

As Johnny slid the knife from his pocket, Clyde put a hand on his shoulder. "It's not worth it," he whispered. "Let it go."

Johnny nodded, letting the folded Buck drop back into his pants.

"Yeah," Chipped Tooth sneered. "Listen to your friend." He bent over, scooped up a handful of bills from the case, then spun around to herd his buddies away.

Johnny smiled as he watched them strut out of the park, joking and congratulating each other on their big win.

"What the fuck are you grinning at," Mario asked him.

Johnny ignored the question and turned to Eric. "You've been hanging out with us lately."

He shrugged. "Yeah?"

"You want in?"

"What do you mean?"

"If you want in this gang, go follow those fuckers. Find out where they live, work, hang out, something." Johnny jutted his chin at JJ. "You go with him."

"Me?" JJ scrunched his face.

"Yeah, you're both the least conspicuous."

"You mean the whitest," said JJ. "Okay, *hhh*-ombre, I'll be your token Caucasian. No prob-*lemo!*"

Johnny smacked JJ's head. "You're so white you're transparent. Now go." He shooed them away. "Hurry. We'll catch up with you at school tomorrow." Eric and JJ jogged after the men.

Clyde sighed. "We're doing this again?"

"Look, I'm not gonna be shit on by a bunch of wannabe Hells Angels," he said. "So, yeah, we're doing this again. Except now there's a lot more of us." He scanned the faces of his gang. "We'll gather information, then retaliate. Someplace where *we* can have the upper hand. Not surrounded by people in broad daylight. Is everyone down with that?"

"Hell yeah," said Rafael. "Otherwise, next time we're out here, it'll be the same old shit."

"Like bullies stealing our lunch money," said Andre. "Fuck that."

"Perfect," said Johnny. "We'll start building a strategy during our homework sessions."

Chico sucked his teeth. "When it comes to homework, he's all, 'do it now, do it now,' but when it's about kicking ass, he's all, 'wait, wait.'"

Johnny laughed. "We'll get all As *and* exterminate those motherfuckers!"

"The Exterminators," said Mario. "That should be our band's name."

"I'm not sure about that one," said Clyde. "But we *do* need a name."

"Something will come," said Patrick. "Don't force it."

Chico slapped Jarrod on the back. "Hey, that's what yo mama said to me last night!"

Jarrod shook a drumstick at him. "Gross!"

Chico grabbed it. "*Mira, tranquilo,* temper, temper."

"I like that better," said Clyde. "Temper. How about it?"

"Shit, that *is* kinda good." Johnny waited for an objection. "Okay, I guess we're Temper."

In the cafeteria, the gang leaned over their lunch trays to hear Eric's report. "First, they wandered around the Village, going into stores and acting obnoxious. You should hear the stupid shit they say."

"Okay, they're dopes," said Johnny. "What else?"

"The guy with the broken tooth—they call him Ron—I think he might be the leader, just by how he talks to everyone. Anyway, across town, half of them peeled off to do other shit, so we stuck with the main guys. They got a bunch of beer and went to this little kids' park in a building on East 12th, by Avenue B. They stayed till like eight-something, but then me and JJ had to get home, so we left."

"Good work," said Johnny.

Eric leaned back in his chair, pleased to have helped.

Johnny looked around the table. "Let's take turns scoping out that park this week, see if they have a pattern."

His brothers nodded.

CHAPTER THIRTY-TWO

Friday after school, Johnny gathered the gang by the East River to work on their fighting technique. They sat in a circle on the grass, but before getting started, they reviewed what they had found.

"Me and Chico passed by that park a few times," said Mario. "Caught some of them in there once."

"Us, too," the Martinez brothers echoed.

"They drink beer and smoke joints," said Chico. "And when they're fucked up, they get so obnoxious."

"Shouting shit at people as they walk by," said Andre. "Even throwing bottle caps."

Johnny and some others grunted in disgust.

"And that park is for *little* kids who live in that building and go there with their families." Mario flicked a hand. "Not those big oafs."

Chico's head bobbed. "They're gonna break the rides."

"Why would they even hang out there?" asked Johnny.

"They've probably been kicked out of every place else," said Jarrod.

Alex tapped his brother, Andre. "The night we saw them, that Ron asshole threw an empty quart of beer against the building. Left all that broken glass laying there for those kids to play in."

Johnny flashed his palms. "I've heard enough. Let's get on with our practice so we can injure these motherfuckers."

The gang remained in a circle, watching pairs of brothers take turns battling it out for two minutes each. After every round, the group provided feedback, which the fighters could implement during their next turn. The one who surprised the gang the most was meek little Mikey Mahoney. When he stepped into the circle, his whole demeanor changed. He locked eyes on his opponent and struck with such ferocity it left them little more to do than block, even during one match with Tito, who was much bigger.

After the round, Johnny had Mikey remain in the center when Tito returned to sit with the others. "What's your deal, man?"

"What do you mean?" said Mikey, still winded from the fight.

"You're always so quiet, but here you're like the Tasmanian Devil."

Mikey looked at the ground.

"Listen, we can't have secrets in this gang. You guys know my shit, even though I hate talking about it. So, what's making *you* so angry?"

He toed the grass with his sneaker.

Johnny stood. "How about you tell me, or I'll beat it out of you."

Mikey's head snapped up. "It's embarrassing."

"I don't give a shit."

Mikey scanned the circle. "Sometimes my stepfather hits me."

"Why?"

"He has a temper when he drinks."

"What do you do that makes him so mad?"

"What *I* do?" Mikey huffed. "It's *my* fault now?"

Johnny smiled at having touched a nerve. "Yeah, what do *you* do that makes him so mad?"

Mikey's jaw tightened. "It's what I won't do."

"What won't you do?"

"I won't let him touch me."

A few groans came from the circle. Johnny tensed as an acidic jolt sickened his insides. He pushed the feeling away and continued. "When did it start?"

"After I turned twelve."

"That's fucked up." Johnny went to Mikey, and they both sat down. "What do you want to do about it?"

Mikey wiped some moisture from his eyes. "I want to get the fuck out of there."

"A lot of us have homes we need to get out of. I'm working toward that. But what do you want to do in the meantime?" Johnny put his hands on Mikey's shoulders. "Do we need to kill him?"

Mikey wagged his head. "No, I—I can't do that."

"I get it." Johnny pursed his bottom lip. "The other option is to pay him a visit. Show him that you're not alone anymore, that you have a lot of people watching your back."

"I like that idea better," said Mikey. "But lemme think about it."

Johnny nodded. "Whenever you're ready, just say the word."

"Thank you."

At the DeMarcos', the original three raided the refrigerator, took turns showering and closed themselves in Clyde's room.

"What's your plan with the Scorpions?" Clyde asked Johnny.

"I plan to let them know they're lucky we don't kill them.'"

"Sounds good," said Jarrod, flopping onto the couch.

Clyde sat on his bed and sighed.

"What?" Johnny snapped. "When those guys came over just to intimidate and humiliate us, how did *you* feel?"

"Pissed off."

"Pissed off? I wanted to rip them to pieces. I know I need to stay under the radar, at least until I'm eighteen. But that doesn't mean I should let everyone shit on me."

"This is your thing now? You got away with beating Shawn and popping that guy on the pier, so now we're gonna bump off everyone who looks at us sideways?"

"I'm not the one looking for trouble, Clyde. *These* people are fucking with *me*. With us." Johnny raked his fingers through his hair. "And it feels too familiar, like all the reasons I left home. If you want to take a step back, I respect that. But after everything I've already been through, I can't."

"Johnny's right," said Jarrod. "If we don't do something, next time we're out there, they *will* take our instruments. How're you gonna feel then?"

Clyde cradled his head. "No. I get it." He met Johnny's eyes. "Once you explain it like that, it makes more sense. I guess the injustice doesn't feel as big to me because I didn't suffer the same kind of shit like you and Mikey."

"Speaking of Mikey," said Jarrod. "I think there was a lot more to his story than, 'My stepfather *wants* to touch me, but I don't let him.'" He wagged his hand. "Not with anger like that."

Johnny crossed his arms. "Mikey's situation and mine are *not* the same."

"I know, I just—"

"My brother tied me up and tortured me. I never said anything about him diddling me." Johnny's head toggled between Clyde and Jarrod. "Is that what you think?"

"I don't think anything," said Jarrod. "We only know what you tell us. But you blacked out a lot of shit, too, so…"

"So what?"

Clyde stood up. "Everybody, calm down. Nobody's making any comparisons about anything. We're talking about the Scorpions, right?"

"Yeah." Johnny sat on the edge of Clyde's bed. "I'm just a little on edge today."

"You know," said Jarrod, smirking, "if we *really* want to hurt those guys, we should hit 'em with a dictionary."

Johnny's eyes widened. "You saw that?"

"That O definitely looked like an A to me."

"Wait," said Clyde. "They spelled their name wrong?"

Johnny nodded. "Either that or they had some drunk do their tattooing."

Jarrod cracked up. "When that guy asked for five dollars, I was gonna say, 'You sure you can count that high?'"

They all laughed.

CHAPTER THIRTY-THREE

Johnny lurched awake as if two cymbals had clapped together. He sat up, blinking, then tried to swallow, but his throat was so dry it hurt. Other parts throbbed, too, like he had tumbled down a cliff. When the dregs of unconsciousness lifted, he saw Clyde and Jarrod perched on Clyde's bed. Both were dressed, hands in laps, fixated.

"How'd I get on the couch?"

Clyde exhaled. Jarrod was unblinking, mouth agape.

Johnny curled into a ball, pressing his face into his knees so hard it muffled his words. "Did it happen again?"

"Yeah," said Clyde. "Bad."

"How bad?"

"Really bad."

"And it went on a long time," added Jarrod.

Johnny unfurled himself across the sofa. "How long?"

"Like four hours," said Clyde. "You seemed worse than after the Shawn fight."

"You were in the corner," said Jarrod, "rocking back and forth, head thrashing, muttering some weird, fucked up language."

"I thought you'd wake the house," said Clyde. "But me and Jarrod just kept talking to you, trying to keep you calm. Then, out of nowhere, you slipped out of it, crawled over to the couch, and lay down."

"You've been sleeping hard for hours," said Jarrod.

Johnny rubbed his face. "What time is it?"

"Like ten something."

The three sat in silence until Clyde started to fidget. "So…" his eyes surveyed the walls. "Did you come to with anything?"

"Huh?"

"We were gonna try to recover some of those memories. Remember? Like, to stop this from happening.

"Fuck." Johnny folded forward.

"What woke you up just now? A nightmare?"

Johnny shot them a scowl. "It was probably because you guys have been staring at me. That's kinda creepy, you know."

"Sorry," said Jarrod. "But we didn't know if you'd flip out again."

"When it happened before," said Clyde, "you had a feeling about shit your brother did."

Johnny sat up. "First of all, Orlando is *not* my brother. *You* are my brothers. He's just some sick prick I had the misfortune of growing up with." He sighed. "Can't we just drop it?"

Clyde leaned forward. "I can't drop it, like you wouldn't drop it with Mikey. We need to figure this out and fix it so it doesn't put the gang at risk."

"He makes a point," said Jarrod.

After several breaths, Johnny tipped his head back and closed his eyes.

"Do you see anything?" Clyde asked.

"No."

"Do you remember talking because you were saying a bunch of shit we couldn't understand."

"What, like Spanish?"

"I recognized some Spanish, but there was other stuff."

"Must've been Turkish, then."

"French, too." Jarrod snorted. "Four whole semesters of French, and this is the only time it's come in handy."

"But it wasn't one language at a time," said Clyde. "It was like you were mixing them together, alternating words."

Johnny covered his face with his arm. "Back when shit was still kinda normal, my mother used to teach me and Orlando languages, in addition to the Spanish and Turkish we were already hearing from birth.

But it was fun, not like work." A lump developed in his throat, and he swallowed it down. "The three of us would get cozy on her bed and take turns reading all these foreign books she collected. Nursery rhymes and storybooks from when *she* was a kid, and her family lived in different countries like France, Portugal and Germany. Before they settled in Colombia."

Jarrod coughed up a grunt. "Meanwhile, I thought *I* was special when my dad cracked a beer to watch Saturday morning cartoons with me."

"You idiot." Clyde swatted him.

"I'm serious." Jarrod scrunched his face. "His favorite was Quick Draw McGraw."

Clyde rolled his eyes and gestured for Johnny to continue.

Johnny sat up, relieved to have the mood lightened. "Orlando and I used to blend the different languages when we played together like it was our own special code. But once he got locked in the basement, I stopped doing it because that's how he'd talk when he was really deranged." Johnny rubbed his scarred wrists. "It's how I knew shit was gonna be especially bad for me." He stood up in front of Clyde. "Is that enough for you, Bob Newhart? Because I gotta pee."

CHAPTER THIRTY-FOUR

Johnny, Clyde and Jarrod lounged around the DeMarcos' apartment all day, watching TV and noodling on guitars, but it wasn't enough to distract Johnny from the contaminated remnants of his episode. The only thing that did work, he found, was thinking about revenge against the Scorpions. So, as evening approached, the trio took turns making calls, rallying the rest of the gang to meet them at Union Square Park in an hour.

When all members were present, they headed toward East 12th Street. Johnny had two brothers run ahead to scope out the kiddie park. They returned, reporting it was empty, so the crew killed time wandering around.

Chico sidled up to Johnny. "You're awful quiet over here, Jefe."

"That's 'cause he's got a batshit crazy hangover," said Jarrod.

Clyde shoved him. "Jesus, you gotta be so fucking harsh?"

"He said we're supposed to let the gang know when this shit happens."

Johnny put up a hand. "It's all right. I like that we're not taking this too seriously. And yes," he spun to face the others, "I had another one of those episodes last night, but I'm fine now." His eyes landed on Mikey. "How about you? You okay?"

Mikey pressed his mouth into a smile. "I'm good."

"Cool."

They rechecked the park a few more times, but it was getting late. They decided to make one more pass before calling it quits.

"They're in there now," said Andre, jogging over with JJ.

196

"How many?" Johnny asked.

"Four."

"What are they doing?"

"Same old shit, drinking, loafing."

"Perfect. Let's go." Johnny's spine straightened as he strode forward. A good ass-kicking would remedy his batshit crazy hangover.

The seventeen members of the Dogs of War entered the playground and spread out, with Chico and Oscar hanging by the entrance as lookouts. Idly rocking on the kiddy swing set was the blond with the broken tooth, the one called Ron. Beside him, the other mouthy guy with the bandana. Another pair sat on the merry-go-round: a jaundiced-looking teenager and a flabby thirtysomething with a buzzcut. Each had a quart of beer in a rolled-down brown paper bag.

Johnny went straight for the swings, eyes on his main target. Ron watched him, puzzled at first, then saw the others. "Oh shit, look who it is," he slurred. "It's those kids from the park. Did you miserable pricks come to serenade us?"

Buzzcut guffawed. "I think these *children* came to ride the rides." He pushed the ground with a foot, making the merry-go-round spin a lethargic half-circle. The teen beside him wasn't prepared for the motion and almost lost his balance.

Johnny's head wagged in disbelief. These idiots might make things easier than he had thought. "We didn't come to do either."

"Then you must be here to suck my dick." Ron grabbed his crotch.

Johnny ignored the comment. "Who's in charge of this outfit?"

"What's it to you?"

"Maybe I want to drop off a membership application."

"Why don't you leave it with me so I can wipe my ass with it?"

Bandana sneered. "Good one, Ron."

"Ronald." Johnny stepped closer. "That's your fucking name?"

"I ain't tellin' you shit."

"You ought to if you don't want to get your ass kicked."

"By who? You cock-sucking cum stains?"

Just what I've been waiting for. Johnny lunged forward and punched him in the cheek. Ron dipped backward, dropping his beer to grab the metal chains so he wouldn't fall off the seat. The bag kept the bottle from breaking, and foamy liquid gushed from its neck.

Buzzcut jumped up to help, but Tito and Rafael restrained him. He struggled in their grip, so Tito punched him a few times in the face. The scrawny teen tried to scramble off the merry-go-round but banged his head on a handrail, making it easy for Alex and Maurice to nab him. Clyde, Jarrod and Leon held on to Bandana, and Patrick went to back up Johnny. The Scorpions were too drunk and outnumbered to offer much resistance. After lining them up on the bench farthest from the street, Johnny's crew surrounded them.

"I want to know who's in charge," Johnny said to Ron.

"What the fuck for?"

"I have a message to deliver."

"And who the fuck are you?" asked Buzzcut.

Rafael smacked the guy's face. "We're the Dogs of War."

Johnny looked at Bandana. "Is it you?"

"Fuck you." He spit on the ground.

Johnny tapped his chin while surveying the park. "Well, well, lookie here. Some *assholes* left a bunch of broken glass over there." He went to it and stomped on a triangular chunk, breaking it into smaller pieces. "This is *not* very safe. Some poor baby could get seriously injured." Johnny scooped up some shards and returned to Ron, then yanked his head back while Patrick and Andre held him from behind. He shoved as much of the glass in Ron's mouth as he could. Ron thrashed, trying to keep his lips closed, but Johnny pressed until he got more pieces inside, cutting Ron's face as well.

As Johnny wiped his bloody palm on his jeans, he caught some contorted reactions from his crew, but he ignored them to refocus on Ron. "Tell me who's in charge."

Ron flicked his head, then turned away.

Johnny punched him in the mouth. Pieces of glass flew from his face, trailed by streams of blood. Ron doubled over, gagging and coughing. Johnny grabbed more shards before singling out the youngest one. He gestured to Alex and Leon, who both clamped down on the guy's arms and tipped his head back. Johnny pulled open his jaw and fed the kid some pieces.

"Anybody else wanna punch this one?" said Johnny.

"I'll do it," said Mikey.

Mario winced at the victim. "Good luck, my man. That little kid packs a serious punch."

The teen spit out as much glass as he could before getting hit, but Mikey swung too fast. The young Scorpion retched, trying not to swallow the fragments.

"All right, who's next?"

"Stop, okay, just stop," said Bandana. "It's him, Ron Porter. He runs the gang."

"For Christ's sake," said Johnny. "Was that so fucking hard? How many in your crew?"

"Only like twenty, but half of them don't even hang out with us anymore because they got jobs and shit."

"And who are you?"

"Greg."

"Looks like Greg is the brains in this club," said Jarrod.

"And old Ronald over here," Johnny offered an open palm, "won't even admit he's in charge of his own gang." He looked up and down the bench. "And he'll let you guys take a hit to save his ass. What a classy motherfucker."

Some groans from the panel suggested Ron's men were not learning anything new.

Ron dribbled slimy fragments onto his chin. "What do you want?"

"I'm just here to let you know that you fucked with the wrong people."

"Eat shit!"

Johnny rocked back and made a swooping roundhouse kick. It connected with the side of Ron's face. Patrick and Andre let go of him, and he dropped to the ground, choking and clawing at his mouth.

"One more thing," Johnny kicked Ron in the ribs. "Lemme get five dollars." Ron was gasping and couldn't respond, so Johnny leaned over, stuck a hand in his pocket. He fished around and pulled out a ten. He pointed to the other three. "Don't fuck with the Dogs of War."

"That was cool," said Rafael as the gang walked toward Washington Square.

"Damn, man, we messed them *up!*" Mikey added.

Johnny marched in front, and Clyde rushed to keep up with him. "Hey, you all right?"

"I'm fine," he said without turning.

Once in the park, Johnny stopped along a darkened finger path. Clyde plunked down on a bench across from him, searching his face.

Chico slid beside Johnny. "You showed *them* motherfuckers."

He went to clap an arm around him when Clyde leapt up. "Don't!"

Chico patted Johnny on the back, then shot Clyde a look. "What the fuck, man? You're a little jumpy."

"I know." Clyde sat back down. "I just thought—never mind."

Jarrod's head swiveled between Clyde and Johnny. "What's up with you two?"

Johnny massaged his neck. "He thinks I'm gonna flip. But I'm worried about *him.*"

"I'm fine," Clyde said. "It's okay."

"Whatever," said Jarrod. "Maybe we should all just go home in case those Scorpions call the cops or something."

"You're right," said Johnny. "What time should we meet tomorrow?"

"My father asked if we could give him a hand moving some shit," said Chico. "If you guys want to come to my place, like noon, we could hang there for the day, lay low."

"Sounds good." Johnny stood. "Everybody did a really good job tonight." He gave the gang handshake all around—a soul clasp for unity, standard grip for honor, finger clamp for respect, ending with a fist bump for respect.

As the original three headed uptown, Jarrod put an arm around Clyde. "I'll bet it's you we find rocking in the corner tonight."

Clyde brushed him off. "That's not funny."

"It sorta was," said Johnny.

"What's wrong with you anyway?" Jarrod asked.

Clyde stuffed his hands in his pockets. "I guess I wasn't expecting you to hurt them like that."

Johnny clicked his tongue. "What the fuck should I have done?"

"I thought you were all about fairness and honor."

"I am, but how long was I supposed to ask the same fucking questions?"

"I don't know." Clyde shook his head. "I thought we'd beat them up, not all that other stuff. What if those guys die from internal bleeding?"

"If they were worried about it, they could've acted different."

"Johnny's right," said Jarrod. "We can't be known as a bunch of lightweights. You saw what kind of pricks they were. Do you honestly give a shit about them?"

"No, but I *do* worry that the brutality could trigger an episode."

"That again?" Johnny rolled his eyes. "You can't sit around waiting for me to flip every fucking minute."

"Easy for you to say. But when you're flipped, it's like you'll kill anybody with your bare hands." Clyde stopped walking. The others did, too. "Maybe if I just understood it more."

"Then go read some psych books in the library."

"It wouldn't hurt," said Clyde. "You don't mind?"

Johnny laughed. "No, not at all."

"And meanwhile," said Jarrod, "we just gotta look the fuck out for each other."

CHAPTER THIRTY-FIVE

When the Dogs of War arrived at the Velasquez house, Lucinda was placing platters of hot dogs and hamburgers on the kitchen table. Condiments, bowls of chips, buns and bottled soda were already set out, along with stacks of paper plates and cups. Luis stood in the center of the dining room, waving his calloused hands like a traffic cop, directing everyone to fill their plates, then ushering them to empty chairs that had been lined around the apartment. Once everyone was eating, he laid out the plan.

"When I asked Chico if he had a few friends who could help today, I wasn't expecting an army!" He grinned. "But I'm happy to have all of you. Thank you for coming." Luis hooked his thumbs in the pockets of his grease-stained canvas pants. "The old man from 5B moved to a nursing home. His family has taken whatever they wanted from the apartment, but there's still a lot that needs to be cleared out. The furniture we'll carry to the street. If it's not salvageable, it has to be broken up for the sanitation men." He swiped a meaty paw across his balding head. "And, if we have enough time, I could use one or two of you to help me fix the plumbing in 2D."

Chico groaned. "Not Mrs. Peterman again."

Luis smiled at the others around the room. "My son is tired of helping me with that job. I swear that woman eats for one but shits for five. Either that, or she's hiding a baby elephant in there!" His protruding belly rose and fell between his red suspenders. The gang laughed with him.

As everyone finished eating, they brought their plates and cups to the kitchen. When Johnny came by the counter, Lucinda pulled him aside. She took his hands and turned them over. "What happened here?" she asked in Spanish.

"No big deal. I was just looking out for my crew."

"I'll bet it was a big deal for the other guys."

"Maybe." He pulled his hands away.

She looked into his eyes. "You are different."

"I might have grown since I saw you last."

"No. Something is different *inside you*."

"What do you see *inside me*?" Johnny tried to hide his annoyance.

"Go ahead, be a smart-ass, but something has changed you."

He expelled a breath. "Is that good or bad?"

"I haven't made up my mind yet, but you're not the same person I first met eighteen months ago. He was a bold and courageous survivor."

"And I'm not those things anymore?"

"You are still those things, but the street has added more." Her eyes combed over him. "Maybe *you've* become the thing that people need the courage to survive."

Johnny twitched a shoulder. "What's wrong with that?"

Lucinda inventoried the gang as they trickled out of the apartment with her husband. "I see what you're building here, this fortress of companions. And it is necessary. Given your circumstances, you need protection, but not just from the authorities and bad people. It is your own self you should be wary of."

"What do you mean?"

"Don't let the ghosts distract you from your goals."

"What ghosts?"

"The ghosts from Miami. Your body is free from them, but your head is not."

"Look, I'm not part of those people anymore, okay? They're gone. They're nothing to me."

"I've made you angry. That is how I know the accusation is true."

Johnny put his elbows on the counter, clutching clumps of hair.

"Do you know what is more painful than the truth?"

Johnny wagged his head between his hands.

"Resisting the truth."

The words made Johnny acknowledge the logjam of emotions in his throat. Behind it was the urge to cry, and he could not do that here.

Lucinda pulled him up to face her. "I understand that you need to be calm and cool on the outside. Just remember that anger is sadness plus resistance. If you are upset, you should not try to avoid it."

Johnny looked at the ceiling. "It's not that I'm trying to avoid what happened to me. There's just so much of it I don't remember." He leaned against the counter. "When I was in that house, I used to black out a lot, but it's still happening, and I need it to stop."

She cradled his cheeks. At fourteen, he was already taller than she was. "Things happened that you cannot tell your boys. But you must confront those things, otherwise, you will never be free."

Johnny squeezed her hands. "I should go help the others."

He tried to turn away, but Lucinda stopped him. "You know I love you like my own. I must because you have my son."

"He's not a prisoner."

"No, but you aren't letting him go."

"I guess not."

"And he'd never leave your gang."

"Lucinda, I would die for any one of these guys."

"Yes. But the problem is they will die for you, too, which is why you need to keep your head together."

He kissed Lucinda's forehead and made for the door.

Upstairs, he joined the procession that was carrying furniture down to the street. He grabbed part of an end table Mikey was trying to manage alone. "How are things at home?"

Mikey coughed out a laugh. "My stepdad was drunk when I came in last night. He got in my face for being late, but I was so pumped up from the Scorpions, I threw my cassette recorder at him. Hit the pervert right in the face."

"No shit."

"Broke the recorder, but he backed right the fuck down."

"You think he'll lay off now?"

"I don't know. But what you said the other day, how you guys are behind me, makes me feel like I don't have to put up with his shit anymore."

204

"That's great, man." Johnny smiled. "If you ever need backup, just let us know."

"I will."

At the end of the day, Luis gave thanks all around and offered up more of Lucinda's cooking to anyone who wanted to help him paint the apartment the next weekend. No one declined.

As the gang poured into the street, Jarrod tapped Johnny. "You staying over tonight?"

"Nah. I'll go uptown. I could use the time to think."

"You sure?"

"Yeah, but I gotta pick up some cash and clean duds from Clyde's for tomorrow. I've got to look good for the DMV."

"Oh right, that thing the Brick set up."

The three of them walked together until Jarrod split off for his building. Once in Clyde's apartment, Johnny packed some clothes into a grocery bag. He also pocketed a bunch of bills from the Twister box.

"You gonna be all right?" Johnny asked Clyde before heading out.

"What do you mean?"

"Are *we* gonna be all right?"

"Of course."

"You said I scare you."

Clyde's shoulders fell. "Look, about that, I'm not scared *of* you, I'm just scared for you. When you become that person, it feels so out of control, like we wouldn't be able to stop you if you decided to do something crazy." He looked at his feet. "And then what if you got caught, and they sent you away?"

"And I disappeared?" Johnny studied the top of Clyde's head. "Just like your dad?"

Clyde's eyes snapped up.

"See? I guess you *are* just as fucked up as the rest of us."

"You asshole." Clyde laughed. "Whatever, as long as we're cool."

"We're cool."

"Sure you don't want to stay? We could think up an excuse to tell Tiff."

"It's all right. Let's save breaking the house rules for when we really need to."

As Johnny approached his building, Lily was huddled on the courtyard steps, smoking a cigarette. He sat next to her. "How's it going?"

She brightened up. "Hey, stranger."

Though her complexion was ashen and her hair unkempt, she didn't appear to be high. "You seem good," said Johnny. "Are you getting your shit together?"

"I'm trying."

"Why are you out here in the cold?"

"My mother's being a bitch again, so I'm waiting for her to go to bed."

"So that hasn't changed. Are you working?"

"Not really." She threw him a flirty grin. "You got twenty bucks you could lend me?"

"I'm not giving you money for drugs, but if you want to come upstairs, we could hang out."

"Could we at least get a few beers?"

"Sure."

They walked around the corner to the bodega, where Johnny bought a six-pack of Michelob and a pack of Marlboros. Inside the apartment, he lit some candles, cracked two cans and put the rest on the fire escape to stay cool. Johnny eyed his bedroom as he handed Lily a beer. His bedding was messed up, and there were cigarette butts in a juice bottle on the floor. He shook out the quilts and blankets one by one. "Do you stay here sometimes?" he asked as he worked.

"Only when it is unbearable at home."

He shot her a stern look. "Just *you*, or you bring other people here?"

She bowed her head. "Sometimes I do."

"What the fuck, Lily? There are like twenty vacant apartments in this building for your junkie friends to get high in. Why do you have to come here?"

"I'm more comfortable here, where you stay."

"But now I have to sleep in this skanky jizzed-up bedding."

"I'm not fucking anyone up here, just hanging out, I swear, like when I'm too high to go home."

"I don't mind *you* sleeping here, but I don't want those fucked up friends hanging around. Go somewhere else." He paused to take a long pull off the beer. The buzz took the edge off his anger.

"I'm sorry. I won't do it again." She bent over to help him flatten everything out. "I'll take all this stuff to the laundromat tomorrow if you want."

"With what money?"

"You could lend me some."

"Yeah, that's not happening."

"You're mean." She feigned pouting.

They sat down on the bedding and sipped their beer. Johnny lit a Marlboro, took a drag, then passed it to Lily. When she reached for it, he noticed the needle marks on her arm. He started to say something but let it go. What was the point? Still, it was hard not to care. She was the first friend he had made in New York City and his first lay.

He watched her drag from the cigarette. That normally crass mouth, so pretty now as her lips enveloped the filter, drawing in the smoke, then puckering into an O to discharge the vapor. Whenever Johnny and Lily had been intimate, it was always at her initiation. He had been too inexperienced to be anything but a passive—and grateful—recipient. However, in the wake of the savagery imposed on the Scorpions and the embarrassment of having been so exposed by Lucinda, all on top of the beer buzz, he felt reckless and uninhibited, like he needed something to disrupt the conflicting emotions.

Johnny put down his can and straddled Lily's lap. She was surprised at first but then dropped the cigarette butt into her beer and pulled off her shirt. Johnny undid his pants and lowered them to mid-thigh. He guided his erection toward her mouth. She began lapping and suckling, but it felt weak, like not enough to shake his mood. He put his hands on the back of her head and shoved himself deeper into her mouth. Lily retched, but he held her hair.

She shoved his hips away. "Jesus. What the fuck's wrong with you?" She wiped her mouth.

"Sorry." Johnny clutched his hard-on. "I was just trying something different."

"Well, don't."

She shimmied onto her back and pulled off her pants. He did the same, then took some time to tongue her neck and breasts before climbing on top. Once Johnny was inside, he thrust into her, over and over, hoping his rotten feelings would spew out with the semen. When he could not ejaculate anymore, he rolled off, and they both lay panting. After a few minutes, Lily went to the bathroom, and Johnny got up to blow out the candles. He found his pants with the money in the pockets and hid them under his pillow before crawling beneath the blanket.

Johnny slept deeply through the night, but when he woke for school, the bed was empty. A jolt of anxiety shot through him, and he slid a hand under the pillow. *I'll fucking kill you.* He released a breath. The pants with the money were still there. Johnny felt a wave of guilt. Did he have to be so hard on her? Maybe she deserved to be cut some slack.

He got up and went to the living room. "That thieving little snatch." Every article of clothing Johnny brought home had been pulled from the bag and rifled through.

CHAPTER THIRTY-SIX

In the school cafeteria, the gang speculated over whether or not the two glass-eaters would have gone to the hospital. If so, their injuries might have been reported to police. No one was sure what swallowing glass could do to a person, but the consensus was it wouldn't be good.

While they debated, Johnny noticed a sketch on the back of Mario's notebook. It was a snarling Shepherd-type dog with glimmering red eyes and a green army cap. The details were quite good.

"Hey, lemme see that." Johnny reached across the table.

Jarrod peeked over Johnny's shoulder. "Wow, when'd you do that?"

"The other day," said Mario.

"That's cool." They passed it around for everyone else to see.

"There's our tattoo," said Clyde.

Mario nodded. "But it still needs lettering."

"How about *The Dogs of War* in a semicircle above the image." Johnny marked it out with a finger. "But written in English or Spanish."

"Shouldn't they be the same, so we're more recognizable?"

"No. I like to keep people guessing." Johnny slapped a palm on the table. "We got the money. Let's research tattoo artists, find one who can copy your design. It's good, Mario. Really good." He looked at the clock and grabbed his knapsack. "I gotta go meet Joe. I'll see you guys later."

Precisely at noon, Joe arrived in front of Roosevelt in a brown 1963 Dodge Dart tricked out with custom rims. He was dressed slicker than usual, wearing shades and a black leather jacket over a maroon cashmere sweater.

Johnny slid into the passenger's seat. "Shit, man, what the hell is this thing? Smaller than what you usually drive."

"I know, right? But this one's mine."

"You got your own car?"

"Hell yeah," Joe shrunk back, grinning. "Who you think you're talking to?"

"No shit." Johnny laughed. "With fake documents, we can all be king."

"That's right." He pulled away from the curb.

"Is there anything I need to know before I go in there?"

"Just what you want the license to say. My uncle already set it up, so his girl, Charmaine, is expecting us. She does her thing, you pay, and it's done."

"Cool." Johnny turned to Joe. "So, what's your deal?"

"I'm on call for my uncle, but it's a lot of waiting around while he does what he does, so I kill time studying."

"What do you study?"

"Business management."

"They have that in high school?"

Joe laughed. "It's college."

"What the fuck? I thought you were sixteen."

"I'm almost seventeen. I tested out of high school and got accepted by Medgar Evers in Brooklyn last year."

"Man, you really got your shit together."

"My uncle helped me a lot. Financially, but also by pushing me in this direction. In exchange, I take care of his accounting."

Johnny nodded. "I'll bet."

Joe drove around midtown until he found a parking space. After pumping some quarters into the meter, he led the way to the Department of Motor Vehicles on West 31st. It was sterile and characterless: a long counter with individual stations divided by thin partitions of faux wood paneling and Plexiglas. A smattering of bored-looking customers waited on rows of brown benches. Fluorescent lights flickered and hummed above.

"That's her." Joe nodded to a voluptuous black woman behind the counter. She had long, straightened dark hair with blonde highlights. She wore a frilly white silk shirt that accented her ample cleavage, a shapely red jacket, and a black pleated skirt. She flashed Joe a nod even though she was helping another customer. When she was done, she flagged Johnny over.

"How you doing today, baby?" she asked.

"I'm well, thank you." He smiled.

"What can I do for you?"

"I need a learner's permit."

"Okay, just fill this out." She pushed a form across the counter. "I see Joey brought you. You've known him long?"

"A while." Johnny filled out the paper as they made small talk. He put April 1, 1958, for a birth date but pointed to the space where it asked for his social security number. "I *lost* my card, and I don't remember the number. Think I could get a replacement?"

"I can help with that," she said, shuffling papers around. "But it'll be an extra hundred."

"No problem. I also *lost* my birth certificate."

She wrote a phone number down on a piece of paper and slid it to him. "Does it need to reflect the information you put on this sheet?"

"Yes, please."

"Why don't you call me after business hours, and we'll talk about it."

Johnny stuffed the number in his pocket. "Thanks."

"Did you take the written exam?"

"Huh?"

"Of course you did." She handed him more papers. "You just forgot to sign." She also passed him a booklet with road rules and regulations. "You'll receive your documents in a week or two." She wagged a few brightly painted fingernails at him.

"Oh, right." Johnny thumbed out six hundreds and handed them over.

Charmaine tucked the money into her jacket. "Pleasure doing business with you. I'll be expecting your call."

"Thank you, ma'am." Johnny smiled and left, grabbing Joe on the way.

"Wasn't that easy?" said Joe once they were back in the car.

"Hell yeah, but how does your uncle know so many fine women?"

Joe shrugged. "You want me to drop you back at Roosevelt?"

"Why bother at this point. Can you hang out, or you got classes?"

"Not till later."

They drove around the city, getting to know each other. Joe was easy to be with, laid back, funny and smart. He talked about his weightlifting goals, the importance of a healthy body, and how he never drank alcohol, smoked or used drugs.

"You sure you're related to Rick the Brick?" Johnny asked.

Joe laughed. "A lot of people say that, but the truth is my uncle is the king of moderation. He'll have a few beers and a toke now and then, but I've never seen him out of control. He says you're either a dealer or a customer, but if you're both, you won't be successful."

"I can see that."

Joe grew serious. "Speaking of drugs, we need to go over those pickups." He pulled a folded piece of paper from his jacket and handed it over.

Johnny opened it and saw two handwritten addresses and some numbers.

"My uncle's business is mostly weed. You'll pick that up once a month at the Harrisburg, Pennsylvania, address. Ten to fifteen pounds or so. The blow comes from Hamden, Connecticut. He tries to stay away from large quantities of that stuff." Joe grinned. "But, as you've seen, if a sweet opportunity presents itself…"

Johnny nodded.

"So, what's your plan for traveling?" Joe's thumbs tapped the steering wheel. "You can't be relying on that learner's permit. You gotta be legit, or you'll get pulled over."

"No, I get it." Johnny cocked a knee to face him. "One of my boys, Tito, he's legal. He works at his cousins' garage in the Bronx. They got cars they lend him whenever he needs. We might even be buying something off them soon."

"Okay, but these people are long-time connections. They're professional, not like those guys at the pier, so don't show up posturing with your whole crew in tow." He raised a brow at Johnny. "You catching my drift?"

"Low-key. No problem."

"Each trip pays a grand. As you know, Rick likes to toss in a little product sometimes for personal consumption. But it's not for resale, understand? You don't compete with the boss."

"That makes sense."

"You got someplace to be reached so I can get with you about the dates?"

"Not really." Johnny tore off a corner of the page, scribbled a number and dropped it in the center console. "But if you leave word at Clyde's, I'll always call you back."

"Check in with me from time to time. My pager number is on that sheet, too."

"Your what?"

As Joe explained how the system worked, Johnny slipped the paper into his jeans. When the business portion of the ride appeared to be over, Johnny asked Joe if he ever had time to hang out.

"I'm pretty busy most days, but occasionally I do."

"We should get together again. Would your uncle mind?"

Joe smiled. "I doubt it. You got my number now. Hit me up sometime."

CHAPTER THIRTY-SEVEN

The last of Johnny's crew had made off for home hours ago. He knew he should do the same, but each time he approached a subway station, he would picture his bleak, depressing squat with nothing to distract him from his own thoughts. To make things worse, Christmas was looming. Decorations were up around the city, and spirits were high, even amid his own brothers. But all it meant for Johnny was the inevitability that his heat and hot water would start cutting out.

He kept walking.

If Lily was around, he could usually get laid, but even that was discouraging. If she wasn't fucked up, she was jonesing. She looked like shit, and the money-grubbing was endless. The last time they had sex, she even tried to make him pay for it. Johnny's feet felt heavier as he trudged. It was all getting so old. Ping-ponging between gang brothers for a meal here and a sleepover there. Never knowing which article of clothing was stored in what apartment. Cash, that continued to accumulate now that he and Tito were making those out-of-state runs, which he couldn't even access at will.

Rich and homeless.

Johnny was tired from walking but could not convince himself to go home. He veered toward Washington Square instead. Using his backpack as a pillow, he stretched out on a bench by the perimeter and nestled into his coat. He would just rest a few minutes, then go uptown.

Johnny woke to the smell of perfume and cigarette smoke. He opened his eyes and tipped his head. Margaret was sitting beside him. She wore a three-quarter-length black suede coat, and her hair and makeup looked all fancy.

"What are you doing here?" he asked, closing his eyes again.

"Me? *I'm* coming home from a date. What are *you* doing? It's a little late to be out on a school night, isn't it?"

"Maybe." He adjusted the pack under his head. "How was your date?"

"It wasn't really a date, it was work. Don't you have a home to go to?"

Johnny flipped through the Rolodex of lies, all of which rolled off his tongue by now, and stopped. He was too tired and despondent to care, and the person asking was an escort who was friends with a drug dealer. "I stay here and there, but I'm between places tonight."

"Interesting." She dragged from her long, skinny cigarette and blew out a dainty stream of smoke. "I always thought there was something mysterious about you."

"Yeah, I'm real *mysterious*, all right." Johnny pushed himself to a sitting position.

"Would you like to crash on my couch? I get the feeling I can trust you, given our mutual friend and all." She tapped an ash on the ground. "And if you prove me wrong, I'll just have him kill you."

Johnny laughed. "I'd have to be one dumb-ass motherfucker to screw up an invitation like that."

"Let's go."

They walked across Waverly Place and up the front steps of a four-story brownstone. She pulled out her keys to let them into the lobby. Johnny's eyes swirled. This was nothing like his building. The walls were covered in matching colored tile, there was a stone mantle with two vases full of flowers, and tasteful oil paintings hung on the wall. Margaret led him up the marble staircase to the penthouse apartment. Inside, she hung their coats on a freestanding brass rack. "Home sweet home. Feel free to look around."

"Thanks."

Johnny stepped into her spacious one-bedroom with its Art Deco décor. The living room, dining room and kitchen were encompassed in a wide area with high ceilings, segregated by a tiled island/bar with fancy stools. The dining table was a round ebony eight-seater with white upholstered chairs. The living room furniture was light-colored pastels with a flat design that sat low to the ground. It was contrasted by big, multicolored geometric art illuminated by track lighting.

Near a row of windows overlooking the park was Margaret's bedroom. It had a black king-size platform bed, matching bureaus and end tables with oversized white ceramic lamps. The abutting bathroom was the fanciest Johnny had ever seen. The shower was as big as a freight elevator, with large plates of earth-toned tile, brass fixtures and a glass door. The granite counter, with its basin sink and wide mirror, spanned the length of the wall.

"Why don't you wash up, and I'll get the couch ready."

When he returned, she had covered the couch with a sheet, set out a pillow, and was unfolding a quilt. "Can I make you a nightcap?"

"A what?"

"I was being facetious. It means a drink." She smiled. "But I'm going to have a brandy and take it to the bedroom so you can get some sleep. Do you need me to set an alarm?"

"I usually wake up on my own, but thanks."

"All right, I'll leave out some things for you to take a shower in the morning. Help yourself to anything in the kitchen. There's plenty to eat."

"Thank you, Margaret."

"Sweet dreams." She dimmed the lights before retreating behind her bedroom door.

Johnny settled into the couch. The apartment was so clean and quiet. He held the pillow to his nose and detected a hint of lavender and oranges. The quilt smelled of lilacs. It wasn't long before he drifted off.

When the morning light woke him, it took a moment to get oriented. He got up and went to the bathroom. On the counter, along with a folded towel and washcloth, Margaret had left a new bar of soap and a packaged toothbrush. Johnny thought this must be what a first-rate hotel was like. He stepped into the shower. There were so many knobs and attachments that it took a few tries to figure everything out. Once the water was set to his liking, he stood under it for a long time.

Johnny emerged refreshed despite having to put on his same clothes. A wall clock read 6:30. He still had plenty of time because Roosevelt wasn't far. He went to the kitchen, turned on a light and looked around. No roaches. He found a bag of English muffins in a bread box and put one in the toaster. While it cooked, he poured a glass of juice and took out the butter. Johnny remembered he was supposed to read a chapter for homework. He pulled *The Call of the Wild* from his backpack and sat at the counter with his breakfast and the book.

He'd been reading for a while when Margaret's bedroom door opened. She walked naked to the bathroom. Her body was as beautiful as her face. She had a nice figure with full round buttocks and breasts. Her skin was smooth and tight, and her tousled black hair looked sexy draping over her shoulder blades.

Johnny closed the book and put his dishes in the sink, then went to the couch to fold the blankets. The toilet flushed, and the bathroom door opened, but instead of going to her room, Margaret shuffled toward him. Johnny was frozen. He didn't want to offend her but wasn't sure which would be ruder, looking or not looking, so he did a little of both. She stopped in front of him and kissed his forehead. "Have a nice day at school, baby." She returned to her bedroom.

He kept looking, even after the door had shut, but then forced himself to refocus on the task of folding. After, he ripped a blank piece of paper from his schoolbook and wrote, "Margaret, thanks again for letting me stay over—JA... PS, your pajamas are really sexy." He placed it on the counter, then fished through his coat pockets. He found one of the grams of cocaine the Brick had given him as a bonus. He wasn't interested in trying the stuff, but he always accepted whatever he was given. He tossed it on the note, grabbed his backpack and left.

Johnny found a bunch of his gang brothers on the school block. He greeted them, then leaned on a parked car and lit a cigarette.

Jarrod pulled open the lapels of Johnny's coat. "Why are you still wearing the same clothes?"

"Huh?"

Clyde peeked over Jarrod's shoulder. "They *are* the same. Didn't you go home last night?"

Johnny stifled a smirk. "I never made it."

"What's that supposed to mean?"

"If I tell you, you won't believe me anyway."

"Now you *better* tell us," Rafael said.

"Rafi's right. Nobody likes a tease," said Chico. "If you're gonna get us wet, at least put a finger in."

Johnny winced. "You kiss your mother with that mouth?"

"No way. My mother is wholesome, but I'll kiss Jarrod's mother."

"If you do, you'll have to go to detox," said Clyde.

"Spill it," said Mario. "Where'd you sleep last night?"

"I stayed at Margaret's." Johnny watched them mentally run through the list of Margarets from school, none of whom they would have deemed fuckable.

Chico's eyes widened. "Oh snap, you did *not*!"

"Wait," said Mario. "That fine piece of ass from the park?"

Johnny nodded.

"What did she charge you?"

"Fuck you, she didn't charge me!"

"Tito's gonna be mad," said Jarrod.

Johnny waved him off. "I was in the park, and it got late. She asked if I needed a place to crash. I slept on the couch, that's all."

"Your game must be getting pretty weak, my brother," said Mario.

Johnny rolled his eyes. "She's like thirty."

"And a hooker," Rafael added.

"An escort," Johnny corrected.

"That means she's experienced."

"For real," said Mario. "A girl like that'll know how to fuck you right. You always want to get with the older chicks."

"Suddenly, *you're* an expert?" Johnny flicked his butt into the gutter. "Margaret's a classy woman. She deserves our respect." He pushed off the car to head into school but looked back over his shoulder. "And she looks fucking amazing naked."

CHAPTER THIRTY-EIGHT

By year's end, Tito was making decent money working full-time at his cousins' garage, so he got an apartment on Nagle Avenue between Dyckman and Academy Streets. It was a one-bedroom on the fourth floor of a roach-infested building that faced the elevated IRT subway line. Every time a train passed, the windows rattled and the TV reception got fuzzy, but rent was cheap, and the shady landlord let him pay month to month without a lease or security deposit.

The gang voted to allocate money for furnishings, knowing they would all be staying there at one time or another. They bought twin beds for Tito's room, a pair of fold-out couches for the living room, and extra mattresses just in case. Secondhand items were purchased, with other stuff found on the street. Tito made keys for all of the brothers so they could come and go at will.

Johnny was grateful for another place to crash, but each one was depressing in its own right. Even Clyde's was becoming claustrophobic. His sisters were getting older, their friends were coming over, and there was always a line for the bathroom. Though Johnny continued to leave Diana money for bills and food, he still felt staying there was only adding to the family's burden. Johnny ached for a place to call home. Something big enough for the whole gang, that wasn't just another rundown shithole. Until then, all he could do was keep looking and keep banking money.

One day in January, the gang was in Washington Square. It was too cold for playing music, so they sat in subgroups, sparking up a few joints.

Johnny, Clyde, Jarrod and Eric were on one of the granite benches, cracking each other up with silly comments about passersby, until Johnny noticed something that sobered him.

"What's up?" Jarrod asked.

"You see that?"

Jarrod looked around. "What?"

Johnny pointed with his chin. "Over there."

Across the fountain were some teenagers on skateboards, practicing flips and jumps. They were bundled up in puffy coats, scarves and knit caps, but it was clear one of them was Shawn. The others were unfamiliar.

"Oh shit," said Jarrod. "Despite massive head trauma, it walks and skates."

Eric nodded. "His motor skills appear intact."

"What should we do?" asked Clyde.

"Nothing," said Johnny. "I've done enough."

"He's got no clue we're here," said Jarrod.

Eric grinned. "That's the fun part."

They watched the skateboarders migrate closer, popping and pivoting, focused on their maneuvers. Shawn attempted an old-school kickflip and missed. The board rolled away from him and came to a stop near Johnny's feet. Shawn started after it but then froze.

Johnny examined Shawn's face as he stood there, and parts of their fight began to flicker in his mind. But it was more like segments of a movie instead of an actual memory. Johnny stared deeper, trying to force more images to come.

Shawn scanned the others beside him. His mouth tightened into a knot when he saw Eric, then dropped open when he noticed the dozen boys assembled behind them.

One of Shawn's friends put a hand on his shoulder. "You all right?" He glanced at the bench of four stoned teenagers. "What the fuck, man. Get your board."

Johnny didn't want to torment Shawn, so he kicked the skateboard back. Shawn caught it with his foot and popped it into his hand, then turned to flee the park, followed by his confused friends.

Chico walked over from behind. "Wasn't that the dude you beat up?"

Johnny struggled to stretch the fleeting glimpses into whole memories. *Clyde said if I could just remember, it might stop the batshit episodes.* He closed his eyes and pictured Shawn's face, saw himself kneeling over the kid, punching him, but the images were too fragmented, like some whacked-out slideshow.

"Hey, you okay?"

Johnny looked up to see Jarrod in front of him. "I just thought I was remembering something."

"What, kicking the shit out of him?"

"Almost. Like maybe if I stared at him a little longer, I could've remembered."

Clyde stood. "What if we go to the place where you fought him? See if that trips your memory."

Johnny swiped his face. "Why not? Beats sitting around here in the cold."

They rallied the others and began the trek toward the West 30s. Once they got to the lot where the fight had occurred, everyone fanned out to give Johnny space. He walked around, pondering the view from every angle. *Visualize Shawn.* Johnny squatted down. He closed his eyes. *Where are those images from earlier?* He clutched his head. *Come on. Please. Something.*

A homeless man, wearing a closet's worth of clothes and pushing a shopping cart full of junk, rattled out from under the West Side Highway. "You kids spare some change? Cigarettes?" His voice was so gravelly it blended with the traffic.

A few crew members dug in their pockets. Others pooled together an assortment of smokes. The man flashed a toothless grin. "Bless you, kids, and have a happy New Year." He veered back across the avenue.

Johnny popped up. "Fuck this." He took off uptown. The others had to jog to keep up.

"Sorry, man." Clyde strode beside Johnny. "It was worth a try."

"I'm just pissed it didn't work."

"Where are you going?"

Johnny stuffed his hands in his pockets. "I just need to keep walking. You guys can leave if you want."

"Nobody's leaving."

After a while, the gang crossed to Riverside Boulevard. On 65th Street, they came upon a condemned twelve-story building that had been ravaged by fire. Half of it was an empty shell of bricks, with rectangular spaces that used to be windows. The other half was in the beginning stages of demolition. The surrounding area was carpeted with debris and construction equipment, closed off by a twelve-foot-tall chain-link fence with DANGER: KEEP OUT signs.

Johnny perked up. "Who wants to go in there?"

"I do!" said JJ.

Chico threw his hands on his hips. "How am I supposed to get my ass over that fence?"

"I'll help you." They both gripped the links, sticking the toes of their sneakers into the holes and shimmied to the top. Johnny vaulted to the other side, but Chico was stuck. Johnny crawled closer, clamping onto Chico's coat, and yanked him over. They both skidded down the fence. Johnny caught his balance, but Chico rolled onto his back. He got up, brushing the dirt from his pants. "See? I told you pussies it would be easy!"

The others scurried over and retreated toward the shadows of the building. Inside was some scaffolding surrounded by piles of wood and plaster, also a corroding stairwell, which several crew members started climbing.

Johnny saw a fire escape on the outer wall. In the setting sun, it was hard to gauge its precariousness, but he decided to scale it anyway. The wrought iron swayed under his weight, and the higher he got, the more it peeled from the building. He kept going until he got to the roof. Several others came up the staircase.

Oscar leaned on the roof's short wall to look down. "This place feels like it could crumble any minute." A concrete chunk loosened beneath his palm. It sailed to the ground with a *poof*.

A handful of brothers remained below, tagging the gang logo on construction equipment with jumbo markers. They looked up and hollered some expletives.

Rafael pulled Oscar away. "I wouldn't lean on that."

Johnny hopped up on the wall and started to walk the perimeter.

"That's not funny, you fucking kamikaze," said Patrick.

"Yeah, man, get down," said Maurice. "You're freaking me out."

The comments fueled JJ, who jumped up and danced a little jig.

"Watch *this*." Johnny did a front handspring on the long side, then took a bow.

Clyde gasped. "I can't watch this shit." He rushed for the stairs. Others followed.

JJ jumped off the wall. "I can't compete with that."

Once Johnny was alone, he stepped to the edge, just like he had on the Brooklyn Bridge. He felt that threatening to jump, using his own body as a negotiating tool, would get his mind to stop betraying him, stop blocking his memory. It felt, in some small way, like taking back control.

Johnny took a long look at the Manhattan skyline.

CHAPTER THIRTY-NINE

A few weeks before Easter, Johnny got a message from Joe to meet him by the arch Saturday morning. When the black Cadillac pulled up, Johnny hopped in the back but was surprised to see an older white man already there. Joe was at the wheel, with the Brick riding shotgun.

"Colombiano, *buenos días*," the Brick said as the car pulled away. "This is Irving."

The man extended a meaty palm. "Nice to meet you." He was brawny and balding in bright-colored business casual clothes, and he spoke with a faint southern drawl.

"You too, sir." Johnny clasped his hand.

The Brick turned toward them. "Irving's an associate of mine. We go way back. I've been telling him about you."

Johnny retracted. "What's to tell?"

The two men guffawed, which Johnny wasn't sure how to take, so he slouched in his seat and kept quiet. Irving and the Brick seemed to have a lot to catch up on. They talked about mutual acquaintances, current politics, and older days, passing time as Joe followed signs toward Westchester County. After almost an hour, he pulled off the main road to pilot through some suburban towns.

The Brick cracked his window and lit a Newport. "Colombiano, listen up, there might be a big job on the horizon."

Johnny straightened. "Oh yeah?"

"Irv and I are trying to put a deal together. If it works out, we're looking at you to make the pickup."

Irving offered Johnny a forged smile. "It'd be a one-time thing, but the quantity is large."

"Much bigger than those runs you've been doing," added the Brick. "Primo shit at a discount price. Hard to pass up."

Sounds familiar. Johnny snatched a glimpse of Joe, but he was zeroed in on the road.

"You'd be dealing with these people I know. Your people." The Brick flicked some ash out the window. "The Colombians."

Johnny expected the two men to have another laugh, but both remained serious.

The Brick stroked his goatee. "It's a lot more risk and responsibility, but you'll be compensated."

Irving rubbed his sausage fingers together. "Like twenty-five grand worth of compensation."

Johnny's stomach fluttered. "Whoa, that's a lot."

"But," added the Brick, "you'll have to travel much farther than you been doing."

"Like, how far?"

He turned and smiled. "Miami. I hear it's beautiful this time of year."

All of Johnny's blood rushed to his feet. The only part of him not riddled with dread was the small section of brainstem reminding him to blink and breathe. "Where about?" he heard himself say, his voice distant and foreign.

"If you really want the particulars," Irving offered, "it's a marina on North Bayshore Drive. Near 395. Right off the interstate."

"I know it," Johnny wheezed.

The Brick did a double take. "Motherfucker, you *what?*"

"I—I know where it is." Johnny didn't know how to drive there from the highway, but he knew he could find it. He had been there many times while wandering the streets. He was familiar with the whole strip.

"You little son of a bitch." The Brick stuffed his butt in the console ashtray. "You got more goddamn secrets than my ex-wife!"

Irving chuckled into his fist.

"Were you a fucking tour guide in a former life?" The Brick waved his hands. "Never mind. I don't even wanna know. If you can get your ass down there and back without getting popped, that's all that matters, you dig?"

"We should have more details in a few days," said Irving. "Dates, times, which boat. But one thing to know about this guy you'll be dealing with…" he circled his ear with a finger, ". . . he's a *little* crazy."

The Brick frowned at Irving. "Crazy's a strong word." He turned to Johnny." Let's just say he uses his own products, so he can be… *erratic*. It's why I ain't done business with him lately." He reached over the bench seat to tap Johnny's knee. "But he'll like *you*. You're young, so he won't feel threatened, and you're sharp. He'll respect that. And you got the whole Colombian brotherhood shit going on." The Brick grinned. "Think about it."

Johnny forced a smile. His brain was swirling so badly that he didn't realize Joe had already parked the car. They were at another gun range, this one, according to the sign by the road, with outdoor facilities and skeet shooting. Everyone was getting out. Johnny did likewise but had to steady himself by putting a hand on the Cadillac.

The Brick opened the trunk and passed out cases of rifles, then led the way inside the sprawling facility, but it was all a blur. The ambient sounds of gunshots and voices blended together as Johnny tried to force the thoughts from his head. *Just decline. Make up some excuse.* But the money. Twenty-five grand. With what they already had, surely that could lock down a permanent place for him and the gang. All Johnny had to do was drive there, make the deal, then hightail it back to New York. He wouldn't even be there long enough for anyone to recognize him. Or have a panic attack.

The Brick and Irving passed through a few outdoor ranges before picking an empty bench to unpack the rifle bags. They were so absorbed in conversation they didn't notice how withdrawn Johnny had become, but Joe did. "You all right?" he asked, passing over some ear protectors.

"Yeah, I'm fine." Johnny secured them on his head.

He pretended to study how the men were handling their rifles, but once the possibility of returning to Miami became real, all his suppressed feelings began to unburrow like cicadas, careening around, screeching. It made him worry he might have an episode. *Not here. Do not flip. Not now.*

Irving grinned, mouthing something to Johnny while handing him a rifle. It was a Marlin Model 336. Johnny felt himself reach for it. The wood and steel made his hands tingle. But there was something about holding it, the weight, its contours, that was calming. Johnny noticed himself breathing again. Some of Irving's words even matched his lip movements when he talked about the gun and how to hold it.

Johnny mimicked what Irving had demonstrated, nestling the rifle's butt into his shoulder. As he lined the target into the crosshairs, a vision of the cellar appeared. His impulse was to push it away until he remembered what Lucinda had said. He was supposed to confront this shit. Maybe that's how he kept from flipping. Instead of resisting the memory, he allowed the images of that room to form in his mind. He could smell the mustiness, feel the stagnant air on his skin, even hear the floorboards creaking as his parents walked above.

Irving adjusted the angle of Johnny's elbow, then stepped back.

Johnny is hanging from the rafters. Upside down. Feet bound, naked. Orlando is pacing, box cutter in hand. A slice is made in Johnny's thigh. Blood droplets are trickling toward the floor. Drying up on his stomach. Orlando is furious. He throws the box cutter.

Johnny pulled the trigger. The rifle lurched in his grip, but the bullet still came close to the bull's-eye.

Orlando returns with the razor. The blade disappears into Johnny's other leg. More blood drops this time. Skimming across his skin before disappearing into his armpit. Orlando is yelling, pounding, stomping.

Johnny squeezed his finger, more prepared for the recoil. The bullet barely missed the bulls-eye. He fired again and again.

Orlando is waving the blade over Johnny's genitals, grinning now. Johnny can't look. He might throw up, pass out. Both. His breath freezes as the razor enters at the pubic bone, cuts toward his belly button. Much more blood this time. A small stream, tickling him as it flows down his chest, the curve of his neck, thinning. It stops at his chin.

Irving took the Marlin rifle from Johnny and replaced it with a different one, saying something incomprehensible as he pointed to a more distant target. The Brick had stopped shooting and was standing with Joe, both of them looking on with arms crossed. Johnny began firing that gun, too.

Orlando is squeaking with excitement, his face stretched into a grin, hands balled together. Johnny lifts his head to see. When he does, the blood rolls off his chin and into his mouth. It is salty, metallic. Orlando jumps around the room, laughing. Johnny can hear him. "That's it, little brother! I win. You can get down."

As Johnny sent bullet after bullet through a single distant hole, his peripheral senses broadened. He could smell freshly mowed grass. Words were making sense. The heat of the sun warmed his skin. He felt a hand on his shoulder and flinched.

Irving was motioning to take off the headgear. "You ran out of ammo, son."

"Huh?" Johnny set down the rifle. "Oh, shit. I was concentrating."

Irving grinned. "I guess so."

"I told you!" The Brick slapped Irving's back. "Didn't I fucking tell you? This kid is like some kind of freak!"

Irving let out a belly laugh. "You didn't lie."

The Brick turned to Joe. "Did you *see* that shit? *Goddamn*! I should've put money on him!"

Johnny watched them rejoice in his accomplishment, but the revelation about Orlando made him feel sick.

"Colombiano, why ain't you jacked up?" The Brick turned his palms to the sky. "I thought we'd try some of them moving targets next."

"I've gotta use the bathroom. You guys go ahead." He mustered a smile. "I'll find you." He made for the main building and located the men's room. Crouching over the sink, he pooled cold water in his hands, then sunk his face into it. He pushed away the impulse to vomit. All those times he emerged from blackouts wondering what happened, now he wished he could forget. Johnny tested out the idea that it was just some ghastly hallucination. After drying off on the towel dispenser, he peeked down the front of his pants for confirmation. The scar was there. But even more disheartening was the murky notion that it still wasn't the worst thing Orlando had done.

CHAPTER FORTY

Johnny had Joe drop him at the DeMarco's apartment, but only Claire and Cecily were home, and neither bothered to acknowledge him. He grabbed something to drink and closed himself in Clyde's room. He lay on the bed, intending to process the Brick's proposal, but was so drained by everything that he fell asleep.

Johnny woke to the door closing.

"Isn't this nice," Clyde said to Jarrod. "He only pretended to have plans with the Brick so he could spend all day sacked out in my bed."

"Fuck you," said Johnny.

"When'd you get back?" Jarrod asked.

Johnny sat up, glancing at the clock radio. "Few hours ago."

"So? What did the Brick want?"

"He took me to another shooting range, a bigger one, with outdoor targets and stuff."

"That's it?" asked Jarrod. "Just shooting?"

"There was some talking too…" Johnny's voice trailed off.

Jarrod perched on the couch. "And?"

"The Brick's looking to partner up with this friend of his, go in on something big."

"Why don't you look excited about it?" asked Clyde.

Johnny's chin fell to his chest. His socked feet made circles on the floor.

"No!" said Clyde. "Absolutely not."

Jarrod shrunk back. "What?"

Clyde plunked down beside Johnny. "You are *not* going to Miami."

229

Jarrod lurched. "He wants you to go to *Miami?*"

Johnny's hands sliced the air. "First off, it's been almost three years since I left. The odds of being recognized from some old-ass missing person poster are just as slim there as they are here. And I know exactly where the deal is going down. It's a high-end marina, which is the last place I would bump into anyone I used to know."

Jarrod tented his fingers.

"It's right off the interstate." *It sounded good when Irving said it.* "And, it pays twenty-five thousand dollars."

"For one run?" asked Jarrod.

Johnny nodded.

"Shit, that *is* a lot of money."

"Agreed," said Clyde. "But how are you gonna handle it, like, emotionally?"

"Look," said Johnny, "all I know is I was really freaked out about it at first, but now it seems worth the risk. Like, for all of us. Think of what we could do with that money."

Clyde and Jarrod's heads bobbled.

"And I won't be alone. Maybe we'll borrow the exterminator van so a bunch of us can go, keep it light, like we're going camping or some shit."

Jarrod looked at Clyde, then back at Johnny. "What's the timeline?"

"The Brick's trying to put that together now. Could go down in the next week or two. He just said to be ready."

"All right," said Clyde. "I'm down. But only if you're really okay with it."

"Me, too," said Jarrod.

During study sessions, the Dogs of War studied maps, calculated the driving time and made lists of things to bring. Along with Tito and the original three, it was decided that Rafael, Patrick and Mario would also make the trip. They were among the oldest and most mature looking, and though neither one had a license, all three had been learning to drive and could take over if Tito needed a break. Over school vacation, Johnny made sure to be in the park every day, just in case word came down.

Mid-week, the crew was swapping dance moves by the fountain when Margaret walked over. She wore skin-tight capris with a short jacket. She crossed one foot over the other and tapped her chin, evaluating, but it was hard for anyone to continue with her watching.

"Don't stop on my account," she said. "It looks like fun."

Mario glided to her and bowed, then offered his hand. "Madam, would you care to tango? A little rumba, perhaps?"

She laughed. "That's the best proposition I've had all day."

He patted his chest. "Me? I'm more of a bump guy, myself." He did a little hop, then threw his hips in her direction. She surprised him by bumping back with hers. They made a few turns, dancing around while the crew whooped and whistled.

Margaret wound down her moves and smiled at Mario. "Thank you. That was very entertaining." She pointed a manicured finger at Johnny. "But it's this young man I need to see."

Snickers resounded from the gang as Johnny exaggerated a pimp walk toward her, hand on his crotch.

Margaret rolled her eyes, then turned so he would follow her. When they were out of earshot, she stopped to face him. "You got yourself one far out crew, don't you?"

Johnny nodded. "I sure do."

"I haven't seen you in a while, but I wanted to thank you for being such a courteous and *generous* houseguest." She put a hand on his shoulder. "That was a very nice little present you left and such an adorable note."

"The pleasure was all mine. It's the nicest-smelling place *I've* ever been, that's for sure." He laughed.

Margaret handed Johnny a business card. It was silver, with black pinstriping around the border. A single phone number was printed in italics, centered, nothing else. "If you're ever between places, feel free to call. I'd be happy to help you out."

He stared at the card. "Oh shit, I mean, thanks, but you don't have to—"

She lay a finger on his lips. "I know I don't. I want to." She kissed his cheek before turning to leave.

Johnny watched her stroll away, long black curls bouncing on her

231

back, pants outlining her buttocks. He stuck a hand in his pocket to calm the tingling in his groin before returning to the gang.

The Brick appeared from the Thompson Street entrance. He strode by without stopping. Tipping his chin at Johnny, he said, "Colombiano, 18th Street Pier, ten o'clock tonight. Joey will have what you need so you can head out tomorrow."

Johnny forced aside a wave of nerves. "Okay, I guess it's going down." He looked at the brothers selected to travel. "Are you guys gonna be okay with your families if you're out of touch for a few days?"

"No sweat," said Rafael. "Since school's out, we've all been crashing different places anyway."

Patrick nodded. "And everyone is set to cover if anyone's parents start calling around."

"Perfect," said Johnny. "If any decisions need to be made while we're gone, Chico's in charge."

"Oh, snap!" Chico brushed his shoulder. "Instant promotion."

Johnny pointed at Clyde. "I gotta swing by your place, get some cash and the gun, but all of us heading south should convene at Tito's so we can get ready."

At the DeMarcos', Clyde told Tiffany he would be staying at Johnny's for the next few nights.

"You're so full of shit."

"I am not."

"You *never* stay at his house." She looked at Johnny. "*He* never stays at his house."

Clyde searched the room. "Yeah, well, his parents are gonna be out of town, so we'll have the place to ourselves."

Tiffany squinted her eyes at them. "What the fuck are you mutts up to?"

Clyde opened his mouth, but Johnny nudged him. "Don't bother." He pulled a folded paper packet from his pocket. "Just give her this."

Clyde took it. "Here. It's cocaine."

Tiffany swiped it from his hand. "I know what the fuck it is, you little twat."

"Will you just cover for me? Please?"

Tiffany eyed the envelope, turning it back and forth. "All right. But you better be fucking careful. Mom has enough shit to worry about without you becoming some teenage tragedy."

Clyde put a hand on his chest. "Thanks, sis."

"Yeah, Tiff, thanks." Johnny winked.

She winced. "Don't do that. It's creepy."

Tito drove Johnny to 18th Street and parked in a dim section by the pier. Promptly at ten, the brown Dodge Dart appeared from under the highway and idled beside them. Joe and Johnny rolled down their windows.

"You ready?" said Joe.

Johnny gritted his teeth. "I guess."

Joe passed a folded piece of paper to Johnny. "This is the marina's address and the slip number where the boat will be docked. The guy's name is Marco, and he does all his business in the middle of the night. You need to be there at one a.m. on Saturday morning."

Johnny nodded.

"And don't be late. He considers tardiness a sign of disrespect, even though he'll probably keep *you* waiting."

"Okay."

"You're picking up ten kilos of coke and two of dope."

"I thought the Brick didn't care for dope."

Joe's fingers tapped the wheel. "I don't ask questions."

"I hear you."

"There's a lot of money here. Three hundred grand. There's also two handguns and a high-powered rifle. He wants to make sure you've got enough protection."

"That was thoughtful."

"I wouldn't go getting sentimental, Johnny. He likes you and all, but business is business. He needs to make sure you and your boys can protect his money."

"I get it."

"He's giving you the heat but said not to be armed when you see Marco. He's easily threatened. The guns are just in case there's trouble before or after." Joe raised an eyebrow. "Or, if you should need to *follow up* with something. You catching my drift?"

Johnny shrunk back. "What, like if he beats me on the deal? Are you saying I should take him out, like an assassin?"

"Use your judgment." Joe reached for the two duffel bags beside him. Johnny pulled them through his window. "Anything else?"

"Just be careful. I've overheard the conversations. The guy is fucking nuts and high *all* the time. But if you can stay calm and don't let him rattle you, it'll be fine." He offered half a smile. "I want to see you come back."

"Oh, I'm coming back, all right." Johnny met Joe's eyes. "There's no fucking way I'm gonna die in Miami."

CHAPTER FORTY-ONE

At Tito's apartment, Johnny looked inside the bags. One contained the bound stacks of cash. In the other was a Winchester model 70 sniper rifle, two Sig P210 9mm pistols, and extra ammo. Johnny added the .38 Special to the mix. If they hit the road by morning, they would be in Miami with plenty of time to prepare for the meet. The group slept as well as they could despite their anticipation and the occasional clatter of trains.

By ten a.m., they were rolling south on I-95. For everyone except Johnny, it was the longest ride they had ever taken. Patrick entertained himself with a stack of *Mad* magazines, Tito brought mechanical periodicals from the garage and Rafael had some *Penthouses*, "for the articles." Mario packed a sketch pad to hone the gang's logos, and Clyde brought an acoustic guitar.

Once out of the city, Johnny offered to drive, but Clyde wouldn't let him. "What if he flips while he's behind the wheel?"

"Right," said Jarrod. "He could go batshit crazy and drive us off a bridge."

Johnny rolled his eyes. "How about I leave all you motherfuckers on the side of the road?"

After midnight, they parked at a truck stop outside of Florence, South Carolina, to crash for a few hours. Some stretched out on the van's bench seats, others huddled on blankets in the back. Everyone was awake by dawn, so they ate breakfast at the twenty-four-hour diner, then filled the tank before resuming their trek.

Johnny held up a newspaper he had bought. "Look, it's April 4th."

"Yeah, so what," said Rafael.

He took out the learner's permit he had received from the RMV. "According to this, I'm seventeen now. When we get back, I can take the road test and get a license."

"Tomorrow is my real birthday," Tito mumbled. "I'll be nineteen."

Johnny put an arm around him. "I promise to splurge on a fancy celebration dinner, with cake and everything, as long as we don't all get shot to shit on that boat."

Clyde grimaced. "Don't even say that."

When they returned to the van, Johnny sat in the second row, strategically flanked by Clyde and Jarrod. "Just in case," Clyde said.

Johnny gazed out the window, noticing the passing cars. More had Florida license plates now. When the van passed a Greyhound bus, it made him recall that first ride, how much courage it had taken, and the freedom he felt despite all of the uncertainty. He had a lot to be proud of. But when he started seeing signs for Jacksonville, Johnny felt a tightening in his solar plexus. *We're going straight to the marina, then right back to New York.* He tipped back his head and closed his eyes. *Don't even look. Pretend we're driving to Albuquerque, San Diego, fucking anywhere.* He distracted himself by listening to Patrick and Rafael behind him, comparing the bushes on various centerfolds. Maybe his little freak-out at the gun range was it, and now the episodes will be done. But the more he tried to convince himself, the more claustrophobic he became.

Clyde tapped him. "Hey, you all right?"

"Huh?"

"You were rocking."

"Sorry."

"I don't need you to be sorry." Clyde twisted in his seat. "I need you to help us out here, let us know what's going on."

Johnny straightened up. "The Florida signs were making me restless, that's all."

Mario hung an arm over the passenger seat. "I'm restless, too. But that's from being stuck in this damn rat van with all you gassy motherfuckers."

"Pull my finger," said Patrick from the back.

Clyde sighed. "C'mon, this is serious."

Jarrod tamped the air. "Clyde's a little high-strung, but some of you haven't seen Johnny in that state. It's pretty fucking scary, so if we can prevent it…"

"Exactly," said Clyde. "This also might be the perfect opportunity to learn how to get a grip on it."

Johnny stuck out a thumb. "Sigmund Freud DeMarco over here."

"You can make fun of me later," said Clyde. "But for now, you gotta tell us everything that pops in your head, no matter how stupid you think it is."

His eyes locked onto Clyde's. "Okay. I will."

Johnny rolled his shoulders and settled into his seat. He tried not to focus on anything in particular, just allowed the flat stretch of highway to blur by. He started listing his feelings as they arose, even finding some catharsis in the process. A lot of them, it was suggested, could have been attributed to the upcoming meeting. But after a while, the abstract sensations began locking on to images.

"Hey," said Clyde. "You're awfully quiet over there."

"Hmm."

"Don't disappear, man. Stay with me." Clyde's tone was authoritative but soothing. "Tell me what's happening."

Johnny was in the cellar again. On the floor this time. Hands tied to the leg of the workbench, the cement cold against his naked body. Orlando was hunting for something on the table above, ripping through the clutter. Objects were falling onto the floor. A paint roller bounced in front of Johnny's face, and he curled into a tighter ball. "He has an extension cord."

"Who, Orlando?"

"Yeah."

"Are you in the cellar?"

Johnny offered a weak nod.

"You're doing great, just stay with me. What's he doing now?"

"Whipping me." Johnny flinched.

"Can't you yell for help?"

"Noise angers my parents. The quieter I am, the faster they release me."

"That's fucked up," said Jarrod.

Concerned brothers looked on.

"He's wrapping it around his fist now." Johnny began rocking again, so Clyde and Jarrod looped their arms around his elbows. "He's punching my back and legs."

"Keep talking," said Clyde.

"Yeah," said Jarrod. "We're all gonna protect you, okay?"

"He's looking for something… a plastic bag. He's putting it over my head." Johnny's breath grew shallow and rapid. "He's tightening it around my neck with the cord."

"It's just a memory," said Clyde. "You're not really there."

Clyde's words became more distant as Johnny strained to see through the blackness. His mouth opened wide, gasping for air, then his body went limp. He could feel Orlando rolling him face down, then straddling him.

"Get the fuck off me!" Johnny pulled against Clyde and Jarrod's grip, thrashing from side to side. "Let me go!" From the back, Rafael locked his hands around Johnny's chest. When his feet started thrashing, Mario scrambled over the front to sit on Johnny's legs. "Let me up! I need to get out!"

"Not until you calm down," said Clyde through gritted teeth.

They wrestled until Tito pulled into a rest area. He parked in a secluded section while the others kept a hold on Johnny. Eventually, the fighting wound down, and his breathing began to regulate.

Clyde blew air through puffed cheeks. "You all right now?"

"Uh-huh."

"Look at me."

Johnny turned, but the rage was so swollen inside of him he could barely see Clyde's face.

"You understand, I just gotta make sure you're *you* and not… whoever."

Johnny ripped his arm from Clyde's grip. "I'm fucking me, okay? Now let me out, unless you want puke all over you."

Mario opened the side door. Johnny climbed over him and Jarrod to scramble out. He staggered to a tree and doubled over. The impulse to vomit continued after his stomach was empty. He gagged up some bile, then spit several times before turning toward the van. His brothers were all milling around outside, sneaking peeks at him, but Johnny could not look at them.

"If you're okay, we're gonna hit that restroom," said Rafael.

Johnny waved a hand. "Go."

Only Clyde hung back. "You sure you're okay?"

"I will be if everyone stops fucking asking."

"What happened?"

"When?"

"After the plastic bag. What did Orlando do to make you freak out so bad?"

"That's not enough?" Johnny stormed in a circle. "He fucking suffocated me. What more do you want?"

"I don't want anything other than your mental health, but that comes with not hiding shit." Clyde raked fingers through his hair. "I think the fact that we didn't fully lose you back there is a good start. Don't you?"

"It's a *great* start, now where the fuck are we?"

"Somewhere outside Jacksonville."

"What time is it?"

"One-something."

"Cool. We'll get a little closer, then stop at a motel. Rest, kill a few hours, and get to the marina around midnight."

"Whatever." Clyde executed a half-assed salute, then spun toward the restrooms.

Outside of Jupiter, the crew rented a no-frills double occupancy room off the highway. They took turns showering and changing. While his brothers did pushups or walked around the motel's property, Johnny was quiet. He thought he had been prepared to start facing shit. Maybe having the episodes was preferable because he didn't have time for these sickening emotions. He needed to be focused for the deal, but it was hard to shake that grotesque image. Of all the feelings bubbling inside him, anger was the most manageable. Anger was a motivator. Fear, shame, sadness? The only things they inspired were inertia and weakness. He sucked in a deep breath, then slowly exhaled. He vowed to give the anger free rein to express itself as long as those other feelings would just go the fuck away.

CHAPTER FORTY-TWO

As the van entered the Miami city limits, Johnny directed Tito through the dark streets. The skyline loomed in the distance, its tall buildings twinkling in the night, reminiscent of Manhattan's. Johnny remembered riding his bike past the rows of palm trees and the little shop where the old man would give him a free soda if he swept the sidewalk. Seeing it all stirred up a whole new batch of emotions, but each time one surfaced, he balled it up and tossed it in his anger well. For the most part, it wasn't Miami he hated. The city had been his salvation when he didn't want to go home, but it was difficult not to associate it with his family.

Johnny suggested they pull into a public lot near the waterfront, then unfolded the note from the Brick. The boat was *The Seven Cs*, a brown and white sixty-five-foot cabin cruiser docked at slip #44. He had Clyde and Patrick scope out what they could while the others waited by the van.

"It's there," Patrick said when they returned. "Go left at the entrance, and the slip is on the fifth pier down."

"It's way at the end," said Clyde. "Everything's pretty deserted at this hour, so it would've been too conspicuous for us to get much closer."

"And there are two guys guarding that little boat bridge thingy," said Patrick.

"The gangway?" said Johnny.

Mario tsked. "City folk."

Johnny ignored the wisecrack. "Probably best not to show up with a mob." He combed his fingers through his hair. "Rafi and Mario know the most Spanish, so maybe they should come in case nobody speaks English."

"What about me?" asked Tito.

Johnny stopped to look at him. "You're gonna need to drive the others home if we don't make it."

"Jesus," said Clyde. "Will you stop talking like that?"

He twitched a shoulder. "I'm just keeping it real."

"Well, don't," said Jarrod.

Johnny grabbed the cash, leaving the guns under some blankets in the back of the van. "These are here, in case you need them for whatever."

"I've shot guns before," Tito muttered.

Jarrod coughed out a laugh. "Why am I not surprised by that?"

"Or the fact that he never bothered to mention it," said Patrick.

Johnny started toward the harbor. "You coming?"

Mario and Rafael exchanged the gang handshake with the others before jogging to catch up to Johnny.

The boardwalk parallel to the shore was wide, with several long piers jutting into the harbor. The office, convenience store and fueling station had closed for the night, but a smattering of distant voices echoed over the water.

Johnny turned onto the pier, pushing aside the instincts telling him not to. He glimpsed Rafael and Mario out of the corner of his eye, both striding beside him, but the strength his Dog brothers always provided was waning now, having been fragmented by his shame. If shit went down and he got killed, so what. As long as he protected his guys.

As they neared the yacht, the two guards took a defensive position in front of the gangway. Both were bronzed, about six feet tall and muscular. They were dressed in short-sleeved shirts with nicely pressed slacks, silver-tipped belts and designer shoes. The gold from their watches and chains glimmered in the moonlight.

"Who the fuck are you?" asked one with a close-trimmed beard.

"We're here to see Marco."

He looked at his partner and laughed. "*Ellos son niños.*"

"I have an appointment," Johnny said in Spanish. "I represent the Brick."

"And what is your name?"

"Johnny."

"Johnny what."

"Just Johnny."

He smirked into his chest, then walked across the stern and through a sliding door. While he was gone, the clean-shaven man folded his arms, sizing up the three teens. When the one emerged, he tipped his chin toward the moon, indicating it was okay. Johnny started up the narrow gangplank, but before Mario and Rafael could follow, a meaty paw blocked them. "Only him."

Johnny turned to his brothers. Their expressions signaled for him not to go alone. "It's okay," he said. "I'll be fine."

On the deck, the bearded guard yanked the duffel bag from Johnny's hand and frisked him. He performed the task rougher than necessary, but Johnny stood compliant. After rifling through the cash, he handed the bag back, then opened the slider.

Johnny crossed the threshold, and the door swished closed behind him. *Holy mother of fucking Christ.* He had seen big fancy boats before but never imagined the insides would be so plush. There were dark wood walls and maroon shag carpets. Dimmed recessed lights glowed from a mirrored ceiling. Portside was a full kitchen with brass fixtures and a rectangular oak table. Starboard was a mahogany bar with ample liquor bottles, a hanging glass rack and white cushioned swivel stools. Hemming the panoramic windows off the bow was an elegant matching white leather couch behind a round glass coffee table. In the center sat a huge triangular marble ashtray that looked heavy enough to double as the boat's anchor. Tasteful art hung from the walls, and smooth jazz piped through a surround-sound system. Johnny tipped an ear toward a narrow staircase leading to a lower level but could not hear anything.

After a few minutes, he sat down on the couch. He set the bag of money at his feet and lit a cigarette. It was not until some twenty minutes later that a man emerged from the stairs. He walked straight past Johnny and over to the bar. He was in his early forties, with a full head of black hair slicked back with gel, dark eyes and a wispy mustache. His posture was erect, but his movements were squirrely. His features were handsome in spite of his complexion, which was pale and pitted from acne scars. He was barefoot, wearing loose summer clothes, white knit pants and an untucked yellow shirt, half-unbuttoned to expose his narrow chest. The outline of a pistol could be seen stuffed into his belt.

Johnny sat unmoving, observing. Did this guy even see him?

Two tall glasses were pulled from a rack and filled with ice. Measured shots of rum were added, followed by a blend of juices. He pumped in a final spritz of soda from the bar's fountain before garnishing each drink with a skewered Maraschino cherry and an orange slice.

The man walked the cocktails to the coffee table and set one in front of his guest. He perched on the opposite edge of the couch, slurped from his glass and looked at Johnny for the first time. His gaze was unnerving. His dark pupils were glassy and twitchy. The energy radiating off him was turbulent. Johnny felt anxiety creeping up. *I've got nothing to fear because I have nothing to lose.*

The man's eyes remained locked on Johnny as he wiped the drink's sweetness from his lips with the back of a hand. "*Escuché que eres un chico colombiano. ¿Cómo te llama?*"

"*Me llama Johnny.*"

"Oh, right, *Just Johnny.* Octavio told me." He sneered. "Sorry about your friends, but I don't like crowds."

"I understand."

"Drink." He pointed to Johnny's glass. "I'm Marco, but you figured that out."

Johnny offered a closed-mouth smile.

"I was told about you."

Johnny tasted the cocktail. It was fruity but strong, and the liquor felt good in his belly. "There isn't much to know."

"Don't be so sure." Marco set down his glass. "I might know things about you even *you* don't know."

"I guess you might."

Marco cocked his head. "Are you patronizing me?"

"No, I just meant—"

"For instance, I might know exactly how this evening ends for you."

Johnny bowed his head. "Yes. I believe you might, and I respect that."

244

Marco sank a little deeper into the couch. "Are you American-born?"

"Yes, but my parents are from Bogotá."

"Have you ever been?"

"No, but I'd like to go." Johnny had never given it much thought, but it sounded like a good thing to say.

"You should. Colombia is one of the most beautiful countries in the world. It has the most beautiful women and the best beaches in all of South America. Its food, culture and music are second to none…" As Marco rattled on about the country's history, geography and politics, alternating between English and Spanish, he got up to search for something. He poked around the kitchen and behind the bar until he located a black pack of cigarillos and a fancy gold lighter. He sat back down and lit one, never pausing from his narrative.

Since leaving Miami, most of the Spanish-speaking people Johnny knew, including his own gang brothers, were Mexican, Puerto Rican or Dominican. It had been years since he had heard the subtle cadence and slang of the Colombian dialect, and it reminded him of his father. The blending of languages, of course, was what Orlando used to do. Johnny's heels started to bounce, so he crossed his ankles and tucked them under the couch. *Nothing to lose, nothing to fear.*

Marco either noticed that Johnny had stopped listening or was tired of the topic because he redirected mid-sentence. "So, why the fuck are you here?"

"I'm here for Rick, the Brick."

"And *he* couldn't make it?"

Johnny shrugged.

"I know why he couldn't make it." He blew a stream of smoke toward the ceiling. "He doesn't like to deal with me anymore. He thinks I'm crazy, doesn't he?"

Johnny didn't say anything. Then he realized it was not a rhetorical question. "Um, I don't know what he thinks. He pays me to make these runs, that's all."

"Well, I *can* tell you what he thinks because I know." Marco took a big pull off the drink, nearly draining it. "We go back many years, he and I. We used to do business. Do you know why they call him the Brick?"

"No."

"Really? He never told you?"

"I guess not."

"The rumor is, a long time ago, his wife caught him with another woman. I'm talking stark naked, balls deep. They started arguing. The fight spilled onto the street, and she hit him in the head with a brick. Knocked him out cold. He went to the hospital and eventually recovered, but while he was there, she decided to get even by fucking one of his friends. When the Brick found out, he shot them both in the face, point blank, in the middle of Lenox Avenue!" Marco spit out a laugh. "No one's ever said a fucking word about it, and he's never gone to jail. *That* is why he's called the Brick and how he got the reputation for being a man you don't cross."

Johnny's eyes widened. "Wow. That's heavy."

"Heavy?" Marco stood to walk back and forth. "That's not fucking heavy! That's self-righteous, egomaniacal, pride bullshit. Who shoots a woman in the face?" His hands were flailing, including the one with the cigarillo, its ash clinging precariously to the tip. "I mean, we've all shot people in the face, right? But not a woman. Not for cheating. Maybe you cut her where she bleeds, but you don't shoot her in the face."

Johnny sucked down more of the cocktail, letting the rum desensitize his brain.

"You, on the other hand," Marco's eyes narrowed at Johnny. "You think it's heavy because he dresses flashy and talks fast, but you don't have the slightest clue about shooting someone in the face."

"I kinda do," Johnny mumbled.

"Say what?"

"I said I do."

"Liar." Marco's tone was snide, childlike.

"I shot a guy."

"What for?"

Spare the details. "Because he crossed me."

"How old are you?"

"Almost fifteen."

"You think you're a tough little motherfucker, don't you?"

"No, not really."

"That's fucking right!" Marco stuffed his butt in the ashtray, then continued parading around. "After all this time, the Brick sends *you* here? Some punk kid? What a fucking insult." His head wagged from side to side. "He's too good for *me*, but not my product. He knows I got the best shit for the best price but thinks I'm too stupid, *too crazy* to get what's going on." Marco stood in front of Johnny. "Who the fuck does he think he is?" He reached behind his back for a Colt .38 and pressed the barrel into Johnny's forehead. "And who the fuck are you?"

Johnny refused to flinch. He locked eyes with Marco and leaned into the gun.

Marco's mouth hardened. "Do *you* think I'm crazy?"

"No."

"Because I'll show you just how fucking crazy I am." He cocked the gun and glared at Johnny. "Your boss doesn't see what I see. I'm the sanest motherfucker in the universe! His mind is flat, one-dimensional. I see things in depth, like a kaleidoscope. Past, present, future, all at the same time. Most people can't handle that level of intelligence, or they can't define it, so they call it crazy." Marco's finger shook on the trigger. Droplets of sweat formed on his brow as the ceiling lights bounced off his dilated pupils. "Have you ever had a gun at your head before?"

"No."

"How does it feel?"

Better than what Orlando did to me. The pistol pressed deeper into Johnny's skull.

"I could reduce you to a stain on the fucking carpet, do you understand?" Spit flew from Marco's mouth and landed on the gun's hammer.

"Yes, sir, I understand that."

"You think I'm crazy too, don't you?"

"No."

"Bullshit."

"It's not."

"I don't believe you."

"I don't think you're crazy, and I can prove it."

247

The anger in Marco's face faded. He took a step back and lowered the gun. "Okay. Go ahead."

Johnny showed his palms deferentially, then stood to lift his shirt, exposing the numerous razor knife scars and lash marks on his chest and abdomen. "The person who did this is crazy, not you."

Marco's brows knitted as he leaned in for a closer inspection. He raised the shirt even higher to see more scars on Johnny's ribs and back. When he was done, Johnny held out his arms to show the disfiguration around his wrists.

"Who did this to you?"

"My brother."

"Your *brother* did this?"

"Yeah, he used to torture me for fun."

"And your parents, they allowed it?"

"Yes."

Marco's lips tightened. "When?"

"It started at ten, but he was six years older." Johnny reached for his glass to drain the watery remnants. "It's why I ran away a few years ago."

"Who does that to an innocent child? That's savage, diabolical." Marco pinched his temples. "Where do you live now?"

"I stay in different places, with friends."

Marco walked to the bar shaking his head. He un-cocked the gun, set it down and took a seat on one of the stools. Johnny flopped on the couch. Everything was already feeling so overwhelming. And they hadn't even gotten to the drug-swapping part yet. Johnny didn't know how to move things forward without upsetting Marco. Sure, it was a fancy yacht and not a dingy cellar, but he felt just as trapped.

"That's not right," Marco said to the bar. "You don't do that to a child." He straightened a stack of cocktail napkins. "Listen, the Brick is a decent businessman. I just don't need his critical, self-righteous bullshit. And it was cowardly for him to send you here."

As Johnny listened to Marco talk, his words started to blend with the jazz, the walls were closing in and the air grew thinner.

"But you are different. Smarter, bolder, more like me. I can see you outgrowing him very quickly."

Johnny felt his peripheral vision narrow.

Marco pulled a plastic packet from his shirt pocket, then reached across the bar for a paring knife. He opened the baggie, scooped some of its powdery contents onto the tip of the knife and snorted it. "Come here, I want you to try this."

"Thank you," Johnny wheezed, "but I don't do well on coke." He didn't think he should admit he had never tried it.

"Come the fuck here and sit your ass down." Marco patted the barstool next to his.

Johnny shuffled over.

"How can I trust you in this business if you don't take a taste? And how can you trust me if you don't try the product?" He scooped up another hit.

"I just don't like—"

"Shut up. It's not coke. Cocaine is for ideas, inspiration, motivation. But *this?* This is the regulator."

There was no room for negotiating, so Johnny leaned forward as Marco raised the blade's tip to his nose. He sniffed, and a blanket of warmth washed over him. He felt calm like he was floating in slow motion. Everything he'd been thinking about vaporized in an instant. His vision widened, his hearing cleared and he no longer felt claustrophobic. In fact, he felt fine. Peaceful, even.

"One more," Marco scooped out another hit for Johnny before taking one himself. They both sat quietly, experiencing the moment.

"What is that?" Johnny asked.

"I call it serenity."

Johnny slumped in the stool, feeling like all the cells in his body were ejaculating. Now he understood Lily's attraction to the stuff.

Marco's voice cut through the tranquility. "By rights, I should send the Brick your severed head, but I'm guessing you didn't know about all the bad-mouthing he's done. He never mentioned that part, did he?"

"No."

"Of course not. To him, you're just another disposable courier." Marco circled a finger at Johnny's abdomen. "Does he know about all of that, what happened to you?" He got up to make two more cocktails.

"No." Johnny looked Marco in the eye. "I don't tell many people."

"It affects you."

"What do you mean?"

Marco set the drinks on the bar, then sat down facing Johnny. "You left home, but it follows you. The abuse. It still fucks with your head."

Johnny poked at his drink with a straw. Was this guy like Lucinda with the telepathic shit? "Yeah. It affects me."

"I see that. It bleeds into everything you do. It gives you nightmares and it is making you push away the people you need the most. You can't let it do that."

Johnny shook his head, not prepared for the wave of weightlessness that followed. "How do you know all of that?"

"I told you. I see everything." Marco waved his hands around the air. "It's the kaleidoscope vision." He snorted out a laugh. "But you can fix it, you know."

"I can?" Johnny cocked his head. "How?"

Marco shrugged like it was obvious. "You have to kill them."

"Huh?"

"Listen to me. When people hurt you or betray you, they need to die." Marco plucked the cherry from his drink and dropped it in his mouth. "It's the only way to free yourself from the suffering."

Lucinda never told me that part.

"You said you already dropped a guy, right? Are you good with a gun?"

"Actually, I'm really good."

Marco scrunched his face.

"It sounds crazy, I know." Johnny slurped from the straw. "But I have this knack for hitting targets. I always have, ever since I was a little kid."

"You *are* a little kid."

They both grinned.

"Really. You're that good, huh?" Marco looked Johnny up and down. "So, if I need you to kill a motherfucker, you'll do it?"

"Of course."

"You answered pretty quickly."

"I mean, you aren't cutting my head off, so I owe you that much, right?" Johnny raised his glass. "And you make an awesome cocktail."

Marco laughed. "You got a safe number to call?"

"Not really."

Marco slid off the stool and glided downstairs. He returned with a black gym bag and dropped it on the coffee table. As Johnny swiveled around, a pager was tossed at him. He barely caught it.

"Now I can get in touch with you. Sometimes, I call internationally, so you better have enough coins for the pay phone when you call me back." He snatched Johnny's bag off the floor, put it beside his and unzipped both of them. He thumbed through the stacks of cash, making a mental calculation, then tipped his bag for Johnny to see. "Ten keys of coke and two dope." He held up a pair of sandwich baggies. "And these are for you, a sample of each." He tossed them in with the rest.

"Marco, you don't—"

"Shut the fuck up. Look, I like you, kid, and I have a feeling we'll be doing business again. Just consider it a welcome gift."

"Thank you," said Johnny. "And if anyone talks shit about you again, I'm gonna set them straight."

"I know you will. Those motherfuckers don't get me like you do. There's intensity in you, the way you look at people, always evaluating. That's smart. And you're charismatic. People are drawn to you." Marco wagged a finger. "You fix that shit about your past, and your future will be very bright. I can see it." He zipped up the bag and outstretched his arms. "Okay, we're good."

Johnny climbed off the stool and offered his hand. "Thank you. For everything."

Marco shook back and winked.

Johnny picked up the bag and went to the slider.

Outside, the guards were reclining on deck chairs, but Mario and Rafael were gone. "What happened to my friends?"

"We got tired of looking at them," said one.

"Okay then." Johnny stepped off the yacht. "Goodnight."

CHAPTER FORTY-THREE

As Johnny approached the boardwalk, Clyde and Jarrod rushed to his side. Jarrod took the bag. "What took so long?"

"We were worried shitless," said Clyde.

Johnny weaved through the parking lot. "Everything's fine."

At the van, the others circled with similar questions, but answering seemed like too much work. He crawled into the front passenger seat, tipped back his head and closed his eyes. His body was still humming.

Everyone piled in, and Tito started the engine.

"Damn, man, we thought you got taken hostage," said Mario.

"How long was I in there?"

"Almost two hours," said Jarrod.

Patrick rifled through the gym bag. "Looks like you did it, though. You got the merchandise."

"Don't be doing that." Rafael yanked the bag from his lap. "We gotta hide that shit." He spun around to stuff it under a blanket.

Clyde leaned over Johnny's backrest. "So? Aren't you gonna tell us what went down?"

"Yeah," said Mario. "Once Ali and Frazier told me and Rafi to hit the bricks, we wondered if we'd ever see you again."

Johnny's brain was too muddy. But even if it wasn't, he felt he would need more time to process everything.

"Hello, earth calling." Jarrod tapped Johnny's shoulder. "What the fuck is wrong with you?"

Johnny lifted his head. "He made me try some of the product."

"He made you do coke?"

"Not the coke."

"You fucking did heroin?" said Clyde.

"I didn't have a choice."

"Was he as crazy as the Brick said," asked Patrick.

Johnny chewed his bottom lip. "He's complicated. But I learned a whole lot of shit in there." He looked out the windshield. "Tito, where are you going?"

"Back the way we came. I-95 North, right?"

"No. Up here, make a left."

"What the fuck are you doing?" asked Jarrod.

"We're going to the house."

"Why?" said Clyde. "What're you gonna do?"

Between directions, Johnny gave a brief synopsis of Marco's revenge theory. "What if he's right? What if killing them puts an end to these episodes? I mean, it's not like they don't deserve it."

"And what if seeing them makes you flip out, and you run off." Clyde massaged the base of his neck. "Then we'll be driving all over Miami, a city none of us know, looking for your ass."

"No, because we'll all go in there together." Johnny sighed. "And besides, I started to have an episode on that boat, but as soon as I got high, it went away. Maybe I'm in the perfect state to deal with them."

"That's some fucked-up logic."

"Tito, turn here." Johnny faced Clyde. "Maybe I'll find out that Orlando is already dead, and that'll be good enough. I just don't want to get all the way back to New York and wish I'd done something different."

"I get that part," said Clyde. "But there are a lot of variables, and you're making it sound way too simple."

"Let's just take a look, see what opportunities present themselves."

It was close to 3:30 a.m. as the van rolled onto 14th Street. Johnny had Tito pull over and cut the lights near 28th Avenue. "It's at the end of that dead end, but we can't drive. Too conspicuous."

Rafael passed the gun bag forward. Johnny grabbed one of the Sigs, Tito took the other and Mario pocketed the .38. They exited the van, looking around, but the area was deserted. The only streetlight was on the corner, so the avenue was dark. He waved for his brothers to follow as he skulked forward. The shadowed outlines of his old neighbors' properties were as he remembered, the flat-roofed houses with fences and birdbaths. With each one he passed, he waited for emotions to surface. But everything was still muted by the drugs. He stopped at the bottom of the cul-de-sac, and his brothers did the same. The decaying house sat under the moonlight, surrounded by overgrowth and fallen tree branches.

"Damn," whispered Patrick, "this place looks abandoned."

Johnny nodded. "It always looked like that on the outside."

"But this is some serious Addams Family shit."

"There's no car," said Rafael. "Do they have a car?"

"They used to."

Clyde leaned into Johnny. "How you holding up?"

"I know this is gonna surprise you, but I'm all right. Really." Fingering the gun in his waistband, Johnny started up the broken brick walkway. He bypassed the front door to peek in the living room window. The blinds were down, but several slats were askew. He cupped his hands around his eyes and pressed into the glass. "It looks empty."

"Like they moved?" asked Jarrod.

"I need to get in there and see for sure." Johnny double-checked the street before tracking around back.

Mario was already there, snooping around. He had squeezed between two overgrown hedges to jiggle a window. "Hey guys, I think it's unlocked."

Johnny muscled his way through the shrubbery, and together, they were able to push it open. Mario gave Johnny a leg-up, and he heaved himself inside, skirting the kitchen sink to climb off the counter. Mario was right behind him.

Johnny stood in the middle of the kitchen. He did not need the absence of furniture to tell him no one was there. He could feel it. The noxious energy had been exorcized. He forced his feet to move around the room as his eyes adjusted to the dark. He opened a cabinet, expecting to see cans and jars lined up symmetrically, labels facing out, but it was empty.

Mario had found the front door and let in the others, who fanned out to look around. Johnny's sedated brain floated through the living room. Shadowy silhouettes played off the walls, making it feel unreal. Watching Rafael crouch down to tie his shoe where Miguel used to sit reading the paper added a time-warping element.

"Where do you think they went?" said Jarrod. "Place looks like it's been empty a while."

"I don't know," Johnny mumbled.

"We could wait around till morning," said Mario. "Knock on a few doors pretending to be friends, ask what happened to them."

"My parents never talked to the neighbors when they lived here," said Johnny. "I doubt they'd say something before moving out." He made a pass through all three bedrooms and could not find one shred of evidence that he or his family had ever lived there. Maybe with more light, he would discover a single hair in the shower, a button on the closet floor, but it wasn't worth someone seeing it from the road. The hallway was darker than the rest of the house, but Johnny could still make out the cellar door. His stomach dropped as he ran a hand along the jamb. The deadbolt was gone.

"Oh shit," said Mario walking by. "Is that where your brother used to—"

"Shut up!" Clyde said to him in a hushed bark, then turned to Johnny. "Wait, you're not going down there, are you?"

Johnny fiddled the knob. "I think I need to."

"Okay, but you're not going alone."

Johnny pulled open the door, and cool, damp air wafted out. He started down the narrow stairs. It was pitch black. He tested each step with his weight, half expecting someone to reach up and grab him. When Clyde and the others followed behind him, that fear subsided.

At the bottom, Johnny swiped the wall where there used to be a switch. A single bulb hanging from the ceiling flickered on. Patrick closed the door to restrict the glow upstairs.

The space was much smaller than Johnny remembered, and everything had been restored. Except for un-cementing the windows, it looked just like it did before Miguel had turned it into a prison. Even the bathroom was gone.

"Damn," said Mario walking around. "Your brother *lived* in here?"

"They took everything out," said Johnny. "That's the only thing left." He pointed to the handmade workbench, now bare. Every single implement of torture gone. He walked closer to lay a hand on the wood and remembered the flashback he had earlier. Hands bound to a table leg, twisting on the floor naked, being whipped by an extension cord. He went to the corner where it had all happened. He tapped the 2x4 with the toe of his sneaker. It buckled. His fingers found the bolt holding it to the table. He jiggled it, and it came free in his hand. The leg dropped to the concrete with a hollow smack. Those vile images—the plastic bag over his head, Orlando on top of him—all seemed so powerless now, here in this dusty cellar, surrounded by gang brothers, diluted by dope.

Marco was right. He couldn't push away the people he needed the most. Johnny tossed the bolt on the table. "He raped me, okay? That happened here, too." He turned to let his eyes settle on each of his brothers. "But maybe we don't have to have a gang meeting about it. Maybe that can just stay between us for now."

"Of course," said Clyde.

"Absolutely," said Jarrod.

CHAPTER FORTY-FOUR

Johnny crawled into the back of the van and stretched out on a blanket. He was asleep before they hit the highway. He slept straight through till dusk, then made good on his birthday promise to Tito. They stopped at a steakhouse off the interstate and ordered a fancy dinner with appetizers and desserts. While they ate, Johnny disclosed more details about the yacht and what had gone down with Marco.

The next morning, he paged Joe from a rest stop in Jersey City and was told to go to a parking lot on 10th Avenue between 17th and 18th. While they waited, Johnny removed Marco's welcome gift from the main stash and put it in the glove box.

When the blue Oldsmobile pulled up behind them, Johnny went to the passenger's side. The Brick rolled down his window. "Colombiano, how'd it go?"

"Fine."

"Fine?" He shrunk back. "That's it?"

Johnny picked at his fingernails. "Yup."

"That's great. I knew you'd pull it off." He produced a brown paper bag from under his seat and wagged it. "I put an extra five in there for you."

Johnny took it, then waved to his crew. The van's back doors opened, and Jarrod passed out the drugs. Johnny tossed him the cash.

The Brick checked the contents before setting the duffle bag in the back seat. "The guns—did you need them?"

"No, but I think I should keep those." His eyes met the Brick's for the first time. "You know, as a little *extra* bonus."

The Brick furrowed his brow. "Excuse me?"

"Because that guy could've blown my fucking head off, given your history and all."

"What'd he tell you?" The Brick cocked an ear but then waved both hands. "You know something? It doesn't matter. You can't believe that cokehead." He brushed some dust from the dashboard. "The guy's got a reputation, you dig? And I ain't the only one who knows it." He settled back to look at Johnny. "You know I appreciate you."

As much as any disposable courier.

"Lemme hook you up with a little product. I just need to measure that shit out first."

Johnny scratched his chin. "If it's all the same to you, Rick, I'd rather have the guns."

The Brick glanced at Joe, who stayed facing forward. "Okay, Colombiano. Have it your way." He rubbed his knees. "You keep that hardware, then I don't have to worry about you in the future." He put an open hand out the window. "As long as we're good."

Johnny looked at it a moment, then nodded. "We're good." He slapped him five before returning to the van.

Jarrod patted Johnny on the back. "We did it! *You* did it. Now we can get the fuck out of here and sleep for two days."

"No can do, brother," said Mario. "We got school tomorrow."

"Shit, that's right," said Clyde. "Vacation's over."

"Might not be a bad thing," said Johnny. "I'm craving something normal and boring."

After dropping everyone off, Tito parked outside his apartment, and he and Johnny carted the stuff upstairs. They each took long hot showers, then sprawled on the couches. Tito turned on the TV and dozed through an old movie.

As Johnny stared at the ceiling, he struggled to match his thoughts with his feelings, but there were so many. His brothers did not seem shocked to learn what Orlando had done, nor had they treated him any differently after his admission. It was only Johnny who felt like he was rotting from the inside out. And how much more shit was still buried? The thought was terrifying. Also, since he never got to *fix his past*, as

Marco had said, what did that mean for his future? But even if his family had been there, would he really have been capable of killing them? Maybe in self-defense, but not while they were sleeping. *At least not my mother, anyway.* Perhaps it was a blessing he never got to find out.

Tito roused from the sofa. He went to the fridge and returned with two beers. "It's a lot." He set a can in front of Johnny and sat down. "But you will be all right."

Johnny felt a reflexive wave of resistance.

"Over time, the pain of what happened will fade. Maybe so slowly that you don't even notice at first. But if you trust and sit patiently, one day you will realize that it doesn't own you anymore."

Johnny swung his feet to the floor and took a swig of beer.

"Do you understand why people want to be in this gang?"

Johnny picked at the tab of the can.

"It's because of your strength. Even without knowing what you lived through, we see it. It inspires us. Others, too. Look how much responsibility the Brick is giving you. And how you were able to put that drugged-up, trigger-happy Marco at ease. Don't ever take that for granted. Those are powerful skills." Tito leaned forward. "Whatever bad things you uncover about your past, you need to know that *this* family—the Dogs of War family—will always be with you."

Johnny poked at the condensation drops forming on the beer can. "Those are the most words I've heard you say since the day we met."

Tito smiled. "Go ahead, be sarcastic. All I'm saying is that you could grow this gang as big and powerful as you want. You see that, right?"

Johnny met his eyes. "Yeah. I see that."

Acknowledgments

There are many people to thank for supporting me on this journey—friends and family, co-workers and writing group colleagues—many of whom read through drafts of this book in various stages of edit, including the first draft, the one that professionals say *never* to show anyone. Thank you all for your feedback and encouragement: Maxine Gordon, Jennifer Wyland, Hazel Belvo, Melissa O'Grady, Jonathan Ryder, Harris Thompson, Terry Williams, Kevan Spoor, Dale T. Phillips, Dan Howard, John Photos, Todd Snider, Jacob Dyer-Spiegel, Jane Goren, Madeline Arnstein, Rich Alves, Madeline Miele Holt, Katie Rhodes, Cathleen Bennet, Kathy Bragg Aspden, Albert Diaz, Stephanie Page, Kara Gamble, Sue Buchanan, Kate McCamy, Meaddows Ryan, Stan Carmack, Heidi Howell, Frantz Degand, Dana and Polly Crowe, Nicole Barrell, Frank Adolfini, Kathleen Murphy, Jeanie Bagley, Hank Henderson, Kathleen Krikorian, Cathleen Bingham, Pam Marin-Kingsley, Linda Wiggin, Sterling, Willow, and Spike.

Huge thanks to the publishing team at Calumet Editions and Ian Graham Leask in particular. Ian understood my vision for this book from the beginning and knew how to help me get there.

The cover image was created by Nathalie Erika Langner, an extraordinary and prolific artist whose talent is only rivaled by her amazing spirit.

Big thanks to the Cape Cod Writers Center. My involvement with the Center and the Books and the World program they produce has allowed me to meet many brilliant authors and literary professionals.

The numerous seminars and annual writers' conferences facilitated by the CCWC have been helpful on many levels.

I am grateful to Cape Cod Community College for their continuing education classes. There, I met Professor James Kirshner, an enthusiastic supporter of writers. His knowledge of the craft and the publishing world, along with his recommendations for resources, steered me down pathways that eventually led me here. Thank you, James.

I found immense value in *Authors Publish*, a website run by Jacob and Caitlin Jans, and Emily Harstone. They offer interesting and relevant, well-run seminars—many for free—on a variety of topics related to writing and publishing. They also provide regular listings of personally vetted publications that are open for submissions in all genres. The majority of my short stories have been published using names from their lists.

The one person who could have helped me the most, whose opinion I would have respected above all others, was my mother, Sally. She was the most well-read, intelligent, and witty person I've ever known. A true shit-talking New Yorker. She did not live long enough to see the first draft, and her absence has been felt throughout this entire process.

None of this could have happened without my beloved Mark. (Well, I suppose it *would* have happened, just not until I was ninety.) Mark not only believed in me from the beginning; he facilitated reshuffling our lives so I could devote more time to *this* kind of work instead of the kind that yields actual money. Thank you, sweetheart. I'll make sure you get a signed copy.

And thank you to the city of New York. No matter how long I stay away, it always feels like home when I return. It's a complicated relationship. I endured a lot of traumas there, but they will never eclipse the beauty, the life lessons, the spirit, and, most of all, the people who helped mold me into the person I am.

About the Author

Alyssa D. Metcalfe grew up in New York City, living in Washington Heights, the West Village, Tribeca (before it was trendy) and Inwood. By the time she was fifteen, she was entrenched in the bar scene and hanging out with addicts, dealers and criminals. It is those experiences that inspire much of her writing. At the age of twenty-seven, she decided she needed a change and went to college, where she attained an A.S. in Equine Studies from Northwest College in Powell, Wyoming, then a B.S. in Animal Science from UMASS Amherst. She currently lives on a small farm on Cape Cod, where she sits on the Board of Directors for the Cape Cod Writers Center.

Made in the USA
Las Vegas, NV
08 March 2024